Praise for the *Planetside Series*

Planetside

"This was a brisk, entertaining novel. . . . I was reminded a bit of some of John Scalzi's Old Man's War novels."

—SFFWorld

"A tough, authentic-feeling story that starts out fast and accelerates from there." —Jack Campbell, author of *Ascendant*

"Not just for military SF fans—although military SF fans will love it—*Planetside* is an amazing debut novel, and I'm looking forward to what Mammay writes next." —Tanya Huff, author of the Confederation and Peacekeeper series

"*Planetside* is a smart and fast-paced blend of mystery and boots-in-the-dirt military SF that reads like a high-speed collision between *Courage Under Fire* and *Heart of Darkness*."

—Marko Kloos, bestselling author of the Frontline series

"The book was an enjoyable read and would likely sit well with any fan of military SF looking for an action-thriller to browse while lying in the sun at the beach." —Chris Kluwe for *Lightspeed Magazine*

"If you like military SF you'll love this or if you like SF mysteries or probably just SF in general. It's a highly impressive first novel that left a real impact." —*SFcrowsnest*

Spaceside

"Highly recommended for military SF lovers, who will savor his perspective and probably want to buy the man a drink."
—*Library Journal* (starred review)

"*Spaceside* is a worthy sequel to *Planetside* and Mammay once again successfully delivered another highly entertaining page-turner. The cleverly mixed mystery and military sci-fi element made this relatively small book packed with a strong impact, and I highly recommend it to readers who are looking for a fast-paced mystery/sci-fi read." —Novel Notions

"This is another wonderfully addictive, fast-moving book from Michael Mammay. Corporate intrigue, interplanetary politics and military action are blended into a cohesive whole that is both satisfying and great fun." —*SFcrowsnest*

"Wow, just wow. This was another exceptional book from Mammay, who has once again produced a fantastic science fiction thriller hybrid with some amazing moments in it. . . . *Spaceside* is an incredible second outing from Michael Mammay, who has a truly bright future in the science fiction genre." —Unseen Library

Colonyside

"Highly recommended for readers who like their heroes cynical, their mystery twisted, and their SF thought-provoking."
—Library Journal (starred review)

"A fine read clearly informed by the author's own military background." *—Amazing Stories*

"With the Planetside trilogy now complete, there's never been a better chance to get into Mammay's work. If you're a military SF fan, you won't regret it." —At Boundary's Edge

"I loved this one. Actually, I've loved this whole series, starting with *Planetside* and flying right through *Spaceside*."
—Reading Reality

DARKSIDE

Books by Michael Mammay

Planetside
Spaceside
Colonyside
Darkside

The Misfit Soldier

Generation Ship

DARKSIDE

A Novel

MICHAEL MAMMAY

HARPER Voyager
An Imprint of HarperCollinsPublishers

DARKSIDE. Copyright © 2024 by Michael Mammay. All rights reserved. Printed in the United States of America. No part of this book may be used or reproduced in any manner whatsoever without written permission except in the case of brief quotations embodied in critical articles and reviews. For information, address HarperCollins Publishers, 195 Broadway, New York, NY 10007.

HarperCollins books may be purchased for educational, business, or sales promotional use. For information, please email the Special Markets Department at SPsales@harpercollins.com.

Harper Voyager and design are trademarks of HarperCollins Publishers LLC.

FIRST EDITION

Library of Congress Cataloging-in-Publication Data has been applied for.

ISBN 978-0-06-332013-0

24 25 26 27 28 LBC 5 4 3 2 1

A NOTE FROM THE AUTHOR

Due to the growing length of the Planetside series, I wanted to provide recaps of previous books for those who want them. These aren't necessary for the enjoyment of *Darkside* but may help with some references and callbacks.

Obviously, these summaries contain **massive spoilers** for the previous books, so if you haven't read those yet, consider this your fair warning to turn away.

Which is more warning than Butler usually gets . . .

—

PLANETSIDE

Colonel Carl Butler is nearing retirement when he's called in by an old boss (and friend), General Serata. The military brass need him to travel to the distant, war-torn planet of Cappa to investigate the disappearance of Lieutenant Mallot, who is not only a soldier, but the son of a high councilor. It's a difficult mission but seems like a straightforward one.

Of course, it isn't.

Cappa Base is anything but friendly to Butler's inquiries, and more than one person is hiding something. The military commander is covering his ass, the hospital commander, Dr. Elliot, stonewalls Butler, and the special forces commander, Colonel Karikov, won't come up off the planet. Not to mention the witness who goes missing or the critical data that disappears.

Butler, along with his security guard, Mac, goes down to the planet's surface in search of answers, but they're hard to find. After a battle, Butler learns of a medical experiment that blended Cappan and human DNA, allowing humans to better tolerate cybernetic appendages. Except a flaw in the process means that patients who undergo the procedure need constant treatment, or they start to go insane. Butler and his team are attacked by human-Cappan hybrids led by Mallot, the man Butler had come to find. They need a leader, and since Butler himself has a cybernetic appendage, they want Butler for the job. Small problem: He has to undergo the medical procedure first. Butler is captured and taken to a medical facility where he's restrained until Dr. Elliot shows up. Elliot won't operate on an unwilling patient, and while she and Mallot are arguing, Butler steals a pistol and shoots Mallot in the face. Realizing the damage she's done, Elliot shoots herself.

Back on the orbiting base, Butler learns that in their dealings with humans, the Cappans have acquired fusion technology that will allow them to spread the war to the rest of the galaxy. He suspects that the powers that be who sent him to Cappa knew that all along, and part of the reason he's there is to deal with it while providing those leaders with plausible deniability.

Butler, being above all else a soldier, understands the mission. Despite serious misgivings, he fires weapons of mass destruction at the planet, ending the Cappan threat but killing millions in the process. He turns himself in to be arrested for what he sees as a war crime.

SPACESIDE

Carl Butler doesn't go to jail due to a political deal, which is pretty messed up in his mind. It does end his military career, however. He quickly lands a cushy job doing minimal work for a defense contractor, but his personal life is not as good. His wife divorced him, he's suffering from PTSD, and he's seeing Cappan-human hybrids everywhere. Half the galaxy considers him a pariah, the other half a hero.

When someone breaks into the network of a rival company called Omicron, Butler's boss asks him to investigate so that their company can eliminate any vulnerability that might make it susceptible to the same thing. Butler uses his contacts to set up a meeting with an Omicron executive, who later calls him and says he's found something big. The contact is killed before Butler can get the information.

In part to battle his own demons, Butler pursues one of the Cappan hybrids he thinks he's been seeing and finally confronts them. He learns that not only has he not been hallucinating, but that a large number of Cappans escaped their home planet and perfected the hybrid process, eliminating the insanity side effect. Brought face-to-face with a Cappan leader, he learns that Omicron is trying to steal that technology for commercial gain. Butler teams up with the Cappans to try to put a stop to it.

He hatches a plan, along with a computer genius named Maria Ganos, to break into Omicron. Unfortunately, he's captured, relocated across the galaxy, and forced to collaborate with Omicron's mercenaries to extort from the Cappan refugees the final pieces of information that Omicron requires to exploit the technology. After they get what they need, they intend to nuke the settlement from orbit.

Following a battle on the surface, Butler kills the leader from Omicron and makes his escape back into orbit. He convinces the crew of the ship to let him target the missiles, as he's already got one genocide on his record. While planning the attack, he uses a subtle trick to minimize the damage to the Cappan colony, and the ship leaves, convinced that everyone is dead.

COLONYSIDE

Carl Butler has fully retired to the idyllic backwater of rural Ridia, enjoying his time gardening and generally not being shot at. That comes to an end when General Serata, also retired, shows up and asks him to do another job. While Butler remembers how Serata set him up in the past, the job itself is to find someone's missing daughter. Having lost a daughter himself in the past, Butler can't say no. That the client is a CEO named Drake Zentas, one of the richest men in the galaxy, is a drawback, but Butler reluctantly signs on anyway.

Butler, along with Mac, Ganos, and a captain named Fader, arrives at the mostly undeveloped colony in the jungle on the planet Eccasis, where he finds an understaffed military, an incompetent governor, and a corporation called Caliber running roughshod over both. When someone tries to blow him up, signs point to a protest group that is trying to save the planet and hates Butler for what he did back on Cappa. But he has no shortage of enemies.

Butler's chief suspect gets shipped off planet before he can question him, but he finds information that brings the circumstances of Zentas's daughter's disappearance into question. Initially, it had appeared that she was killed by the planet's alpha predators: large green apelike creatures called "hominiverts." But it could have been more sinister: Someone at Caliber has found a way to control the animals and drive them into a rage, causing them to kill.

As Butler works to get to the bottom of the mystery, a sting operation goes sideways and he's captured and taken to an underground facility. There, Caliber is scheming to have hominiverts overrun the entire colony, an excuse to allow Caliber to exterminate them (which is illegal, especially after Butler's "genocide" of the Cappans) and move on to full-scale mining operations. Caliber forces Butler into service, and he fights against the raging beasts using an army of killer drones before turning the tables on Caliber and stopping the hominivert attack.

Realizing what he's done, Zentas tries to execute Butler, but Butler escapes, subjecting himself to the hostile atmosphere of Eccasis in the process. Mac leads the cavalry to the rescue, and Butler exposes Caliber for their crimes.

CHAPTER 1

RETIREMENT IS GREAT. I say this because when you begin to contemplate it, there is no end to the line of people who want to tell you otherwise. *You'll be bored,* they'll say. *You'll wish you were still working so you'll have a purpose. So that you'll have people to talk to.*

Lies.

Bored? Please. There are an infinite number of entertainment options available, streaming to any number of possible devices, and more books than one could ever possibly read. So many books. There are endless places in the galaxy for travel, though being the recluse that I am, that thought isn't particularly appealing to me. And people? I can live without them. I've got Mac and a few other local friends, and that's all I need.

I don't know where the lies came from. Maybe it's a conspiracy among people who are still working to trick you into being as miserable as they are. Maybe it's the leftover propaganda of some long-dead capitalist who needed a workforce. But no matter. Not working beats working every day of the week.

I'd gotten pretty good at it.

It had been two years since I'd last been dragged into action, and I preferred to keep it that way, living back on my modest parcel of land on Ridia 2. The military never called again, and if they had, I wouldn't have answered. I didn't miss any of that stuff. I know I've said that before, but this time I meant it. Anything I possibly owed them, I'd paid in full multiple times over. I still talked to General Serata once in a while, but not about official things. We might chat about a show we both liked, or some sporting event, but never anything important. Neither of us wanted that. I had no illusions that the military had forgotten about me—they hadn't, and they wouldn't. Couldn't. I knew too much. I assumed they monitored everything about me that they could, which didn't bother me, as long as they did it from a distance.

Mac had a tougher time with his transition, though some of that might have been because he hadn't had as long to come to grips with it. His retirement came pretty suddenly, and I think he missed the life. Unlike me, he hadn't been looking forward to being done with the military. Still, he was finding ways to compensate. He enjoyed socializing more than I did, so he often hung out with a group of veterans who called Ridia 2 home—a lot of us settled on the out-of-the-way planet because the relatively low cost of living made a military pension go further.

But Mac spent most of his time at the gym/dojo that he ran with another guy. I worked out there twice a week, because when you're old like I am, you have to lift some weights or you waste away to nothing. Mac approved and made sure that I had a good routine. There are benefits to knowing the owner. Technically, he also worked for me, providing for my security needs. I didn't think I needed much. He disagreed, and I acquiesced. Either way, I liked having him around, and I happily covered his costs.

About that. The money. I'm not really allowed to talk about it—

nondisclosure agreements and all that—but let's just say that after my time on Eccasis, Caliber worked out an arrangement with the government to pay me for my troubles in order to avoid even more lawsuits than they were already facing. Which meant I got money.

A lot of money.

And given that I was pretty much set before it ever happened, well, now I had the kind of money where you do what you want and don't really think about it. For me, that meant large college funds for my grandkids, subscriptions to every streaming entertainment service I could find, and a nice garden in a backwater part of a backwater planet. What can I say? I'm pretty simple.

Speaking of Caliber, I'd like to tell you that Zentas paid for his crimes, but if I had money, he had *stupid* money, and the truly rich rarely suffer consequences. On the surface he took some hits. He pulled back from the public eye and put someone else in charge of the company, at least nominally. Most important, for me at least, he never fucked with Carl Butler again. I didn't for a minute think he'd forgiven me for messing up his plan, but as long as he stayed away from me, I'd be okay. And so would he.

Mostly I tried to stick to a routine, and Wednesday afternoon around four that routine involved meeting Mac at Moop's for drinks. Moop's was our local tavern, a sturdy log building that had a dumb name but good beer. I stole that line from Moop, the guy who ran the place along with his wife, Martha. There weren't many people there yet when I arrived—maybe three or four tables occupied—on account of it only being four, which goes back to that whole thing about not working being better than working. Mac was already waiting in our booth.

"You order yet?" I asked.

"Just water. Figured I'd wait for you, and hydration is important."

Which was also his way of saying, "You're buying."

I held up two fingers to Moop to order. He knew our routine too. It rarely changed. "Is Cassie coming?"

"Not today. She had a late client." Mac had been dating a dental hygienist—or, I should say, *the* dental hygienist; she worked at the only dentist office in our area. He'd been seeing her for four or five months. I told him it was a bad idea, because if he ever broke up with her, where was he going to get his teeth cleaned? He took it as a joke, which it was. Mostly. Seriously, the next dentist is over a hundred klicks away, and it's not like you'd want an ex putting a dental instrument in your mouth. "She did mention that she has a friend she wants you to meet."

"I told her I didn't want to be set up."

"We're in the middle of nowhere. How else are you going to meet somebody?"

"I'm not," I said. "That's kind of the point." Moop arrived with two beers, and I hoped that would put Mac off the subject, but no such luck.

"My therapist says people are important."

"That's why he's not *my* therapist," I countered.

"Come on. It'll be fun . . ." Mac's voice trailed off, and his eyes went to the door. Sure, he gave me crap about never dating, but he was good at his job. I didn't bother to turn around. He'd let me know if we had an issue. "Who's that kid?" He said it more to himself than to me, but it got my interest, and I turned to look. There was a girl with light brown skin in jeans and a dark green sweatshirt standing in the door, silhouetted by the outside light. She looked like she was maybe twelve or thirteen, but that was a guess. I'm not very experienced with kids, and those are awkward years.

"Never seen her before."

She'd definitely seen me, because when our eyes met, her face lit up and she headed our way. Mac didn't stand, but he slid closer to the outside of the booth. Apparently a young girl didn't rate the full treatment in his mind. Not yet.

She stopped a few steps short of us and eyed Mac warily before turning to me. She stood maybe one and a half meters tall with short brown hair cut in a bob, all pointy knees and elbows. I re-affirmed my age estimation. "You're Colonel Butler." I couldn't read her tone—there was no awe or hero worship in it. More flat and even. Matter-of-fact. She wasn't asking.

"I am," I said.

"Move along, kid. Pick somebody else to do your research assignment on." Mac saw it as his job to keep dangerous people away. That worked for me. His take on the girl was a fair assess-ment. She wouldn't be the first kid who wanted to interview me for a school project, and every so often a reporter would come around wanting to talk. And once, a reporter had tried to use a kid. I almost had to give that interview just for the ingenuity. Mac put the kibosh on it, said it would encourage others. As usual, he was right.

Confusion crossed her face. "I'm not doing research. I came from New Gaston because I need Colonel Butler to find some-body."

New Gaston? That was . . . far. I don't know how far. Far enough where you don't think about how far it is because it's too far to worry about. The other side of the planet. Nine, maybe ten thousand kilometers. I said I'm not experienced with kids, and I'm not, but a twelve-year-old that far from home on her own triggered even *my* protective instincts. "What's your name?"

"Eliza. Eliza Ramiro."

"Do your parents know you're here, Eliza?" I tried to keep my tone from sounding condescending, but I'm not sure how you do that with that question.

"My father is the one who is missing. I stay with my aunt."

She hadn't answered my question, but I could tell from the way she held herself when she said it that her aunt didn't know about the trip. But it's hard to push a girl who just told you that her father is missing. I mean, I'm an asshole, but not *that* much of one. But I did need to keep her talking until I got a better handle on her situation. "How did you get here from New Gaston?"

"I flew and then I took a bus to Eroka, which is as close as I could get to here. From there I hired a bot car."

"I meant how did you pay for it?" I said. "That had to cost a lot."

She smiled, clearly proud of herself. "I crowdfunded it."

"Crowdfunded?"

"That's right. I took donations for travel costs and the cost of hiring you to find my dad."

I wanted to tell her that I didn't actually do that kind of thing, but that wasn't the most important issue here. I had to address her desire to hire me before moving on to what I saw as the real problem: a young girl who had run away from home. But maybe I could find a compromise. "Would you be willing to call your aunt and tell her where you are?"

"I need to tell you about my father. Something has happened to him."

"I believe you. So I tell you what—if you'll call your aunt and tell her where you are, and let me talk to her, then I promise that I'll give you my full attention while you tell me about your father's disappearance. It's not like your aunt is going to come pick you up right away."

She considered it for several seconds, her face scrunched up as every emotion she felt flickered across it. "Deal."

"Good. Have you had anything to eat?"

"Not recently. I'm saving money for other expenses."

"Okay. Have a seat. Dinner is on me." Mac got out of his seat so that she could get in on his side, while I signaled Moop to bring Eliza a menu. Once we had that set, I gave her my device to call her aunt. After five minutes of getting the understandably agitated woman to calm down, I assured her that Eliza was safe and would remain that way, and when she didn't believe me, I got Martha, Moop's wife, to talk to her and also assure her of that. Eliza seemed indifferent to the conversation and was halfway through a burger and fries by the time we got around to discussing her real reason for being there.

"So. Tell me about your father."

"My dad's name is Jorge Ramiro. He works for Jacob Whiteman. Have you heard of him?"

"I haven't," I admitted.

"He's a famous archaeologist," she said, as if it was common knowledge. Maybe it was, and I was just behind on my *Archaeology Digest* subscription. "They were doing an exploratory dig on Taug."

"That's a moon, right? Orbiting Ridia Four?"

"Ridia Five," she corrected.

I never could keep all the moons around the two gas giants in our solar system straight. There were like forty of them, all told. "And that's where you think he disappeared?"

"That's where I *know* he disappeared."

"When was the last time you heard from him?"

"Eleven days ago."

Mac looked like he wanted to say something, so I nodded to him to go for it. I had no real ideas. "I don't mean to be a jerk here, but is there a chance he got busy and didn't message?"

Eliza turned to him and gave him a death glare. "Not *my* dad. He sends me a message *every day.*"

"He's never missed?" I couldn't help but flash back to all the times I hadn't messaged my kids when I'd been in the military. All the times I didn't message them *now*.

"Three times, all when he was on a ship between locations. But he always told me that the day before it happened."

"Do you have any idea what might have happened to him?" I asked. It seemed like the logical question, because *I* certainly didn't have any clue.

"That's what I want to hire *you* for." She said it like it made perfect sense, and in the eyes of a child, maybe it did. But contrary to my reputation, I didn't actually find people. Sure, there had been a couple of very high-profile events where I was supposed to. But both of those were military things—or at least military adjacent—and both of those people were dead. I'd killed one of them myself—I guess that counted as me finding them, though probably not the way that the people who sent me wanted. It's a long story. Regardless, I didn't exactly have a great track record, and I didn't even know where to start with a civilian case.

I also didn't know how to break it to her. She was sitting there, so earnest, so confident, sure that I could do this thing. But I couldn't *not* tell her. "I'm sorry, Eliza, but I really don't do that."

"But you *have* to. I can get more money if you need it."

I considered that, even though I didn't care about the money. As I said, I had plenty. She hadn't even mentioned an amount though, so her jumping to the idea that she needed more seemed flawed. But then, a photogenic kid with a missing dad would always get attention, and I wondered if we could translate that into something with the media that might help her. Because while I didn't find people, I *did* have a few contacts in the press. "Have you considered taking it to the net to see if someone knows anything?"

"I thought about it," she said. "But I didn't, because if somebody did something to him, they might come after me, too."

It was good thinking for a kid—for anyone, really—being safe with what she put out into the galaxy on social media, but at the same time, it was a bit paranoid, and a bit illogical since she'd released it into the world via the crowdfunding. I'm as big a conspiracy theorist as the next guy—I've seen enough wild stuff where I pretty much have to be—but she seemed a bit out there. Despite what she said to Mac, the most likely answer was that her father had just stopped messaging. Or he'd met someone and taken off. I try not to think the worst of people I don't know, but, well . . . they're people. And a lot of people are shitty. Even ones with resourceful daughters. "What about a private detective? Someone who does this kind of thing professionally?"

"You don't think I tried that first? You think the first thing I thought of was flying halfway around the planet in the hopes that a celebrity hero would find my dad for me?"

Actually, I *had* thought that. In my defense, I have no idea what goes on in the minds of twelve-year-olds. But her sarcasm was justified. "You couldn't find anybody?"

"Nobody would take the case. They didn't want to travel to the outer solar system."

"And you think I do?"

She hesitated at that—the first time I'd seen that in her since she'd arrived. That endeared her to me even more, because it showed that she could reevaluate things when presented with new information. There are plenty of adults who can't do that. But then resolve took over her face again, and it became clear that this girl wasn't going to accept no for an answer. She'd also already proven that she was the kind of person who would do something drastic. You know, like fly ten thousand klicks to hunt down a man she didn't know and try to convince him to find her missing dad. I didn't want her to do anything else rash until we could get her back to her family, so I decided I could at least poke around. It didn't *require* travel. If the guy was still alive, no matter where he was, he'd leave some kind of evidence. As it happened, I knew someone who could track that kind of thing.

"I tell you what," I said. "I'm not taking the job, and I'm not making you any promises."

She started to protest, but I held my hand up to forestall her.

"But," I continued, "I'll do a little initial looking and see what I can find. Okay? We can talk again tomorrow."

She considered it for a moment, and I thought she might cry

(which could have been me projecting—again, twelve-year-olds aren't exactly my forte), but she steeled herself and nodded. With that settled and her meal finished, I shuffled her off to Martha, who had offered to put her up in their guest room. Our town didn't have a hotel, and I certainly couldn't put her up at my place, if only because of how it would look for an old man to be taking in a young girl. I promised to talk to her the next day, figuring that would be enough of an incentive to keep her from running again while we organized her trip home.

With that done, I ordered another beer.

A man has to have his priorities straight.

CHAPTER 2

I GOT HOME FAIRLY late, but I had questions that I needed a computer genius to look into, and Ganos would be awake. She's a ridiculous night owl, plus it's an hour earlier where she is. She and her partner, Parker, had moved to Ridia about eighteen months prior, finally caving in to my insistent requests. She didn't have as many enemies as I did, and if you asked her, she'd have told you that she could take care of herself. I made it about me so that she could keep that illusion. With a computer, she was the baddest of the bad, but that wouldn't do much if someone with a gun physically showed up at her door. I sold it to her that I needed her nearby, just in case. I had exaggerated a bit, but at the same time, it *did* make me more secure, and it gave me an excuse to pay for their move without it seeming untoward.

I texted first, so when I called, she answered after one buzz. "What's up, sir?"

"Something weird came up today."

"Weird as in we need to pack and get out of town as quietly as possible, or . . ."

"Nothing like that," I assured her.

"You've said that before."

"Fair point. But no, this is about a little girl."

"Whoa, whoa, sir. I don't want to hear about—"

"Grow the fuck up, Ganos," I said, but I was laughing as I said it. "She apparently got crowdfunding to hire me to find her missing dad."

"Give me a second," she said. "Yep. Here it is. Nice. She raised forty thousand. You don't come cheap."

"I don't find missing persons for any price."

"Yet here you are on the comm with me, about to ask me to find one . . ."

"The girl ran away from home. I made a deal with her that I'd take a preliminary look in return for her going home to her aunt."

"No mom?"

"She didn't mention one. It didn't seem cool to ask."

I waited through a moment of dead air on the other end of the line. "Mom died two years ago. Ouch. Okay. So what's the plan?" asked Ganos.

"Dig around a bit and see what you can find. Odds are good that her dad disappeared the way that most dads do and there's nothing special about this situation."

"Wow, someone was hurt as a child."

"This isn't about me."

"Right. He could have met someone, and suddenly, it became convenient not to have a kid."

"I hope not, but yeah. Something like that. See if you can find him. Send me a bill for your time."

"This one's on me."

"Yeah?" Something in her voice tipped me to the fact that there was more to that than she was saying, but I didn't want to press.

"Let's just say that I knew a dad like that once."

Someone had hurt her, too. It made me angry, but I didn't know what to say. I hadn't exactly been father of the year to my own kids when they were younger. I'd never be able to make it up to my daughter, who had died in military service on Cappa. I was still trying to make it up to my son and his kids. But I didn't want to compare that with whatever lay in Ganos's past. There were all kinds of ways to screw up as a parent, each unique in its own horrible way. All I said was "Thanks."

"Sure thing. You want me to call you with what I find?"

"Can you send me a file? I'm going to bed, and I'll look at it in the morning."

She snickered. "You're old."

"I really am."

—

I was lost in a building. I didn't know what building, only that it had that vague quality to it that screamed, *I am a military building!* I was behind or late for something, and I didn't know how to fix it. I was supposed to be processing out of the military today, but I didn't have any of the prerequisites completed. I hadn't turned in my gear or even had it cleaned. But I was a colonel, and I'd been called back in after retiring, so maybe they'd cut me a break. Because bureaucracies are always great at making exceptions for things.

I passed multiple offices with soldiers lined up down the wall outside each door, and finally one of them pointed me to the right place. The door was closed, so I knocked before opening it and peeked inside.

"Sorry I can't stand to greet you," said a woman with a thin, pale face and dark hair seated behind a government-issued desk. I didn't know if she meant she physically couldn't stand at all, or if something was preventing her at the moment, and it seemed like the most absurd thought to have right then. Something was off, and I didn't know what. I'm not good in these kinds of situations . . .

I forced myself awake.

My clock said 0445.

I hadn't dreamt like that in a while, and while I found it interesting that my stress dreams had gone from combat things to administrative, I still wasn't happy about it. I'd learned how to push myself out of them a lot of the time now—to force myself to wake—but they still left me disconcerted. I needed more rest, but I didn't want to go back to sleep because I'd dream again, so I swung my feet to the floor, hesitating at a slight twinge from my robot foot that thankfully passed, and sat on the edge of my bed for a bit, somewhere in that state that might be sleeping, might not, but you can never really tell on your own.

After a time, I got up and made coffee before checking my security system to see if anything happened in the night. Assured by the AI that ran it—I called him Todd now for some reason that I've forgotten—that all was well, I fired up my terminal to see what Ganos had sent me. Sure enough, I had a message from her. Not that I ever suspected I wouldn't, but her efficiency always impressed me.

Sir,

So . . . this guy is gone. Like gone gone. No trace. This is no deadbeat dad situation. I checked bank transactions, credit records, travel out of any space-

*port remotely near Ridia 5. Nothing. And before you
ask if this is legal or not, let me tell you what I always
tell you:*

Stop asking questions you don't want the answer to.

*Bottom line, there are only three possibilities with
this guy. Either he's dead, he's incapacitated, or he got
a pro-level change of identity. Which got me thinking,
so I checked. He didn't get a pro-level change of identity. I *really* can't tell you about that one. Just trust
me. I know some stuff.*

I *did* trust her. If Ganos said the man was dead or incapacitated,
there was a really good chance he was dead or incapacitated. She
had contacts in her world well beyond anything I had, and I had
a standing policy: When you bring in an expert who knows more
than you, believe them when they tell you something. Even if
he somehow *wasn't* dead, the fact that he *looked* dead meant
something.

Her message continued:

*I found one weird thing, and it was in his public
social media of all places. He didn't post regularly,
but I found enough there in the past to establish a
pattern of life. And then it stopped, except for one
post that showed up probably four or five days after
he disappeared that might as well have screamed
"This is a fake post that shows that I'm alive." It was
deleted four hours and forty-two minutes after it*

posted. Yes, I found the deleted post. Nothing is ever really gone on the net.

I love how she knows what my questions are going to be and answers them before I even ask.

Anyway, I'll leave it to you to figure out what that means. But it sure does look sketchy. I'll pack my bags for Ridia 5.

—Ganos

I laughed at her joke. We weren't going to Ridia 5, despite the oddities that she'd uncovered. If he was dead and there was no report, that *was* suspicious but not unheard of. That moon mostly hosted mining operations and had a small population. I'd been to places like that, and the reporting wasn't always perfect. Sometimes people died and nobody knew, or it didn't get into the system. At the same time, I couldn't help but think about the previous times I'd seen things like this and how some of those had turned out. The difference was, this one wasn't associated with me. My only connection to it was through the girl, and even with my biggest tinfoil hat on I couldn't imagine her being part of a conspiracy against me.

While I wasn't going to Ridia 5, it intrigued me enough to do some research on my own. And by *on my own* I meant involving another someone else. I didn't have anything close to Ganos's skills with a computer, but even as detached as I'd become, I still knew some people. I decided to reach out to General Serata. Yes, he and I didn't talk about business things anymore, but I could ask him for a favor. He owed me that. After all, he did set me up to commit genocide that one time. And he dragged me into a plot to have me do it again that almost got me killed. On second thought, maybe I *shouldn't* have reached out to him. But it was easy, and he'd get me an answer faster than any other way I had.

Hopefully it would go smoother than things involving him had in the past. A guy can dream.

> *Sir,*
>
> *How are things? I'll cut to the chase. I need a favor. Looking into something for someone here on Ridia 2. There was a man—Jorge Ramiro—working on an archaeology project on the moon Taug, which orbits Ridia 5. We've dug into it and the guy has disappeared. I've checked all of the things you'd expect, and bottom line, I think he's dead. Except that there's no record of it. Wondering if maybe that's an oversight. Could you run it through channels out to Ridia 5 and see if you can find anything out?*
>
> *Thanks,*
> *Carl*

I didn't have to spell things out for him. He'd trust that I wouldn't ask if I hadn't done the background work the same way I trusted Ganos. But I didn't expect a response that morning. It was too early to do anything else, so I did some work looking into the archaeologist, Jacob Whiteman. It wasn't a hard search.

As Eliza had said, he was famous. Not only archaeologist famous but known to some in the general public as well. I didn't know how many archaeologists—or academics of any kind—could say that. Probably just the one. But this guy had spreads in mainstream news as well as style magazines. One article title caught my attention: "Making Archaeology Look Good." Which was a pretty good headline, since it was mostly a photo spread of the admittedly good-looking Dr. Whiteman doing various things that appeared like they might have something to do with archaeology but would probably make other archaeologists laugh. I wondered about what happens when a bunch of them get together. You know they have inside jokes. And I bet they hate this dude.

Could I get myself invited to an archaeologist party and find information that way? No. That was ridiculous and went to show that I really *wasn't* cut out for this kind of thing. Did archaeologists even have parties? I kept searching, and one thing that stood out was that I couldn't find anything recent about him. A couple of sources mentioned him, so he might still be out there, but they were notably academic and might have been in the works for years. None of them were specifically *about* him, and none tied him to a date. There had been nothing of him in the mainstream media for more than five months. Which got me thinking. If Ramiro worked for Whiteman, could they both have disappeared? Maybe some sort of archaeology accident. I didn't know what that would entail, but in my head I pictured a cave-in. I was probably romanticizing things. But if they'd both gone missing, that would make the likelihood of a simple breakdown in reporting a lot less likely. Since I'd already asked Serata to look into that, I'd get an answer one way or another.

But now I was curious.

Ganos wasn't up yet and wouldn't be for several hours, so I dashed off a note asking her to run the same sort of analysis on Whiteman that she had on Ramiro. It never hurt to check the simplest things first. And then I started digging deeper on my own.

What I found made me stop and stare at the monitor. I'd given up looking into the people and left that to my pro to handle, instead looking for information about the moon itself. Two primary mining operations operated there run by two different consortiums: Caliber and Omicron.

Well . . . shit.

I'm sure that those two massive corporations had many things in common, but the one that felt biggest in my mind was that they had both tried to kill me on various occasions. It was probably a coincidence.

Except I don't believe in coincidences.

Now I was *very* curious.

CHAPTER 3

MAC'S GYM WAS a flat-roofed building tacked on to the end of a row of storefronts headed by a chain grocery seller, and from the outside it looked more like a place where you'd go to get your taxes done than a multifaceted fitness/self-defense studio. With the tinted windows, it didn't look like a gym at all except for the white sign with red letters that said, simply enough, "Mac's Gym." I'd mentioned the marketing flaws to Mac on more than one occasion, but he just shrugged and said, "The people who want to find it will find it. The people who don't weren't serious anyway." As a business strategy, it left a little to be desired, but it fit the man who ran it.

I'm not sure if he turned a profit or not. I guess I should have cared, given that I was a silent partner in the venture, but I had silly money. Inside, a few people lifted weights in the back and a few more used the cardio machines at the front left, the rhythmic slapping of feet against treadmills providing the soundtrack for the place. I nodded to Sandra, a short, machine-tanned woman who showed off her jacked arms in a one-size-too-small tank top as she worked the front desk, and I continued farther inside to the mats where I found Mac. That he was grappling with a student—or maybe a customer—didn't surprise me. That he seemed to be losing . . . that got my attention.

Mac was on his back and barely holding half guard as a dark-skinned, muscular woman on top of him pressed at his knee in an attempt to pass. A few seconds later, she escaped his legs and gained side control. A few seconds more and she drove an elbow toward Mac's face that he couldn't block, pulling the blow back just before it reached his forehead.

"Shit!" said Mac. "Good fight."

The woman popped to her feet and offered Mac a hand up, which he took. She had broad shoulders and stood a couple of centimeters taller than Mac. "I'm a little rusty."

"Didn't look that way to me," I said, grinning at Mac.

"You want to take a run at her?" he asked.

"I don't want to take a run at *you,* and you just lost. So no, I do not." Say what you want about me, but I know my limitations. Having my ass handed to me wasn't on my list of things to do today.

"That's why you're the brains of the operation. This is Sergeant First Class retired Angela Barnes. Back in the day she was the runner-up in her weight class—what was it again?"

"Seventy kilos back then," said Barnes. "I couldn't make that weight now."

"Runner-up in the all-military MMA tournament at seventy kilos."

"Impressive." I held out my hand. "Carl Butler."

She snorted, taking my hand in a firm grip. "I know who you are, sir."

"Right. I forget about that sometimes. What brings you to our corner of Ridia?"

"Mac wanted to talk to me about taking a job."

I chuckled and gestured to the mat. "So this was an interview?"

"Of a sorts," said Mac. "I had to make sure she could still go."

"Are you going to teach MMA here at the gym?" I asked.

Barnes glanced to Mac, who shook his head slightly. I don't know if they thought they were being subtle, but something was obviously up, and I was being intentionally excluded. "Spit it out," I said.

Mac sighed. "I'm hiring her to work security for our team when we go to Ridia Five's moon."

I was genuinely confused. "But we're not going to Ridia Five."

Mac smirked. "Sure, sir. We'll call this a contingency hire then." He looked to Barnes and casually waved it off, letting her know that she still had a job offer. He didn't even try to hide it.

"You think your read is that good?"

"I saw the way you looked at that girl, sir. And Ganos messaged me."

"That traitor," I muttered. "If we go—and I'm *not* saying that we are—you think we'll really need another security person?"

"You think we won't? I've got two more people coming in this afternoon. Different specialties."

I gave him a look.

Mac met it, not backing down even a little. "Answer me this: When was the last time someone *didn't* try to kill you?"

I had to admit, he had a fair point. I turned to Barnes. "You heard him. I'm pretty much a walking target. You sure you want in on this?"

"Yes, sir. I could use the money. You know how it is. Debts."

"Yeah, I get it." I turned to Mac. "This is going to cost more than the forty thousand crowdfunding, isn't it?"

"Absolutely, but it's not the people that are going to break the bank. It's the chartered transportation."

"Charter?"

"Yes, sir. Unless you think we're going to put all our toys on a commercial ship and take fifteen days to get there."

Another good point. Mac had clearly thought about this more than me. "Fine. Do the preliminary work, but don't sign any contracts for the transportation."

"Right—seeing as we're not actually going."

"We're *not* actually going."

"Roger," said Mac, keeping his doubt out of his voice this time even though he still didn't believe me.

"You can hire Barnes for a stint. She can always work here at the gym."

"I can definitely do that," she said. "As long as it's not too hard on Mac's ego."

Mac laughed. "I guess you're hired, then. We'll talk pay and sign some nondisclosure stuff in a bit."

Barnes grinned. "Nondisclosure? What goes on in this gym?"

My device buzzed. A message from Serata. I checked it, because maybe we could clear this up right here.

Checked the official logs on the moon. No record of Ramiro's death. No record of him at all. Officially, he was never there. Hope that helps. Not sure how to follow up.

It didn't help and it did. It absolutely didn't provide any answers. But sometimes knowing what you *didn't* know was as important as knowing what you *did*.

Shit. Maybe we *were* going. Mac must have been able to read it in my face, because he laughed.

—

I got my workout in because I'd made the trip to the gym, and once you do that, you might as well, and I waited until I got back home before I checked what Ganos sent me. Nothing would have surprised me, which I shouldn't say, given how many things in my life *had* at some point, but we'd reached a spot where I was prepared for almost anything. If she told me that she found multiple Whiteman clones working for both Caliber and Omicron, I'd probably have shrugged it off. Her real report was much easier to accept: She'd found Dr. Whiteman alive, and as of two days ago, he was on Taug. He'd charged a purchase three days ago and made an off-moon call from his personal device two days ago.

The real takeaways from her message were: one, never mess with Ganos, because she knows everything, and two, be really suspicious of any electronic device you use. But those things I already knew. I asked her if she could hide the fact that the girl had raised funds to hire an investigator, but, as I suspected, that was out there and she couldn't do much about it. I hadn't been named in that, but it did let any potential bad actors know that *someone* might be looking into the situation.

Bad actors. Listen to me. I was already seeing shadows, already trying to protect myself.

But I couldn't rule it out. The crowdfunding could possibly account for Ramiro having been scrubbed from the records. If somebody saw that, maybe they initiated a cover-up. Maybe he'd never actually been on Taug, and somehow he'd avoided Ganos's search. Maybe it had been a massive clerical oversight. But both of those things seemed less likely than him having been there. Besides, if he *hadn't* been there, then that opened up other questions. I didn't *want* to track down a dad who was avoiding his daughter, but him being a deadbeat would at least be better than him being dead.

Maybe.

But no matter how I looked at it, all paths seemed to lead to Taug. Or maybe Mac was right, and I was just subconsciously steering myself that way. I like to think I'm self-aware, but can you ever really know? The facts were the facts though. You could scrub someone from the system—though not easily—but not from people's memories on-site. If Ramiro had been there, someone would have seen him. Also, Dr. Whiteman was there, and I couldn't think of a better place to start searching for Ramiro than asking the good doctor some questions, which would work best in person. Even if he would take a video call, the delay measured in minutes, not seconds, which made things difficult. Especially because there was no substitute for looking someone in the eye when you asked them hard questions. But one doesn't simply show up on a moon like Taug. It required access, and that meant I needed another favor from Serata.

And that presented a new problem.

When I'd only needed information, I had nothing to lose. He

could get that at no cost, and so I wasn't incurring any debt. Access for me and my team would mean calling in favors on his part, and that meant he'd owe them in return. More important, it meant that I'd owe him, and that wasn't a spot I wanted to be in again. But here we were. It was that or go tell a little girl with a big heart that nobody knew what happened to her dad.

It wasn't really a choice at all.

I DID HAVE to talk to Eliza before we set out in order to share the reality of the situation with her and put a cap on her expectations. We probably wouldn't find anything meaningful, and she needed to know that. People want to have hope, no matter how misplaced it is, and I think that's even more so in children. Life hasn't let them down as many times yet. Despite that, I had to try to make her see. It was the only responsible thing to do. In retrospect, I shouldn't have had the talk on the way to the airport/spaceport. We both *did* need to travel that way, but it was a long drive, and sitting in the back seat with her, I couldn't escape once I shared the difficult truth with her. At least I could make sure she got onto a flight home.

"I want to be really clear about what we're likely to find," I said.

"I understand," said Eliza. But did she? Did any of us?

So I had to make it bluntly and painfully clear. "We found no signs of him in our initial search."

She hesitated. "But you're going out there to find him."

"We're going out there. We're not likely to find him."

"But there's a chance."

"There's always a chance. However, in this case, it's not a very good chance. I'm so sorry. But I don't want to give you false hope." I waited a moment for her to respond. She didn't, so I added, "He's most likely dead."

I was prepared for her to cry. To yell at me and tell me I was wrong. To scream, to go catatonic, to go into self-denial. Really anything except for what actually happened. A dozen looks passed across her countenance in as many seconds, but then her face grew hard, and she aged twenty years. The girl disappeared, replaced by the look and demeanor of a mature woman. "If he's dead, it's better to know than to wonder." She said it so flatly, with such an intense look on her face, that I couldn't help but believe her.

I nodded. "We'll find out what we can."

She went silent for a long time. Several minutes. I thought maybe she'd said everything she had to say, and we'd ride the rest of the way in uncomfortable silence. Finally she spoke. "If you find out that something happened to him . . . if someone is responsible . . . I want them to pay."

I don't know how she made that leap, from her father likely being dead to foul play. I had no idea what was going on in that little head, and I didn't know enough about such things to try to draw it out. She'd need a therapist for that. All I could do was nod and say, "Okay."

"Promise me," she said.

Like a fool, I promised.

CHAPTER 4

THE FLIGHT TO Ridia 5H—also known as Taug—was reasonably pleasant. Because if you're going to charter a flight, you might as well charter a good one. That meant, unlike with a military flight, we didn't have to sleep in orange goo. We also had an onboard chef who produced restaurant-quality meals. It took six days at a constant 1g acceleration, with about five minutes at the halfway point where we had to strap down for the ship to flip and start burning to slow us down.

It gave me plenty of time to meet the team Mac had assembled and go through our gear, which was, like the ship, a little over the top. We had nine footlocker-sized containers full of gear, and that didn't count our personal bags, but did include spacesuits, armor, electronics of multiple types, and more than a few weapons. I think Mac thought we had some sort of diplomatic immunity or something, which we probably didn't, though I didn't know how much they'd check us. I didn't see any need for the stuff on a moon that had about seventeen thousand total residents at last count, but then, you never did see the need until it smacked you in the side of the head, and I had agreed with Mac's opinion that it was better to have it and not need it than the opposite.

There were six of us. Along with Mac, Ganos, and Barnes, whom

I'd met briefly at the gym, we'd acquired Alanson and Castellano. I designated the three newbies as "the ABCs." As one does. Alanson was an older guy—and by older, I mean about my age—and the only member of the team who hadn't served in the military. He'd been a contractor specializing in drones and surveillance equipment, and Mac assured me he'd been around enough people who had been there and done things to know the job. Castellano was the baby—a year or two younger than Ganos—and had recently come to Ridia after serving two tours. He was our sniper. I don't think I can reiterate enough that we were overprepared. If we needed a sniper, things had gone well past shit to whatever the next level beyond shit was. I probably would have pushed back on Mac about that, but C had worked for a guy who knew Mac, and Mac wanted to help him out with some good-paying work, so I let it go. If nothing else, C was young, and he could carry things.

We spent the trip exercising, swapping stories over good whiskey, and playing a lot of cards. Personally, I did more of the latter two than the first one, even though I lost a good bit to B, who could read people at a card table way better than she had any right to.

—

As we came into the landing facility on Taug, the gas giant Ridia 5 loomed massive in our view, all red and yellow and gray, and we took turns cycling up to the pilot's compartment to see it firsthand. The moon itself was less exciting, made up mostly of grays and tans and browns, rocky and forbidding. Even the small sea had a grayish hue to it. Taug had a thin and somewhat breathable atmosphere that was thick enough to filter out some of the radiation that reflected from the planet it orbited, and from research I knew the gravity to be about 0.16 standard, which would make for an interesting and lightweight stay.

The spaceport was on the surface since the low escape velocity from the moon didn't require ships to stay in orbit, but landing and launch windows relied on the specifics of the orbit around the gas giant and its massive gravity field. It was a good thing that people smarter than me had all that figured out. I focused more on the social dynamics. Civilians managed the landing facility, but I expected the military exerted some influence, considering the proximity of their installation on the moon. Given the favors that Serata had called in to get us access, they'd definitely be expecting us, but what I didn't know and Serata hadn't told me was what kind of reception to expect.

Of course I'd done my homework. The military commander on the moon was a lieutenant colonel named Parnavic, a combat vet with an average record. He wasn't a star, but was an above-average performer, which fitted him for this mid-tier command. It wasn't an important spot but being his own boss without direct oversight carried a bit of cachet with it. His rank put us in an odd spot, given that I'd been a colonel and thus had outranked him, but I'd also been retired for some time. That gave him a lot of leeway in how he wanted to treat me. He could do anything from giving me full honors to treating me purely like a civilian and the annoyance that I was sure to be. Either way, he probably wouldn't be happy to see me. The reception to my landing might tell me just how unhappy he was.

After landing on Taug's surface, we soon descended into darkness as an elevator took our ship into the underground facility. Some domed structures dotted the surface, clustered mostly in this one area with others extending out toward the sea, about twenty klicks away, but most of the actual business of the moon colony happened underground. There had been a lot of natural passages from the start, which settlers had expanded and stabilized throughout the seventy or so years that people had been actively mining the rock.

After what seemed like a long time, the door finally opened with a hiss, and I waited inside at Mac's insistence while he and Barnes disembarked down a gently sloped ramp. I don't know what risk he assessed in a mostly empty hangar bay, but I found it easier to acquiesce than fight about it.

A few civilians moved throughout the bay, mostly tending to the ship, but they ignored our presence beyond their duties, and a uniformed soldier—a sergeant—was the only one specifically waiting to meet us. Mac and Barnes approached her, and the three of them chatted for a couple of minutes before Mac finally signaled for the rest of us to disembark. The sergeant departed before I reached her, and Mac met me at the base of the ramp.

"What was that about?" I asked.

Mac grinned as he responded. "Not much. She gave us directions to where we can rent a cart for our equipment and on how to reach the hotel." He flicked a link to a facility map to me, which I had already but accepted in case they had updated it. Taug had exactly one hotel for visitors, conveniently located near the spaceport. Businesses based here and the military managed their own facilities.

"So why are you smiling?"

"Just something that Sergeant Voss told us about her commander."

"What's that?"

"He did his research on you before we arrived—which, of course he did—trying to figure out if he should meet you himself, or what. You know, standard officer nonsense."

"Sure," I said, not taking offense, since he didn't mean any.

"Apparently the book on you is that you don't want any undue attention, so he decided to send someone out to act as our point of contact and tell us how to get settled."

I frowned. That seemed . . . kind of normal. "I don't get it. What's funny?"

"Oh," said Mac. "Just that the sergeant probably wasn't supposed to *tell* us that. Kind of ruins the point of it, don't you think?"

I chuckled. Okay. Sure. The commander had forgotten the basic rule of non-coms. They didn't give a shit about officer politics. "Does this mean we're free to do what we want?"

"It seems so. She gave us her contact info and a couple others', and we can message when you want to visit the base. She said the commander will make time for you at your convenience, and I got the impression that she meant it."

"Good to know." And it was—I came to find a missing person, not start a pissing contest. If that's how Parnavic felt, too, all the better. "Let's get a cart, get to the hotel, and get settled. Ganos, you need anything?"

"The hotel's info says you can pay for an upgraded net connection. I'll test that and see what it'll do. Once I know that, we can figure out if it's enough or if we need to set up our own system to get me the bandwidth I want."

"Roger. Getting her what she needs is priority one," I told Mac. Three of the cases of equipment were hers, and she'd assured me she had prepared for any configuration she might find here, but that she wouldn't know for sure what she could do until she saw it herself.

The "hotel" was not a freestanding facility—I hadn't seen any of those in the underground complex—but a set of five corridors that branched off a central administrative area where we checked in. It felt more like being on a space station than on a planet, except that space stations had more gravity. Here I had to fight to keep from bouncing as I walked, which was doubly important because of the low ceiling. Someone had definitely knocked themselves out by accident somewhere in the history of the place, but there wasn't much to be done about it. Physics, and all that.

We had six rooms in a block, three on either side of the corridor, and Mac switched us around from what had been assigned, probably to hide my actual location but also to put Ganos and me in the center with a security person on either side of each of us. We all had identical rooms, so it didn't matter beyond letting me know that they weren't treating me like a VIP here. But the sergeant who had greeted us was right: I kind of liked it. There might be times to throw my weight around, but only when it got us something we actually needed. This wasn't one of them.

The civilian hotel room would have been at home in any military facility with its utilitarian layout featuring a bunk, a desk, a wall locker, and a small latrine with a shower. The lack of metering on the water said a lot about the infrastructure and was the most interesting part about the place.

Mac huddled with the team in the corridor, so I used the time to unpack and to reach out to the commander for a meeting. Nothing said I had to check in with the military command first, but given my connections, they seemed the most likely to be accommodating. That wasn't a very high bar, given how little I expected from Caliber and Omicron. Step two would be to track down Dr. Whiteman and to look for other evidence that Ramiro had been here. Easy stuff, but first things first.

GETTING A MEETING with Parnavic turned out to be even easier than I thought, and twenty minutes later I headed out with Barnes walking with me. I'd tried to insist that I didn't need an escort, but Mac wouldn't have it.

"You ever serve on something as small as this place?" I asked her, as we made our way through a maze of corridors.

She looked up from the map on her device that showed us how to get to our destination. "No, sir. Nothing like this. I was mostly a station rat. I worked supply, but once I got on the MMA track, they kept me in places where I could train. That usually meant big depots."

"That makes sense," I said. That she admitted freely that she'd avoided combat zones scored a point with me. A lot of soldiers who hadn't seen major action lied about it or at least tried to draw attention away from how they served. But there was no shame. Everyone had a job, and all of us went where we were told.

A short major with a round face, pale skin, and a big smile waited at the entrance to battalion headquarters. "Colonel Butler, it's good to have you," she said. "I'm Major Christine Xavier, the XO here. If you'll come with me, Colonel Parnavic is finishing up a call in his office."

"Good to meet you, Xavier. This is Barnes."

"Nice to meet you . . . Ms.? Sergeant?" Xavier struggled without losing her smile.

"Barnes is fine," said Barnes, without smiling in return. If she was trying to play a stereotypical heavy, she was absolutely nailing it.

For my part, I wanted to assess the unit's reaction to my being there to get a feel for where I stood, and Xavier's meeting me didn't tell me much. Parnavic hadn't met me at the door himself, which could indicate a power move to show that I didn't matter. But he'd sent his XO, which is what he would have done if he was trying to show me respect but was legitimately tied up. There's a small chance that I was overthinking things. What really hit me, though, was that I'd been out of touch with the military for too long. So much so that my palms were sweating, and my heart beat hard in my chest. That was new. I'd faced down all kinds of the worst stuff in my career, and here I stood, nervous going to meet a battalion-level commander. I hoped this wasn't a sign of things to come—that I just needed to get back on the horse and I'd fall into stride.

The headquarters itself mimicked the design of the rest of the base except with more polish on the floors and more pictures on the walls. Put a military unit anywhere and they'd figure out how to make it look like every other one in the galaxy. It consisted of two long, parallel corridors with a short connector that, if I could have seen it from above, would have made it look like a capital *H* with the commander's office in the hallway farthest from the main entrance at the top corner.

A giant, dark-skinned man blocked the way to our destination— the unit's sergeant major—and he stepped forward, big hand outstretched to me. "Colonel Butler. Sergeant Major Davenport. You don't remember me, but we served together on Falania. That was . . . shit, what, twenty years ago? Damn, I'm old."

I had him by at least a decade and he looked more than fit, but he meant well. And when I thought about it, he was right, that I didn't remember him. I'd definitely been on Falania—that I wouldn't forget—but I'd been so many places, and met so many people. Hopefully he had good memories of that time. "We're both old, Sergeant Major. One of us more than the other. It's good to see you again."

Davenport sized up Barnes with the practiced glance of a senior non-com. She wore civilian clothes, which meant no name tag, but there was no mistaking her bearing. "You can wait in my office while your boss meets with mine, Sergeant . . ."

"Barnes," said Barnes.

"It's right across the hall, and I promise we won't let anything happen to the good colonel here while he's under our roof."

Barnes looked at me and I gave a small shrug. When a sergeant major says you can wait in his office, you wait in his office. It's not really a suggestion. The two of them disappeared, and the XO brought me to the commander's closed door and knocked.

"Come," he called from behind the door.

"Sir, Colonel Butler's here to see you."

By the time I got through the door, Parnavic was up and around his desk to meet me, hand outstretched. He was tall, with dark skin, a swimmer's build, and a firm grip. "Good to meet you, sir. Justin Parnavic."

"Good to meet you too, Parnavic. Please call me Carl."

"Sure thing, Carl." That would make him uncomfortable—it makes everyone uncomfortable when someone senior does it—but Parnavic didn't let it show. "Call me Justin. Can I get you some coffee?"

"Coffee would be great, thanks."

"Feel free to sit," he said, leaving it to me to choose my spot. His small office held a desk, a sofa, and a meeting table with six chairs crowded around it, but he had his own coffeemaker on a side table behind his desk, as if he always wanted it close at hand. I decided on the table for no reason other than that I didn't feel like sitting on the sofa. After he got two cups of coffee, he joined me, taking the seat directly across the table. He knew how I took my coffee without asking, meaning he'd definitely prepared for this.

"So, Carl. What can I do for you?"

"I'm looking for someone."

"That much I've heard."

I took a tiny sip of my coffee, which was still a bit too hot to drink. "The last place we've got any record of him is here on Taug."

"Yeah. I didn't know about that initially but looked into it later."

"When you found out I was coming," I said, so he wouldn't have to.

He nodded. "There's no record of him being here, so I'm curious why you think he was. Obviously you wouldn't be here if you didn't have a reason."

"I do," I said. I liked Parnavic already. There was a familiarity to talking with a senior officer where you could both assume that the other person had a basic level of competence and had done their job. But I didn't like him so much that I wanted to tell him everything yet. I also didn't want to insult him, so it was a fine balance. "How deep did you dig into it?"

"We get arrival information routinely, but we don't normally monitor individuals. When we learned of your interest, we checked those rosters and didn't find Ramiro, so I had my XO pull the manifests for every ship that has entered the port. The most likely case is that he was never here. But if he *was* here, the second most likely would be an error between the port and us."

"And that's clean too," I said, taking his point.

"It is. Why are you sure he was here?" It was a fair question, and the one I'd put off the first time with my own question. And I still wasn't going to answer it.

"You'll have to take my word that I've got a good reason for that belief, and it's more than 'a kid really believes it.'" I couldn't come right out and tell him that Ganos had found evidence without bringing her methods into question.

"I understand." Parnavic took a sip of his coffee. I wasn't sure he *did* understand. I wouldn't have if our positions were reversed. I'd have been pissed at the lack of information. But he was too much of a pro to say anything. "So where do we go from here?"

"I'd love to have one of my people take a look at your system to see if she can find evidence of tampering."

Parnavic chuckled. "Ganos?" Of course he knew about her . . . and her capabilities. "I don't think I can do that. To be perfectly frank, I can admit that I wasn't super excited about you coming. Who would be?"

"Right," I said. "I get that."

"When I found out *she* was on the manifest? That's when I actually got worried."

Smart man. "I had to ask. How about allowing her to talk to your network people? Ask a few questions about what they've checked and not checked, maybe point them in some directions they haven't thought of."

Parnavic considered it the way someone might consider a live snake. As if somehow her even walking in his headquarters might be dangerous—which, it might be. Who really knew what she was capable of or what might give her a leg up. My asking put him in a tough spot, and I respected that. For one thing, if Ganos pointed them at something they hadn't checked and they then found it, it could bring into question Parnavic's own work. In fact, it somewhat helped his situation if we didn't find Ramiro at all, since if we did, it would probably trigger a formal investigation. I was about to assure him that I'd do my best to keep everything quiet when he said, "Sure, we can set that up. Maybe my people will learn something."

I nodded, my estimation of the man rising with each passing minute. I'd still do what I could to not make him look bad if anything came up, even though I hadn't had to say it out loud. "Thanks. I appreciate that."

"What else can I do for you?"

"Do you have access to security cameras on the moon?"

"Public areas, sure. Nothing inside of corporate-owned spaces of course."

"The port?" I asked.

"Probably. I haven't checked. If we don't have them, I'm sure we could requisition them."

I hesitated. My next question might question his competence, which I didn't want to do. But I had to ask. "I'd have thought that might have been the next logical step. Run the videos through an AI, see if Ramiro turned up."

"Would have done that if I had the resources. They don't exactly give me a surplus of computing power out here. What you're asking is no small task, especially not having a date to cross-reference the inquiry to. We'd have to check every feed forever." He was fishing for information with that one, wanting me to share what I knew about dates.

"I think we can safely tie it to a smaller window. Maybe three weeks."

"Dozens of cameras. That's still a ton of data. Unless you know what ship he traveled on . . . Do you have a record of his departure?" His voice went up with that, hopeful.

I shook my head. Ganos had checked. "No, we looked. There's no record of him even getting on a ship. Which is another reason this whole thing is off. He had to have gone *somewhere,* even if it wasn't here."

"If you want the camera data, we can get it for you."

"Yeah. We'll give it a try."

He made a note. "We'll make that happen. What else?"

"It's a long shot, but do you have any way to get to Dr. Whiteman?"

Parnavic shook his head. "I've heard of him, of course. But he's got nothing to do with us and we don't run in the same circles. Sorry."

"It was worth a try. Okay, well I guess the meeting with your net techs and the camera data is it then. Is there anything I can do for *you*?"

"Try not to blow up the moon?" He didn't smile, so I couldn't tell if he meant it as a joke or not.

"No promises," I said.

BACK AT OUR rooms, Mac had been at work while I visited with Parnavic. I didn't have an assistant for the mission, so he'd taken some of that on himself and wanted to go over notes with me and Barnes. "I tried to get you a meeting with Whiteman," he said.

"How'd you do that?"

"Looked him up in the directory and called him."

"Huh. That's convenient," I said.

"Not really. Whoever answered the line said he was out on a dig."

"Bad timing."

Mac shook his head. "Nope. It's bullshit. I checked."

"Yeah?"

"The site they've been working at went dark about two days ago. It'll stay on the dark side of the moon for about fifteen days, and nobody plans an expedition during that time."

"They couldn't bring lights?"

"They could. It's been done. But as a matter of habit, they haven't. I think it's more about power generation than anything else, as they mostly use collectors that pick up reflected radiation from the planet."

"Outer planets are weird like that," I agreed. At this distance, the sun didn't really provide light, though some did reflect from the gas giant, leaving the "bright" side of the moon in perpetual twilight and the dark side in night. "If we give Whiteman the benefit of the doubt, he might have someone screening his calls to avoid media and stuff."

"Or he's dodging us," said Mac.

"That's a bit paranoid."

"Is it? We'll see." He smirked. "I decided that to find out, I'd go over there and beat his door down until he agreed to see me."

"And you're back already?"

"Didn't go. Because I looked up where his office is, and what do you think I found?"

"No idea," I said.

"His offices are in Caliber's corporate compound."

"You're shitting me."

"Wish I was. Given that the last time I saw Caliber they tried to kill us, I decided I'd wait and see what other leads we got."

"Colonel Parnavic was pretty forthcoming, but the stuff he's getting for us is going to be a lot of work to get through, and even if we find something in the video, it's only going to prove that Ramiro was here, not tell us what happened to him," I said.

Mac thought about it. "So where's that leave us? Wait to see what Ganos finds?"

"That's going to take some time." I paused. "You know what we could do?"

"Please say go to the gym," said Mac.

"In this gravity? What's the point?"

"I always wanted to bench-press four hundred kilos."

I laughed. "Noted. But seriously . . . we did come all this way."

"That's what it's going to say on my tombstone, isn't it? 'He'd come all that way, so why not?' Go ahead. Lay it on me. Might as well get it over with."

"We could go over to Caliber and walk in. What's the worst thing that could happen?"

"Historically speaking?" asked Mac. "They could kidnap you and force you to fight an illegal war against indigenous fauna."

"That seems far-fetched," I said. "I don't even think this moon *has* indigenous life."

"Only at the microbial level," said Barnes.

"That's hardly the point," said Mac.

"We'll be careful," I said. "We can bring all of the ABCs. It's not like they're going to abduct us *all*."

Mac pretended to scowl. Or maybe it was a real scowl. It's hard to say. "Their compound is about four kilometers away. There's a regular tram that makes the trip from the port, but I didn't want to take that, so I secured two vehicles."

That brought me up short. "So you're fine with going, but you wanted to make a whole thing about it."

Mac shrugged. "It was inevitable. Like us coming to this moon. I hate to break it to you, but you're pretty predictable."

"Wait," I said. "You have vehicles?"

"Yep. They're off-road things. I guess some people like to explore the uninhabited parts of the moon. These things are pretty cool. Atmospheric filtration, low center of gravity, fat tires."

"Where did you get them?"

"You can rent them at the spaceport, just like anywhere else."

"Really?" I hadn't even thought of that. "How much?"

Mac looked away.

"Really?" I asked. "Come on. How much?"

"Like fifteen or twenty times more expensive than a rental on Ridia. I put it on your tab."

"This trip is going to break me."

"I can take them back," Mac offered. "We can stay here and open one of those expensive bottles of whiskey you brought."

"Eh. You got 'em. And we *did* come all this way."

"I'll round up the others."

CHAPTER 5

I T TOOK US almost an hour to get ready to go, as we had to prepare before venturing outside on Taug. The moon had an atmosphere, but it was too thin to completely protect from the high levels of radiation reflected from Ridia 5, and the low levels of oxygen could induce hypoxia in a few minutes. And that didn't even account for the microorganisms in the environment. All of that meant we had to wear protective suits. They weren't bad—basically like wearing coveralls and formfitting helmets with oxygen-concentrating filtration built in. We each wore an oxygen canister on our hip for backup as well. Only four of us went in the end, with Barnes and Castellano accompanying me and Mac in one of the vehicles he'd secured. Mac left Alanson back with Ganos, as he was the most tech savvy of the group, and Mac didn't want to leave Ganos by herself.

The electric vehicle sat low to the ground, coming up barely to my armpits, and it had a base so wide that it was almost a square. Fat tires rounded out the complement of things that would keep it from flipping over in the low gravity. Castellano drove with Mac riding shotgun, while Barnes and I took the two seats in the back, which were big enough to be pretty comfortable. It took us longer to get through the line of vehicles waiting to leave through the vehicle airlock than it did to make the short trip over to Caliber, where we waited in a much shorter line with two vehicles in front of us, as there were separate entrances for commercial and passenger traffic. I expected to be questioned as we entered, but the guard waved us through the airlock, and we followed a well-marked road through a decontamination station and into a sealed underground parking facility.

"Huh," I said, popping the seal on my helmet. "That was easy."

"So far. It's easier for them to control us now that we're inside their bubble," said Mac, as if he'd expected nothing different.

We found a space easily in the half-full parking lot—most people probably used public transportation. After stripping off our outerwear, we headed to the only door, which led to an elevator we took to the only floor available: the lobby. The elevator door opened onto a hallway with a scanner and a cheerful-looking security guard.

"Right through here," she said. "You have any weapons?"

"No," I said, at exactly the same time that Mac said, "Yes."

"No weapons in the compound," said the guard in a monotone voice, as if this kind of thing was commonplace. "Either go back and leave them in your vehicle, or you can check them into one of the lockers here."

Barnes glanced at Mac, who looked at Castellano, and all three of them pulled out small pistols and handed them over. I hadn't even noticed they were carrying them. The scanner was unintrusive, and soon after that we found ourselves in a big, square room with a low ceiling. Windows comprised almost all of one wall, darkened by a protective film that kept out the radiation. The expense of that display made it clear that this was not a temporary headquarters. Three separate sitting areas spanned the room with fashionable but utilitarian sofas and chairs, and a workstation sat in the center with a man and a woman surrounded by a circular counter, both absorbed in their multiple screens.

"So . . . we just walk up to reception?" asked Mac.

"Unless you want to pick a door and go." There were two doors on one side of the room and one door on the other. I had no idea what lay on the other side of any of them, or which one led to Whiteman's office though. I didn't really have a plan, because I honestly hadn't expected to get this far. It surprised me that nobody seemed to care about our presence.

"There's only one security guard, and there's four of us," said Mac, as if he was contemplating it. "We're unarmed and she's got a stun stick, but I like our odds. Doors are probably coded shut, though."

I flinched at the mention of the stun stick. I'd had a bad interaction with one—it messed with the robotics in my foot. Either way, a brawl seemed like an option best left for when more rational attempts failed. "Reception it is."

The pale-skinned man looked up as I approached, Mac flanking me while the other two hung back. "How can I help you?" he asked.

"I'm here to see Dr. Whiteman."

"Is he expecting you, Mr. . . . . ?"

"Butler. No, he's not."

The man's eyes went wide at that, perhaps unused to people just popping in. Given the expense to get here, I could see that. "If you'll take a seat over there, I'll ring him and see if he's available."

We stared at each other for a few seconds, and then I did as he said and went to take a seat on one of the sofas. He approached us after only a couple of minutes. Standing now, the tall man towered over us, dressed in a tan jumpsuit that somehow looked both comfortable and fashionable. "I'm so sorry, sir, but Dr. Whiteman isn't available."

I stood so I didn't have to look up at him as much. "Any idea when he *will be* available?"

"He's not answering at all. I took the liberty of calling operations to see if they could track him down. Mr. Toney—he's the deputy director of operations—took an interest personally for some reason."

"Is that normal?" I asked.

"I . . . you'll have to ask Mr. Toney. He'll be right down."

I had a lot of questions, but it felt like asking them would put the nice man on the spot, so I smiled and nodded and waited for Toney. I didn't have to wait long, as a short man with a ruddy face appeared from the side of the room with the single door and hurried across the lobby to me.

"Carl Butler," he said as he reached me, awkwardly holding out his hand.

I stood and in one motion returned his handshake. "That's right. I'm afraid you have me at a disadvantage, Mr. . . ."

"Toney. Andrew Toney. Deputy director of operations for Caliber here on Taug."

"Nice to meet you, Andrew. Is it a big venture here?" I knew its size exactly, but I like to use an innocuous question to establish rapport.

"Not too big. About two hundred corporate employees and another three hundred or so sub-contractors, depending on the day. The mining operations are mostly automated, but somebody has to do maintenance and repairs." He smiled after delivering his clearly rehearsed pitch. "I understand that you're looking for Dr. Whiteman."

"That's right. Do you know where I can find him?"

Toney dry washed his hands, uncomfortable with the question. "Maybe we should talk in my office."

I shrugged. "Sure. Lead the way."

He started back the way he'd entered and I followed, my entourage tagging along behind. Seeing that, Toney said, "Your people can wait here. I don't think we'll be long."

"Boss isn't going anywhere alone," growled Mac.

"It's not far," said Toney.

Mac stared at him, unmoving.

Toney fidgeted. I got the feeling that he wanted to say something else but wisely thought better of it. "Does it have to be all of you? My office is rather small and there's no waiting area." I felt a little bad for him. He posed no threat, but Mac wouldn't care about that in the least, so I kept quiet.

Mac gestured with his head and one hand, and Barnes and Castellano broke off and went back to the sofa. "We're good," he said.

Toney hesitated for a second, but then nodded and led us through the door. Mac had been right about the doors being coded. Toney had to swipe his badge and put his thumb against a pad to open it.

He hadn't been lying about his office. It was maybe two and a half meters by three, with a desk and two chairs facing it. Not much of a space for a deputy director, but perhaps they had limited workspace. It fit with everything else on Taug, other than the large reception area. I took one of the chairs, leaving the other for Mac, but he remained standing and leaned against the back wall, arms crossed in front of himself in a posture that might as well have screamed hostility. This wasn't lost on Toney, who stumbled as he moved around his desk to his own chair.

"You showing up here asking about Dr. Whiteman is a bit . . . well, the timing of it is awkward."

"How so?" I asked. I wasn't being coy—I had no idea what he was talking about. Not that I'd have wanted to give anything away if I did.

"We, uh . . . don't know where he is."

That caught me off guard a bit. "Is that normal? He works for you, right?"

"He works *with* us. We rented him office space, and more significantly, his archaeological work is on land that we have a long-term lease on for mining."

My mind focused for a second on the lease for mining—how would something like that even work? Where did you lease a moon from? But that was hardly the point at the moment.

"When we called for him, someone told us he was out at his work site."

"That's possible," said Toney. "Or it's what he told his paid answering service to say."

"So you think he's *not* out at the site?"

"I really can't say. And I'm not being obtuse here. I simply don't know."

"When was the last time he was here at his office?"

"About twenty-five days ago."

I nodded while I thought. Twenty-five days was suspiciously

close to the eighteen to twenty days we estimated that Ramiro had been missing. Ganos's information established that Whiteman was still on the moon well after Ramiro's disappearance, but I didn't have specifics about *where* on the moon. She probably had that data, but I hadn't paid attention to the details. I definitely wasn't sharing that with this Caliber crony. I believed Toney really didn't know Whiteman's location, so it might be information we could bargain with later. "Do you have any suspicions?"

"We don't," he said, and for the first time in the meeting I sensed deception. I decided to press him on that and see how he held up.

"Would you tell me if you did?"

"Why wouldn't I?"

"I can think of a lot of reasons. You knew my identity before I introduced myself. I assume that means you're aware of my past dealings with your corporation."

He straightened a pen on his desk. "I did some quick research. So yes, I'm aware in general, though I'm not up on all the specifics."

"I'd tell you, but I'm not sure if my NDA covers Caliber employees or not. I don't want to get into legal trouble."

"Of course not." Toney sat back in his chair, trying to look comfortable, and I got the feeling that whatever he asked next was his real purpose for the meeting. "Can you tell me why you're looking for Dr. Whiteman?"

I considered what to share. "I didn't know he'd split from you. In fact, until I arrived on Taug, I hadn't known he was working with you at all. Though given your mining lease, now that I hear it, it makes sense."

"You didn't answer the question," said Toney, a hint of a smile tugging at the corners of his mouth.

I returned the smile. "I'm not specifically looking for *him*. We think he might have information on something else we're interested in."

"The disappearance of Mr. Ramiro."

I stared him down for a second. "That's right. What do you know about that?"

"Nothing at all. The request that the military received for your visit had his name on it."

"Are they in the habit of sharing those sorts of things with you?"

He shrugged. "Not officially. But it's a small moon. People talk."

"That explains why you were expecting me."

"Here, today? Not at all. On Taug, yes, and I don't think it's too much of a leap for me to have predicted that our paths would cross at some point during your visit. After all, Ramiro worked for Whiteman, and the fact that he had an office here isn't a secret."

"Why do you have that relationship? Whiteman rents space here—that part I get. But what's in it for you letting him run an archaeological site on your land?"

"Not a lot. The thing is, we have a *lot* of leased land, and only a small percentage of it is suitable for mining. The rest is pretty much worthless, so it costs us nothing to let him explore. If he happens to make a discovery that has value? Maybe we get some good press out of it. It's risk-free."

I nodded. That was plausible. "So let's cut to the chase. Why am

I here in your office? You could have simply had the receptionist send me on my way. You want something."

"Very astute, Mr. Butler. I want to know if we can work together on this. You want to find Ramiro. We want to find Whiteman. There's at least some overlap there."

"There is," I allowed. But as I thought about it, I had a question: *Why* did they want to find Whiteman? He'd claimed that the relationship was mostly worthless, but me being here in his office showed the lie in that. I could bring that up and use it to push the topic, but I was playing from behind, and winging it could potentially give away more information than I gained. Better to retreat and reassess, and if I was going to do that, I didn't want to make Caliber any more of an enemy than they already were. "Here's what I can do. I'm going to keep looking for Whiteman. If I find him, I'll let you know."

Toney studied me for a few seconds. "Thank you. For our part, if we hear from him, we'll let *you* know. And as a gesture of good faith, we'll authorize you access to any of our leased lands. If you want to go out and see Whiteman's work site, we won't try to stop you."

That he thought he *could* stop me caught my attention, but I decided to take the gesture in the spirit in which he made it. For now. No matter what happened, I'd never believe that Caliber had my interests at heart.

But I could pretend.

IT WAS EVENING by the time we made it back to our hotel rooms, and while Mac sent someone off to retrieve food, I met with Ganos and discussed her part of the operation. In this environment, her skills outweighed most anything I could do, so as she went, so went the mission.

She'd set up two folding tables in her room that held a total of three monitors and other various equipment. She had so much stuff jammed in there that she barely had a path to the bed, let alone room for me to stand in there with her.

"You want me to take a couple of the storage boxes to my room so you have more space?"

"Mac'll get it," she said. "How was your meeting?"

"Interesting. I'll fill you in. How are things here?"

"Well, there's good news and bad news. First, the good. The connectivity here is solid, and I can do almost anything I could do from my home station, albeit somewhat slower."

"Nice. What's the bad?"

"The bad is that everyone here—the military, Caliber, and Omicron—are all running closed nets. So being here on the moon with them doesn't get me any closer to breaking into their internals than I was from home apart from less lag time."

"But you *can* break in, right?"

"With enough time, maybe. But the risk of getting caught is high. If we could get into a workstation on any of their internal nets, things would get a lot easier."

"How do we do that?"

"We need physical access. I'll try to talk the military into letting me have that when I meet with them tomorrow, but I wouldn't hold out a lot of hope in that regard."

"Me either. The commander knew your name, and he'll have warned his people that you're dangerous."

She looked up and smiled, and I shook my head at how being

a galactically known threat touched her. "Aw. Thanks. We'll see. Maybe I have a few fans on the net team here."

"You have fans?" I asked.

"You don't?" She winked. "With the corporate side . . . you know how that goes. They've got people almost as good as me working specifically to keep people like me out."

"So what *can* you access? If I know that, I'll at least know what I've got to work with."

"The security on the public net here is laughable, so anything that touches that. That includes if someone from one of the corporate or military nets contacts someone off moon that's on the public net."

"Does that help us?"

"Probably, but not predictably. For example, whatever Caliber is telling their corporate HQ about your visit today is almost certainly going point-to-point through their own system, and so I can't get it very easily."

"I'm sensing there's a *but*," I said. "What's the other good news?"

"The people we're looking for—Ramiro and Whiteman specifically—probably aren't using those nets, because if they were communicating, it would probably be to someone outside of the corporations."

"There's been a falling out between Whiteman and Caliber. They say he's not on their compound, and I believe them. Let me know if you can find him anywhere, even if it's just a purchase or something."

"Can do. That won't take long. What else do you need?"

"We're going to get a big dump of video—hundreds of hours

from I don't even know how many cameras. Can you automate something that helps us go through it to see if we can get a hit on Ramiro?"

Ganos turned away, clicked something on one of her screens, and turned back to me. "Well, it depends. Remember a few years back when we tried to sneak into Omicron with me wearing a disguise and we got caught?"

"Yeah." How could I forget?

"After that, I learned a lot about facial recognition. It's hard to fool with a physical look, but there are electronic means."

"Okay. What's that mean to us?"

"It means that with the processing power I brought, sure, I can help go through the video. But if he had equipment for electronic deception and wanted to hide himself, the software will struggle to beat it. But we can mitigate that by looking at potential matches manually."

"Which would take time," I said.

"Right. A lot of it, depending on what we find."

I thought about it. "But he'd have to be doing that himself, right? Trying to hide?"

"Pretty sure. Yeah," said Ganos.

"If he didn't try to hide himself, could somebody go through and hide him after the fact?"

"I mean . . ." She thought about it. "*Anything* is possible. But that would involve scrubbing every feed, and that's a massive investment in time and resources."

"Got it." That may or may not have mattered, but I filed it away as something to revisit. "What if we want to look for Whiteman, too?"

"We can do that. Sure. Though looking for two is a lot more work than looking for one. It's probably best to do them sequentially. Who do you want to prioritize?"

I thought about it. Ramiro was the target, but finding him on camera didn't really get us closer to actually locating him since he hadn't pinged in weeks. Whiteman, on the other hand, held more potential. Depending on where we found him and when, it might let me go back to Caliber armed with information I could leverage. Or maybe we'd get lucky and find him. If I could talk to him, it might break open Ramiro's case. "Let's look for Whiteman."

"Can do," said Ganos. "As I said, it's going to take some time. Could be hours, could be days. What are you going to do in the meantime?"

"I think we're going to go darkside and check out Whiteman's worksite."

CHAPTER 6

WE DIDN'T LEAVE the next day, because the trip spanned over a thousand kilometers and the round trip via ground would take over twenty-four hours in travel time alone. So I sat on my hands and paced a lot while Mac and the others looked for the best way to approach the journey. In-atmosphere flights darkside were hard to come by, so that meant we needed overnight camping gear as well as extra batteries and generators so we'd have enough power to get there and back.

With a bunch of down time, I wanted to take a physical picture of Ramiro and head to the port to see if anybody remembered seeing him, but Mac had tasks for all three of the ABCs. I didn't want to interfere with that, and I didn't want to go to the port by myself. I'd promised Mac that I wouldn't put myself in needless danger, and while this didn't seem like a particularly dangerous thing to *me,* he wouldn't agree. I was trying to be good.

By the time we were finally ready to depart, I had enough pent-up energy to power a small turbine. My team had packed both vehicles with supplies, the most interesting being the box of goodies that Alanson brought. It seemed as if he had every kind of drone imaginable, along with multiple ways to tap in to their video feeds. The coolest interface resembled a virtual reality helmet.

"What's that do?" I asked. I had a vague idea, but it's always fun to hear pros talk about their equipment.

"It allows me to scroll through up to six drone feeds at a time," he said.

"Wow. Six is a lot."

"Yeah. But with six up, I give up a lot of manual control of their flight and leave it to AI, so I'll probably limit it to four up at any time."

Still, that seemed like overkill for a two-vehicle mission. Standard military procedure would have us do it with one. *Maybe* two. "Why would we need four drones up?"

He stared at me for a few seconds, as if trying to figure out if I was seriously asking that question, before responding with "Why *wouldn't* we?"

I had no answer for that, so I let it go and loaded into my vehicle with Mac and Barnes. Alanson and Castellano took the other with C driving. We cleared the compound through a seldomly used airlock that Mac had coordinated via the military, and headed on our way.

Travel on Taug left quite a bit to be desired, because about ten kilometers outside of the spaceport, the paved roads transitioned to a less improved surface—more trail than road. The low, scrubby vegetation, which comprised most of what grew on Taug, had been cleared and someone had scraped off the surface layer of sediment, so that the "road" consisted of the underlying rock that dominated most of the moon. Thankfully our vehicles had fat tires and excellent shock absorbers. The porous, rough road surface allowed water vapor to seep up through it from underground oceans and return on the rare occasions when it rained, which gave the horizon a continuous hazy quality that made it hard to pick things out at a distance. Not that the horizon held much beyond a rocky hill every now and then. Occasionally we passed a mining site—that's why the roads existed in the first place—and heavy machinery dotted the landscape to either side of us.

The computers in our vehicles had maps, of course, which kept us on the right route, but we supplemented that with a running update from Alanson, who passed us information from his drone constellation about approaching areas. His voice had become almost a constant, so much so that, along with the whine of our electric engine and the rough ride of the vehicle, it had me nodding my head, in and out of sleep.

Something in his tone snapped me awake when he said, "We have a problem." I hadn't been in a situation with a *problem* in a while, but muscle memory kicked in, and I had to hold myself back from immediately responding to allow Mac to do his job.

"What've you got?" asked Mac.

"Lost one of my forward drone feeds."

"How often does that happen?"

"Occasionally," said Alanson through the speakers in my helmet. "But rarely enough where this warrants attention. It could be a lost signal, but it shouldn't be. Not in this terrain and with so little interference in the frequency spectrum."

I didn't completely understand that, but Mac wouldn't have hired Alanson unless *he* knew. If he called it a problem, it probably was.

"Fuck!" said Alanson. This time, his tone left no doubt. "Lost a second feed. Something is taking out my drones."

"What can do that?" I asked, before Mac had a chance to respond.

"This is all off-the-shelf stuff, so they're visible with even an unsophisticated radar and vulnerable to any number of attacks. Something could be jamming our signal. Or it could be a directed EMP or a laser took them out."

"What's your best guess?" I asked.

"I'm not picking up any drones but ours, so if they're up there, they're stealthed. The easiest answer is military."

"Yeah," I said. The military had all kinds of things to take down drones a lot more sophisticated than Alanson's, but I couldn't envision them harassing us. Parnavic hadn't protested our trip. If he had his forces attacking us, it was the height of passive-aggressive. "Any chance we've entered a restricted area?"

"Negative," said Mac.

"Dust trails. Front left, about three kilometers," said Barnes from the driver's seat. "At least two vehicles. Maybe three."

I checked the digital map and saw an intersecting road just under three kilometers ahead of us.

"Drone three is down," said Alanson.

"I don't like this," said Mac. He reached down beside him to grab a weapon and pulled his civilian version of a Bitch assault rifle out. "Slow down. Let's not race into whatever's in front of us."

A streak of light ripped out of the sky and slammed into the road behind us, followed by a flash and a deafening crunch a split second later. Barnes wrestled with the vehicle, trying to keep us under control.

"What the fuck was that?" shouted Mac. No response.

"Full halt," I shouted back. I leapt from the vehicle before we fully stopped, the low gravity keeping me from hurting myself as I landed six meters behind and sprinted through the dust and smoke. I triggered the light on my helmet, but it didn't help with all the particulate matter in the air. There! Our second vehicle lay off the road on its side in the scrub vegetation, its top two wheels still spinning.

"Vehicle hit!" I shouted into my comm, even though I didn't need to shout for them to hear me.

"Those dust trails are still coming," said Mac.

"I'm more worried about whatever came out of the sky," said Barnes.

"You two handle it," I said. "I've got the wreck."

"I don't know who that is approaching, but I've got a notion to not let them get close enough to find out," said Mac.

I let that pass as I reached the vehicle and leapt the three meters up to the side that was now the top, an easy jump in the low gravity. On his side and twisted around, Castellano was struggling with his seat belts. "Can you hear me?" I asked. Nothing.

Castellano looked at me, uncomprehending, and then a couple seconds later he flipped something and spoke. "You copy?"

"Yeah, I got you now."

"We had comms running through the vehicle. When it died, I didn't think to switch it back to direct. I'm fucking stuck."

With a flash of inspiration, I hopped down to the ground and shoved the vehicle back onto its wheels. It bounced and then settled, and while the bent frame and crooked wheel said it wouldn't be moving anytime soon, at least it would be easier to get the passengers out. Alanson was initially unresponsive, and when I tried to revive him, he cried out in pain.

"What hurts?" I asked.

"Right arm. I think it's broken."

"Can you get out of the vehicle? I don't think we want to hang around."

"Yeah. Can you help me with my belts?"

By the time I had him free, C had reached our side and helped me pull him from the vehicle. "Either of you see what happened?"

"Rocket hit about three meters in front of us," said C. "Good thing Mac had slowed us down, or it would have hit us directly."

"Right." Thank goodness for luck, though we couldn't count on that continuing. "We might not be out of hot water yet. Possible contact to the front."

"Roger that." Castellano went to the back of the vehicle and quickly started assembling a very large weapon with the practiced hands of thousands of repetitions. Alanson wobbled a little but steadied himself by grabbing on to a case that had been strapped into the back seat. He fumbled with the latch, trying to get it open with one hand.

"What is that?" I asked Castellano as I moved to help Alanson.

"Thirteen-millimeter sniper rifle. Custom job."

"You just happened to have that with you?"

"I'm a sniper." Castellano didn't look up as he answered. "Mac said to be prepared."

I worked the latch for Alanson, and he fished a disc-shaped drone from its foam-packed slot inside the case and started powering it up.

"You don't think they'll knock it down?" I asked.

"They might. But if I can get one picture of what's approaching, it'll be worth it." He set the control pad for it on the case so he could operate it with one hand and then flung the drone into the air. It hovered for a second until he pushed something on the screen, and it zipped off. Castellano hurried up to the front vehicle and I hustled after him. Mac and Barnes had pulled it off the road and were taking up positions in the scrub. I went into the operational rover for my Bitch, and then joined them. I checked my magazine and chambered a round of guided ammunition.

"They still coming?" I asked, as I took up a prone position among the others about fifteen meters up the road from the vehicle.

"Yep," said Mac.

"Let's try to wait and see if Alanson can get a visual before we start blasting," I said.

"We wait too long, we might not get an option," said Mac. "There are more of them than there are of us, and we don't know what they've got for weapons."

"They don't know what *we* have, either," I said.

"We don't have air support," said Mac.

"True."

"No sign of any air activity," said Barnes, scanning the sky with the scope of her weapon.

"There were no signs before that rocket, either," said Mac.

"I've got eyes on the convoy," said Castellano, who probably had a much better scope than the 4x I had on my Bitch. "Eleven hundred meters and closing. Lead vehicle has four pax. Can't make out the ones behind it due to dust."

"You got a shot?" asked Mac.

"Can you disable the vehicle without killing anybody?" I asked.

"Probably," said Castellano.

"Odds?" I asked.

"Depends if they've got their seat belts fastened."

"They're not military," said Alanson. "One hundred percent confidence."

That cleared any hesitation I had about engaging them. "Take the shot," I said.

Castellano's rifle cracked a half second later, deep and powerful. Through my scope I saw the vehicle skid, pop off the ground several meters, land on its wheels, and stop. Two other vehicles swerved around it, one on either side, but they skidded to a stop as well. It was hard to make out at this distance, but at least some of them dismounted.

"Range?" asked Mac.

"873," said Castellano. "You want me to take them down?"

"Negative," I said, before Mac could answer. "Let's see what they do. If they don't take the warning, we've still got time to act since they've got a vehicle down."

"So do we," Mac reminded me.

"I could take out another vehicle, just to be safe," said Castellano.

"Hold on," I ordered. The last thing I wanted to do was escalate this, and there was still a chance that we'd fired on some innocent people moving to a mining site. Given the drone activity and the rocket, I *doubted* it. But I couldn't be sure.

"I've got visual on weapons," said Alanson. "Long rifles. At least six, maybe more."

"Anything else?" asked Mac. "Rockets?"

"Can't see any, but there's a lot of dust," said Alanson.

Mac looked at me without speaking, not wanting to put me on the spot in front of the others. I knew what his choice would be, but it was my call. I stalled, hoping for another sliver of information that might give me a better chance at making the best decision before events forced me to act. It felt like a minute passed, the two of us with our eyes locked on each other, but it was probably a matter of seconds.

"They're bugging out," said Castellano.

"Confirmed," said Alanson. "They're loading into the two working vehicles. Looks like they're abandoning the wreck." The net went silent for several seconds. "Yep, headed back the other way."

"We need to get a look at that disabled vehicle," I said.

"We need to get the fuck out of here," said Mac. "For all we know, they're backing off and recalling whatever fired that rocket at us."

I hesitated for a second, but not much longer than that. "Roger. Let's RTB."

"Roger. Return to base. Everyone jam in the one vehicle," said Mac. "Cross load the most expensive stuff and leave what we can't fit."

"I've got pictures of the disabled vehicle," said Alanson. "They aren't great, but we can enhance them back at base."

"Good," said Mac. "How's your arm?"

"Hurts. Once we're out of danger, I could probably use a shot of painkiller."

"Roger," said Mac. We wouldn't be out of danger until we were sitting back in our hotel, but I let that go. The man had fought through the pain when it mattered.

"We going to abandon that one?" I asked, pointing to our own wreck, knowing the answer.

"No choice," said Mac. "Don't worry. I got the added insurance when I rented it." He let that hang for a few seconds before we both started laughing.

Paying for the vehicle was the least of my concerns. Someone had attacked us, and I didn't know if it was personal or if they were trying to stop anybody who tried to head out the way we did.

Not going to lie. I took it personally.

—

Once we cycled through the airlocks to get back into the contained compound, I headed straight for military headquarters, leaving Barnes to download our equipment and taking Castellano with me. Alanson insisted he could make it to the medical treatment facility on his own, and I had no reason to doubt him. To Mac I gave a more important mission: get the data to Ganos. We had video from some of Alanson's drones, and I had a feeling that if I didn't act quickly, someone might try to confiscate that. I didn't think the military had any specific authority in that regard, but then, whether they technically had it or not didn't matter. If they decided they wanted our data, or even our equipment, I probably couldn't stop them from taking it. Part of me was surprised that a military detachment didn't meet us the minute we got back through the airlock. But they didn't, which gave us a chance to hide stuff, and Ganos was our best resource for that.

It turned out that my thought about a detachment meeting us wasn't that far off, as Lieutenant Colonel Parnavic himself met me before I'd made it two hundred meters out of the parking facility. He had a lone soldier as an escort and neither seemed to be armed with anything more than sidearms, so they probably didn't intend to confiscate anything. At least not physically. Parnavic could give me an order, but he wouldn't, because you don't give orders you can't enforce unless you really have to.

"Carl!" he called, well before we reached each other. "I heard that you were back. What happened out there?"

"I was hoping you could tell me." I tried to keep my tone neutral, but I failed to hide the bite in my words.

Parnavic pulled up short, a few paces before we reached each other. His escort, maybe sensing that we needed some privacy, faded back a bit. "We don't have real-time coverage across the entire moon. We had reports of an explosion and we sent drones to scout out the area, but we didn't find anything significant. All I've got so far is a report of a disabled vehicle."

Only one? That didn't fit. I studied him for a few seconds. If he was lying, he was really good at it. I decided to take him at his word. "Somebody fired a rocket at us and took out one of our trucks."

"Holy shit! Is everyone okay?"

"One injury. He's already headed to medical, and he'll be fine. What's more interesting was what did the shooting."

"What was it?"

"Nothing we could see. Best guess is a stealthed drone."

Parnavic thought for a couple of seconds, putting the pieces together. "Ah. And you think it was military."

"That *did* cross my mind," I said.

"Well, I can put that one to bed in a hurry."

"How's that?" I asked.

"I don't have any stealthed drones. In fact, I don't have any *armed* drones. This isn't a combat zone. Why would I need them? I'm here to keep mining companies from breaking the law. If I see something, I shoot it with a camera, not a gun. We pass it up and somebody gets fined."

I nodded. He wouldn't lie about that. I could verify it too easily. "Well, somebody has something armed. I have to believe that they're breaking about a dozen laws with that, so you might want to check it out."

"Yeah. Definitely. We'll do what we can, but unless we find some pretty damning physical evidence out there, I don't know how much good that'll do. It's not exactly hard to smuggle something onto the moon, and my rights to search and seizure are pretty limited."

I almost asked him the point of him being here, but forcing him to say it would make me sound like a dick. The military maintained a presence at any frontier outpost, and in theory, they had authority. But in practice, corporations could run legal circles around them. I'd seen it play out before firsthand, so I don't know why it surprised me now. Someone had an armed drone, and my history with Caliber and drones gave me a prime suspect. But while Parnavic had limited search authority, I had none at all. So unless they confessed—which seemed rather unlikely—I'd never be able to prove it.

"What do you need from us?" I asked.

"If you and your people would write statements about what you saw, it would help me out a lot. It'll give me some ammunition to request more resources."

"Sure. We'll get those to you." Not that I thought that him getting resources would happen on a timeline that would do me any good, but keeping things friendly made sense for now.

"And, if it's not too much trouble . . ." He hesitated.

"Spit it out," I said.

"How much video did you get?"

"I'm not sure yet. Something shot down some of our drones—nothing fancy, just off-the-shelf civilian stuff—and I don't know how much we got downloaded before we lost those feeds. But we've got some footage." I thought for a second. "You said your drone picked up one disabled vehicle."

"That's right."

"No other vehicle out there? Maybe a kilometer from the first one?"

"I'll check, but I'm pretty sure no. Why?"

"We left our wrecked rental, but we disabled one of theirs, too. It should still be out there."

"I'll order another pass," he offered. I appreciated that he didn't even blink at me mentioning taking out one of their vehicles.

"Sure. Thanks." I didn't think they'd find anything. Sometime between us leaving and Parnavic's drone arriving, somebody had probably evacked the truck that C had shot. The question was who. "Anything else I can do for you?"

"I'd love to get my hands on your video footage. See what my people can make of it."

"Sure. I'll get a copy of it over to you as soon as possible." Doubtless he'd have preferred the original, but also doubtless that he knew I wouldn't give it up. Someone had tried to kill me—or, at a minimum, those adjacent to me—and I wanted to know why.

CHAPTER 7

T ELL ME YOU have good news," I said as I entered Ganos's room. She had cleared some of the clutter, but empty cases still crowded the space, made worse by Mac standing in front of a screen tracking file progress. Ganos sat in an ergonomic chair—I have no idea where that came from—in front of her three monitors.

"Well," she said, "that's going to depend a lot on how you define *good*."

"Is anything you say going to actively try to blow me up? Because as long as it doesn't, that would be a step up."

"I mean . . . not right now. Mac's backing up the footage from your trip though."

"Alanson's still at medical," said Mac, explaining why he was working the task.

"Run it down for me. What have you got?" I asked.

"Two main things," said Ganos. "First, I got a hit on Whiteman. He's here and he's alive. Turns out it is *really* hard to exist on this moon without being perceived. That's something I'm working on, by the way. I'm generating some false credentials in case we want to go somewhere without leaving a ridiculous trail. It won't stop a visual scan. Though we could maybe make that harder for people as well, if we . . ." Her voice trailed off as she drifted deeper into thought.

"Ganos?"

She looked at me. "Yeah?"

"Whiteman?"

"Right. He scanned through an access point, which gave me a date, time, and specific location. From there, I did a simple camera search to find him. It was innocuous. He wasn't doing anything." The smirk on her face said she was holding back the good part.

"But," I prompted.

"*But,* I followed him from camera to camera, and we got this picture." A low-resolution photo appeared on one of Ganos's monitors. "I filtered some of the stuff out, and we ended up with this."

The higher-definition photo had a good view of a man getting out of a vehicle in what looked like an underground parking facility. "I assume you know this camera's location."

"Oh yeah." She paused for dramatic effect. "That is the parking facility for the Omicron compound here on Taug."

"Oh, shit," I said.

"Yeah."

"External camera?" I asked.

"Yeah . . . about that."

"Internal? I thought you said you couldn't get into the corporate nets."

Ganos deliberately looked away. "I said it would be hard. And that they'd probably catch me. But once I had Whiteman's trail and saw where it led, I got really curious, and I couldn't resist."

"But you only broke into their parking area, right?"

"Sure. Because that's totally how something like this works."

"Really?" I was pretty sure she was messing with me, but I really don't understand this stuff.

She sighed, as if I'd ruined something for her. "No. Not really. All of their stuff is on the same net. But it seemed important enough to put some energy against it, and what are they going to do if they figure out I infiltrated their system? Report me? Who are they going to tell? Besides, I didn't break anything."

I could see a one-sided conversation with Parnavic in my future that involved me begging for him not to expel my associate from the moon. That would be fun. Dealing with a pissed-off Omicron representative was probably also on the docket. But given the results she'd delivered, I'd live with the consequences. "So Whiteman is ghosting Caliber, who he has a contract with, and is working with Omicron, who is, at least on this moon, their direct competitor."

"At a minimum, he's visiting with them. And it wasn't a short visit. Either that or he left by other means. Because that vehicle didn't move over the next twenty-four hours."

"When is this footage from?"

"Three days ago."

"So right before we arrived."

"That's right," said Ganos. "I'm not sure if that's significant or not."

"Me either." I couldn't make anything from the timing, but the location was definitely important. What to do with the information still required some thought. I could go to Caliber with it. They'd for sure be interested, and their reaction might be informative. It might even convince them that I was working with them. On the other hand, they might have fired a rocket at me. So I had reasons to share with them and reasons not to, but honestly, I really just wanted to put the two corporate beasts in one cage and see if they'd fight. What can I say? I have issues. I also didn't want to be hasty. Once I spent this informational coin, I couldn't use it again, so I wanted to make sure we got the most value for it.

"What else have you got?" I asked.

"Had my meeting with the military network folks."

"How'd that go?"

"About like you'd think. Someone had put the fear of the Mother into them about me, and I could barely get them to even speak. Like if they talked to me, somehow I'd invade their network via a brain-to-brain interface or something. They aren't letting me get *near* their systems, let alone on them. They won't even tell me what they're *running*."

"Why is that?"

"They probably think that if I knew their setup it would help me break in," she said.

"Would it?"

"Well . . . yes. But that's not my current plan."

I laughed. "I'm sure that would totally reassure them. Did you get anything from the meeting?"

"Maybe. I asked a bunch of technical questions about what they did to check for system breaches surrounding Ramiro's missing information—or *if* they'd checked. They wouldn't answer those questions, either. But they took notes, which means someone required them to report everything I said, or, more likely, that they haven't run everything I told them about, and they'll go back and do it now."

"Will we know if they do?"

"Only if I break in and look or if their commander tells you," said Ganos.

I nodded. "Do me a favor. Text me the things you suggested to his team so I can prod him on them later."

"Can do."

"That's it?"

"For now. I'm setting up the search for Ramiro. It's going to take a lot more processing power than looking for Whiteman, because I don't have anything to narrow the time and location. Basically, we're going to be looking through multiple weeks of footage from every camera feed. It's an order of magnitude more than what we had to do for Whiteman."

I sighed. "Okay. I'll leave you to it. Hopefully it'll be useful beyond proving he was here. But that'll be a start."

"I'm sure something will come up. It always does. What are you going to do?"

"I'm going to get a late dinner and then maybe sleep on what you've got on Whiteman. Maybe inspiration will hit me."

"Hold up. I've got like forty-five seconds left here," said Mac. "I'll walk with you."

I wanted to say that I could make it to the mess hall and back to my room without an escort, but I wanted to talk to Mac anyway, so I let it go.

"Boom. Done and sent," said Mac. "Let's go find some chow. You want me to bring you a plate, Ganos?"

"Yep. Fries please, if they have them."

"Roger."

MAC AND I walked in silence for a bit as we headed for the DFAC. I still didn't know the way beyond knowing we had to cross into the military area. The moon's facilities looked too much alike, generic and made by the lowest bidder. Mac led the way without having to refer to his device, but his silence worried me. "What's on your mind?"

"Just thinking through options," said Mac.

"For what?"

"Someone doesn't want us to get darkside. We don't know why they don't want that, but if they don't want it, there's a good chance that we *do*. And there's an even better chance that *you* do."

"You're right about that. But that's at least on hold until we have a reasonable chance at a different outcome. Plus, I don't think anybody is going to rent you another vehicle."

Mac laughed. "I don't know. I'm very willing to spend your money in vast quantities. Here's the thing though: If we wait, we're giving whoever it is time to hide whatever it is that they don't want us to find."

"Yeah. But what could that be? If it was his body, I have to believe they'd have it well gone by now."

"Right. But that's even more reason to go find out. There's something here that we're completely not seeing, and maybe once we see it, everything changes."

"Possible. So how do we get there?" I asked.

"I'm thinking military escort is our only option. Can you talk Parnavic into it?"

"I don't know. On just a hunch? Probably not. He's friendly enough, but he's wary of working too closely with me, I think."

"Smart man."

I laughed. "Fuck off."

"So we have to find something that will make him want to go out there with us, but you think he's more likely to go on his own?"

"Or to deem it outside his purview, which it probably is. If I had to guess, he'd task satellites to get pictures."

"That'd be a start. Think he'll let us see them?"

"Maybe. But only after his people have looked at them first, which pretty much negates the value. If there's something to see that shouldn't be there, we can't be sure we'll get it."

"So maybe we need to talk Caliber into taking us," said Mac. "We find out more about Whiteman working with Omicron and use that to whet their appetite."

"That could work. But there's like a forty percent chance it was them that shot at us, isn't there?" Toney had told me that they wouldn't try to keep me from getting to the site, but I didn't fully trust that.

"Can't rule it out," said Mac. "They're certainly no strangers to having unreported military-grade equipment."

"Neither is Omicron."

"We've got to trust somebody," said Mac. "Going it on our own didn't work. And I don't think I'm going to be able to scrounge up something that can engage a stealthed drone."

"So we probably start with Parnavic. But if he says no, we're stuck?"

Mac considered it. "You do what you always do."

"What's that?"

"Start shaking stuff until something falls out."

—

I'd accomplished the mission, though I found that I had only a vague recollection of the details. It had run long, though—right up until my contracted date—and I had to re-retire. But I hadn't done any of the paperwork, and the military wasn't going to let me go without it. I had gear to turn in and forms to fill out, not to mention the medical tests. And I couldn't find any of the right offices. Lines of soldiers stood outside of rooms waiting for their turns, and I asked them where I needed to go. They were polite, as soldiers usually are to colonels, but they simply didn't know. I had a unique situation, and maybe there was someplace special I had to go.

Surely they'd give me more time to clear. After all, being back in the military after retiring was an anomaly, so there could be exceptions. But I had so much to do. How was I getting paid? Was I still getting retirement money and also drawing an active-duty check? The more I thought about it, the more things changed. I was in a different building, but still lost. Always lost. I found a doctor who would sign off on me as a favor, which also felt wrong.

I don't know when I realized it was a dream this time. Certainly well before I was able to wake up and leave it, though eventually my subconscious wised up and struggled into wakefulness. That I'd had this—the administrative nightmare—twice now meant something. At home I got it maybe once a month, and I hadn't been able to tie it to anything specific. But given the current situation, stress seemed like a possible culprit. I suppose someone somewhere would try to analyze it if given the chance, but not me. I had a tough time sleeping at the best of times, and here, in the low gravity and strange environment, it was far from the best.

I swung my legs to the floor and stopped, waiting for the twinge in my foot, but it didn't come. Maybe the low gravity kept the pain away. Weird how you miss those kinds of things, even if they're bad. After that, I sat there on the edge of my bed in the dark for I don't know how long. Maybe I dozed. When I finally checked the time, my device read 0535, which seemed like a reasonable time to get up. My room didn't have coffee, so eight minutes later, having showered and dressed, I opened the door to find Barnes waiting in the corridor.

"Morning, sir."

"He had you out here all night?"

"Three of us split it, sir. Alanson got the night off because of the injury. I drew the good shift. Came on at oh four hundred."

"Is anybody else up?"

"I don't think so. Ganos was still working when I came on, but she crashed about an hour ago."

"That does sound like her. Can you come with me to get coffee?"

Barnes considered it for a moment, which meant that she had two tasks: me and Ganos. "I think it'll be fine. Give me a second to ping Mac and let him know we're going."

There were more people in the mess hall when we arrived than I would have expected for the early hour—sixty or seventy people busy at various parts of their meal. That probably indicated a larger-than-usual staffing on the night shift, for whom breakfast would function as dinner. Day and night didn't really mean anything on Taug itself, but in the military facility, they used standard time. Shift work always messed with my head. I headed to the fancy coffee machine with a lot of options and selected a dark roast, black, which streamed into a recyclable mug. Lifeblood secured, I took a slow walk around the low-ceilinged room, observing faces and name tags on the off chance that I might know someone. Barnes understood the mission and trailed far enough back as to make me accessible. I probably wouldn't find anyone, given how long I'd been out, but it didn't *seem* like that long for some reason.

I didn't recognize anybody, but somebody recognized me. "Are you Colonel Butler?" they asked from a table behind me.

I turned to see five soldiers at a rectangular table with attached benches that would seat a dozen. "I am. Who's asking?"

A young woman stood up. "Corporal Diana Westhouse, sir."

"Did we serve together?" I didn't think we could have, because she looked like she might be twenty, and I hadn't served with any twelve-year-olds that I recalled.

"No, sir. My dad served with you. I recognized you from the news."

Westhouse . . . it didn't ring a bell. I hated that I'd forgotten so many of the people I served with. I also felt really fucking old. "How is your father?" I asked, afraid for the answer because he could be dead. He hadn't died working for me, though. That I'd remember.

"He's good. Been retired for about ten years now and settled back on Ferra, managing a logistics hub."

"That's great. I'm having trouble placing him. I'm sorry."

"Oh, totally fine, sir. I can't remember half the people I've served with, and you've probably got a hundred times as many."

I forced a smile. "It was good to meet you, Westhouse."

"Hey, sir . . . do you think I could get a picture? My dad would love it."

"Sure thing."

Barnes appeared and accepted Westhouse's device, snapping a few shots as the two of us posed together.

"You okay, sir?" Barnes asked, after we'd cleared the door of the mess hall.

"Yeah. I'm good." But I wasn't good. It had been a small thing, but the engagement with Westhouse had put a thought into my head that wouldn't leave. Something I used to know, but that had maybe slipped my mind since I'd been away from soldiers for so long. We did what we did for people like Westbrook—the soldiers. Her job here on a moon in the middle of nowhere might matter and it might not, but either way, she was happy to do it. Her dad had served, and now she did. And that put another aspect onto my mission here: What would Westhouse expect from me?

I knew what she wouldn't expect. She wouldn't expect me to sit back and do nothing. That didn't mean I had to make a direct charge into bad odds, but maybe there was another way I could go straight at the problem.

CHAPTER 8

"**Y**OU REALLY THINK this is going to work? That we're going to knock on the door, ask to see Whiteman, and they're going to get him for us?" asked Mac. He had a point. He, Barnes, Castellano, and I had made the trip to Omicron headquarters in our one remaining vehicle, and now sat in the same parking facility we'd tracked Whiteman to as the two of them checked their kit one last time before we headed inside.

"You said it last night. Shake stuff until something falls out. Sure, they're probably going to tell us that he's not here, but what's the downside? Even if we don't find him, we put them on notice that we know something's up. Maybe they'll feel the pressure and make a mistake."

"Maybe. Or maybe we're just warning them to be more careful."

"Also possible," I said, thankful that Mac didn't mention the actual worst thing that could happen. The thing that *did* happen the last time I'd investigated Omicron. They probably didn't remember that, though. It had been more than four years.

We left Castellano in the vehicle—something we'd thought about after our Caliber visit, not wanting to leave it unsecured—and Mac, Barnes, and I headed for the elevator, which had only one button and took us to the main floor of the facility, disgorging us into a small vestibule. I didn't see much beyond that, because four armed security guards blocked my view. Okay. Maybe they *did* remember.

"Colonel Butler," said one of the security guards—probably the lead—a tall, thin woman with dark hair pulled into a bun.

"That's right."

"Per the terms of your legal agreement, you are not allowed to be on Omicron property."

A bunch of things flashed through my mind in a hurry. The four guards carried holstered sidearms. Barnes had a Bitch, but it was strapped to her back. Mac had a sidearm. All I had was my rapier wit. In a gunfight, it would come down to how fast Barnes could unsling her weapon, but regardless, we were effectively in a dead end unless we retreated into the elevator, which seemed like a horrible idea. So a gunfight would be bad. Not that that should have been the first thing that jumped to mind, but old habits die hard.

I also didn't want to retreat without an effort, so I used the only tool available to me: pure bullshit and confusion. "The agreement states that I'm not allowed on Omicron-*owned* property, but since we're on an unincorporated moon, all property here is legally considered to be leased, not owned, so the document in question doesn't apply."

I had no idea if any of that was true. I hadn't read my agreement with Omicron in years. I might not have even read it when I signed it, trusting that my attorney had. The only thing I remembered about it was the payout, which had been in the seven figures. Hard to forget that part. Given the reaction of the guards, though, they had no idea either. That made sense, as they'd almost certainly been dispatched to simply send me away. Now they stood, frozen, glancing back and forth at each other while still trying to keep an eye on the three of us. They'd noted Barnes's weapon for sure, as she got most of the attention.

We stood there in silence for several seconds until a pale-skinned woman hurried up behind the guards. She wore a skirt suit, but had on low, rubber-soled boots, which were much more suited to function than fashion. The guards turned to face her as she approached, which gave me a chance to take in the space behind them, small and windowless with a low roof—a far cry from the much nicer reception room at Caliber. I didn't know what that said about the respective companies, and as the woman made her way through the guards and to the front, I didn't have any more time to consider it.

"Colonel Butler, I'm Francesca Alexander. I apologize for the confusion. Of course you're welcome here." She looked at the guards and waved them back. They immediately complied, with only one sticking around, and she at a distance. Francesca wasn't breathing hard, which likely meant that she hadn't run far.

"Nice to meet you. I assume you're an attorney?"

"I'm not. I'm the VP for operations. If you're not familiar with our org chart, that means I'm second in charge of everything Omicron does on this moon."

Interesting. An idea was starting to form at the back of my brain, but it still needed time to percolate, so I stalled. "You apparently knew I was coming."

She gave me a flat smile. "We picked you up on camera as you entered our parking facility."

"That's a pretty quick reaction. You should give your people raises."

"We've got a good team," she said. She was lying. For whatever reason, they'd staged this. The guards had accosted me to make a point, and then the benevolent executive swooped in to earn my gratitude. I was almost disappointed that my made-up contract nonsense didn't actually matter. But I could play along with whatever they wanted instead of calling it out. Them going to such lengths told me a few things. First, that they had someone watching me and had picked me up when I left our facility, if not before that. Second, and more interesting, they cared enough to play the game. They wanted me here. They had to. Because if they hadn't, it would have been too easy to stop me in the garage, before I'd even stepped on the elevator.

The question, as it always seemed to be, was *why*.

I couldn't answer that without diving deeper, but at the same time, I couldn't appear too anxious, or it would put them on guard even more than they already were. I decided to play out my original plan, see where Alexander wanted to take things, and adjust from there. "Since you're here—I know this is way below your pay grade—but I'm looking for Dr. Whiteman. Any chance you could point me to him?"

"That doesn't ring a bell," she said. I had to give her credit. She didn't even flinch. If I didn't know that they had him on the same cameras that saw me, I might have even believed her.

"Any idea who might?"

"I can put out some queries. Do you know in what directorate I'd find . . . them . . . in?"

"Him. Jacob Whiteman. He doesn't work for Omicron that I know of, but he has ties here."

"Still not ringing a bell. But I'll see what I can find. Why don't you come to my office? It may be that we have other things to talk about as well."

I didn't have to look at Mac to know that he was bristling at the idea of me going deeper into the lair of the beast. Alexander would have seen that as well, and I could use that to further the game.

"I'm not sure I should be going into a building filled with armed guards. The last time I did that at an Omicron facility I ended up on a ship to a planet in the middle of nowhere." I kept a smile on my face while I said it, but that didn't change the fact that both Alexander and I knew that I spoke the truth.

She smiled back. "That puts us at somewhat of an impasse, don't you think? Unless you propose that we have a meeting right here in the elevator vestibule."

I looked past her, not quite shrugging, as if seriously considering the idea.

"I can personally guarantee your safety—not that I think you need that guarantee, given your own security personnel." She nodded to Mac, but I kept my eyes on her, so I didn't see how he reacted. "You have my word. You're free to leave whenever you choose. But we should at least explore whether we can help each other out."

"Okay," I said, giving in to the inevitable end of the stalemate. Hopefully that made her think that I took her word as something valuable, and she'd be better disposed to me because of it. Probably not though. I was trying to manipulate her, and I would have bet a lot of money that she was doing the same with me. That was fine. Even if I didn't get what I specifically came for, I might still learn something useful.

I walked beside Alexander, with Mac and Barnes trailing behind us. No Omicron security followed us, and surprisingly, nobody said anything about my escorts carrying weapons. I didn't know what that meant, but it would make Mac more comfortable. The narrow, colorless halls had doors on either side at varying intervals, and we went through two badged doors and took a couple of turns before reaching a set of two elevators. They only went down, and we descended three levels to the bottom floor. The decor on the lower level had improved from where we'd entered, but only slightly, as some non-original art prints graced the walls. We walked down a wider corridor to a large outer office that used furniture to divide it into three separate waiting areas. We headed to the one on the left where a short-haired woman sat behind a desk.

"Will you need anything?" she asked Alexander.

Alexander looked to me, and I shook my head.

"Is it okay if your escorts wait out here?" she asked me. "My office is empty. They can check, if they want."

Mac immediately headed for the door to the inner office.

"Mac," I said, bringing him up short. "It's fine."

He kept a neutral expression, and I couldn't tell if he had actually wanted to check the place or if he'd been playing a part. But he respected *my* role, and that's why I would never want anyone else at my six. He had a job to do, and he was good at it, but he didn't let that override the mission.

"Lead the way." I gestured to Alexander to go in front of me, which she did. The inner office was bigger than I expected, with an open area in the entryway, a large desk at the back, and a conference table to the right that would seat a dozen. Alexander headed for the table, and I followed, surprised when she went around and took a seat in the middle of the far side instead of at the head. There was nothing for me to do but to take the one across from her. If there was any doubt before that this was a negotiation, this dispelled it.

"I'm not going to bullshit you," she said.

I doubted that, but I appreciated the sentiment. "Okay. That would be refreshing."

"We know you were at Caliber."

I nodded slowly, giving myself time to think. If I wanted, I could call her out on Omicron keeping tabs on me, but I didn't know if I wanted to force that much confrontation that quickly. I could always come back to it. "Your sources are correct. I was."

"What's the nature of your work with them?"

That was not where I expected her to go at all. I tried to keep my face from showing it, but almost certainly failed. "I don't have any work with them. I wanted the same thing from Caliber as I want from you. A meeting with Dr. Whiteman. You're suggesting that you didn't already know that?"

"I'm not suggesting it. I'm straight-up saying it. Relations between Caliber and us aren't exactly cordial. They're not sharing information."

"For you to ask the question, you had to have some suspicion, though. Are you vetting a source?" Her question to me would make sense if they wanted me to confirm or deny something someone else told them. Knowing if they could or couldn't trust that source would be useful information for her.

"Not that I'm aware of, though I can't rule out that one of my subordinates might be using this situation for that type of thing." She stopped, as if considering what to share. She would have to give me more if she wanted anything out of me in return. "I'm trying to figure out how much of a problem you're going to be for us."

I laughed, taken aback by her bluntness. Maybe she hadn't been lying when she said she wasn't going to bullshit me. "I don't know how to answer that."

"Well, historically speaking, the answer is a lot. But we can let that go."

I wasn't so sure, but I let her continue. If someone wants to give you information, I've found that it's best to let them.

"But if you're working with Caliber . . . well . . . knowing that potentially changes some things."

"Like what?" I prompted.

"I'm not sure." She seemed sincere in that. "But if we have to, we'll figure it out."

Now I got to consider how much to share. As hard as I thought about it, I couldn't come up with any reason that pretending to be in league with Caliber helped my cause. Telling the truth might not help it either, but I decided to gamble. "I will tell you with one hundred percent certainty that I'm not working with Caliber."

"But you've had ties in the past."

"I am not at liberty to say."

"That sounds like bullshit," she said.

"It does. But it doesn't change that I'm not at liberty to say in a very legal and binding sense."

A light came on in her eyes. "You have an NDA."

"I didn't say that."

"You *can't* say that."

"I am not working with them in any way here on Taug."

"But you were at their compound."

"And now I'm here. As I said, I went there for exactly the same reason that I'm talking with you. I'm looking for Dr. Whiteman."

"So you say." Her tone pissed me off a little, implying that I was lying. It probably shouldn't have, because I *would* lie to her. But I wasn't.

"Yes, so I say. And *you* say you haven't seen him."

"That's right."

"Bullshit."

She studied me for several seconds, which I didn't expect after I called her a liar. "I haven't seen him."

She didn't quite emphasize *I,* but I found myself believing her on that front. "Okay. But somebody here has."

"What makes you say that?"

It was a good question because it put me in a bind. To answer, I'd have to tell her how I knew that he'd been here, and she'd get information from that. As much of a pain as that was, I appreciated being up against a true professional. Someone who had the same skills I did. That didn't mean I intended to play fair. On the contrary. I wanted to win, and if that meant I had to change the rules, I would. I'd be giving her information only if I told the truth. "Caliber told me that at last sighting, he entered your facility four days ago."

She narrowed her eyes at me. "Who at Caliber told you this?"

"Andrew Toney."

"When did he tell you?" She fired the question off immediately, a classic interrogation technique designed to not let me think through another lie.

"Three days ago, when I visited them. Which you know about." And fit with the timeline we had for Whiteman, which placed him here four days ago.

"What proof did he offer that Whiteman was here?"

"He didn't. But he seemed sure of his information," I said. She studied me, as if not quite believing. That was fine; I just needed to give her a push. "But from what he said, I inferred that they had a picture of Whiteman entering."

She flinched slightly at that, though maybe she didn't realize it. Maybe she knew their cameras were vulnerable, but jumping to unsupported conclusions could cause me to miss something. I decided to push her some more, in a slightly different direction, and see what else I could shake free.

"Are you sure he wasn't here?"

"I'm not," she admitted.

"Would you be willing to check if he's here now?"

She smiled. "What's in it for me?"

Well, that advantage I'd enjoyed was certainly short-lived, but I couldn't help but smile. Alexander and I understood each other. "What do you want? I don't have much."

"I'd love to know more about the origin of that alleged picture," she said.

I'm sure you would. Obviously that wasn't happening, since the truth would implicate Ganos, and then me by association. "I'll see what I can find out, but I can't promise Caliber is going to cooperate."

"Why do you want him?" she asked. "Whiteman."

"Means to an end," I said. "I'm looking for a missing person named Ramiro, and the last known info I've got on him had him employed by Whiteman." It seemed safe enough to share that public information. If Alexander didn't already have it—which she should—she'd be able to get it as soon as I walked out.

"Hmm." Alexander looked confused at that, and I had to allow for the possibility that she didn't know about Ramiro at all. Maybe I'd overestimated her preparedness. I didn't think so, which led me to wonder if maybe I'd misread her now and she was a really good liar. I was spinning myself in circles.

"Have you heard of him?" I asked.

"I haven't."

"If I find him, I'm off Taug the next day and forever out of your hair."

She chuckled. "Bribes won't work."

"Of course they will," I said, returning her smile.

She tapped her chin. "Let me offer a bribe of my own, then."

"All right."

"I'd pay a lot to know what's going on with Caliber right now."

"I'm afraid I'm actually *not* susceptible to that kind of bribe. I'm not in this for the money."

"Oh bullshit. Everyone's got a price."

I shrugged. "I really don't."

"So you're all the way out here in the ass end of the solar system looking for a missing person out of the goodness of your heart?"

"What can I say? A little girl is missing her dad and I'm a softie."

She wanted to catch me in a lie, but that couldn't happen when I was telling the 100 percent truth. I think that frustrated her. Liars are often confounded like that—they can't believe someone else *isn't* lying.

"Maybe we can help each other," she said finally. Or rather, said again—I wondered if she was starting to get a bit desperate. "You help me figure out what Caliber is up to, and I'll help you find your missing person. I've got a lot of resources—a lot of eyes—all over this moon."

"I'd love your help in that, but honestly, I don't know how much I can help you there. I assume Caliber is up to the same thing you are here: mining. I'm not your best bet to figure out if they've got some new reserve that they've hit or something." I didn't really know what the two companies were competing over, but that seemed like a good guess.

"I'm more interested in anything they're doing *outside* of mining operations."

"You think they've got something going on?" I asked. It wouldn't be surprising. Zentas had left power, but I'm not naïve enough to believe that they'd turned over a new leaf and gone completely clean.

"I think so. Yes. But I'd like to *know*. I'm told you're pretty good at learning things like this."

"Don't believe everything you hear," I said, wanting to get off that subject. I didn't want to be working for one company against another, especially when both of them sucked. "But while we're talking about what we want from each other . . . what do you know about what happened when I tried to visit a mining site yesterday?"

"That was you?" she asked. This time she was absolutely full of crap, but calling that out wouldn't help me, so I let it go.

"It was."

"I heard about an incident. The military was up in arms about it, but I didn't hear all of the details. We got the report though. I can call for it."

"I'll save you the trouble. I was headed out to Dr. Whiteman's last dig site to see if I could find him there, or any clue to the whereabouts of Ramiro. We didn't make it to our destination. A stealthed drone shot one of my vehicles." Given the odds that her company had something to do with it, I wasn't sure that I had told her anything she didn't already know.

"Holy shit," she said. "Is everyone okay?"

"Yeah. We got lucky."

"Where did it happen?"

I pulled up a map on my device and slid it across to her. "I'm not really as interested in the where as I am about the who."

"Military seems like the most likely, if it was a stealthed drone."

"I thought so too," I said. "I've mostly ruled that out."

She studied the map. "This is Caliber-leased land. Or at least it's a road running through it. The road itself is probably community. So if it's not military, well, I don't like to cast aspersions . . . but the logic *does* dictate . . ."

"Of course not." Except she clearly did want to cast them. She wanted me at odds with Caliber in the worst way, and I wasn't completely sure why. It could be on general principles, creating problems for the competition. But it might be something more specific. If I knew that, it would go a long way toward helping to find my next step forward. Don't get me wrong. I came to Taug to find Ramiro, but I wasn't *against* screwing over Caliber. Or Omicron. Or both. Preferably both.

"So there's no cross-use of leased land?" I asked, because I wanted to know but also because I could use the innocuous question to deflect suspicion.

"There's no cross-use, but it's not something we enforce. Certainly not with weapons. There's no big value to spaces that aren't fit for actual mining operations, so there's no reason for anybody to worry about who drives where."

I took my device back and scrolled the map to Whiteman's dig site. "What about right here?"

She took it back and studied it. "That's Caliber lease as well. I'm sure of it. But it's worthless land."

"There's no active mining?"

"That's right. Nothing to mine. We've all got scans of the whole planet, which is what drives the bids for rights. It's not a hundred percent informational parity situation, but it's probably in the high nineties. The slight deviations are what might lead to one of us outbidding the other for a parcel. But on the other hand, it might also be random. A hunch, or a need to fill a line on a chart."

"Interesting. Could you get me out here?" I pointed to the location I'd already marked on my device.

"Would you trust me if I said yes?"

Probably not. But that wasn't the point. I was testing her. "I want to go there, and I couldn't get there on my own. The military won't do it. As you mentioned, Caliber is the suspect. So you're my only option."

"You really want to find this guy that bad, huh?"

"Call me stubborn."

"I'm sure people have called you that." She smiled to show that she didn't intend offense.

"People have called me a lot worse."

"I'll run it up the chain. See if we can give you a ride out there. I'm sure that would go a lot better if I had something in return that I could show the bosses."

I didn't believe that she had to send it anywhere outside of her office to make the decision. She didn't want me to go out there. I knew it in my gut. I was formulating my follow-on question when a knock sounded at the door, and then Mac poked his head in without waiting for a response.

"Sir, we've got to go," he said.

"What's up?" I asked, before Alexander could get anything out.

"There's a problem back at the rooms."

"What—" I let the question die when Mac gave me a minute shake of his head. Not something to discuss here. Got it. I stood. "Ms. Alexander. Thanks for your time. I'll be in touch to see if we can help each other with our respective projects."

She stood as well, but I was already moving, forgoing the niceties of shaking hands. Mac wouldn't have interrupted if it wasn't important.

We didn't run on the way out, but we moved about as fast as humanly possible *without* running. Alexander's assistant hurried along with us to open doors, so we couldn't talk freely until we reached our vehicle.

The whole time, I was thinking one thing:

Ganos.

CHAPTER 9

MAC WOULDN'T EVEN speak until we cleared the parking area and reached open terrain. Probably a little paranoid, but I absolutely understood that sentiment. "Alanson messaged. They had a problem back at base. Someone was stalking Ganos."

Shit.

Sometimes I hate being right. "Is she okay?"

"Yeah. He called security, they sent a team over from the base, and the guy disappeared. Alanson has more but said that we should wait to get it in person."

"Got it. Good call to pull me out of the meeting." That I hadn't gotten to the bottom of anything with Alexander annoyed me a bit, but honestly I'd probably been at a dead end anyway. This gave me time to regroup.

The drive back took about fifteen minutes at the low speed limit of the inter-compound area, but then we spent ninety minutes waiting to get through the airlock due to traffic and an ill-timed malfunction. We hadn't pre-cleared our reentry through a military gate the way we had with our departure. So when we approached Alanson outside of Ganos's door, standing with a Bitch in his hands at the low ready, it had been over two hours since we'd gotten his message. He opened the door for us, and we all jammed into her already crowded room.

"We are so fucked," said Ganos.

I tried not to laugh. It wasn't funny—not at all—but the way she said it took me back to so many other times she'd told me similar things. Not that she was ever wrong. As I've probably mentioned, I have issues. "How, specifically?"

"Which way do you want to know about first?" she asked. Not good.

"Order of priority," I said.

"Somebody sent a contract killer after us."

I stared at her. I'd been prepared for a lot of things in that moment but hadn't even seen that one as a possibility. "I'm going to need some context."

"Kirk Bingham—not his real name—is a dark-market, for-hire hit man."

"I thought those were a myth."

"The ones *Joe Public* might find are. Not this guy."

"Where is he?"

"Not sure now. But he was in the corridor outside," she said.

"You're sure?"

"As sure as you're standing here."

"I had a couple of tiny drones out there covering us," said Alanson. "I figured there were already cameras, but people might know about those. They wouldn't know about mine. I was right."

"We got a picture and I ran it against some databases that we don't talk about," said Ganos, picking up the story seamlessly. "This is a bad dude."

"I didn't want to take on a professional while I've got a broken arm," said Alanson, as if I were accusing him of something. I wasn't, but I liked that he knew I'd have wanted that info. "I barred the door, called base security, and then messaged Mac for you to get back here. That's when it got weird."

"It gets weirder than an underworld hit man crawling around?"

"The second I called it in, he took off," said Alanson.

"So either he was listening in to you or to security," I said.

"Had to be, right? That's why I didn't want to give you any more information over the comm. There's a good chance our comms are compromised."

"Smart. But it also puts us behind in catching him. Did you send a drone after him?"

"I did, but only after I had secured the door. By then, there was no trace," Alanson said.

I nodded, appreciative that he'd thought of that even if it didn't yield results. I hadn't worked with him before, so knowing he could think on his feet was useful. "Has security said anything?"

"Yeah. Ganos forwarded the picture to them, and their cameras never got a clean look at him—as if he knew their locations or had them spoofed. But they did mark someone in the corridor that fits the time frame. He was hard to track, but they marked him again at airlock six about eighty minutes ago."

"Shit. Let's go," I said to nobody in particular, trusting Mac and whomever he wanted to follow. "Ganos, call security and have them meet us at airlock six. We need to catch this guy." We probably *wouldn't,* but it was worth a try. Stranger things had happened.

Twenty seconds later we were jogging down the corridor. Moving quickly in really low gravity can be tricky, and I winced as I bumped my head against the ceiling, after which I shifted into a longer sliding stride, following Mac's example, which he seemed to do effortlessly. We had to slow as we hit some congestion in the corridors once we exited the hotel area, but Mac cleared us a path, and a few minutes later we pulled up to a half squad of military personnel holding a perimeter around the airlock, backing up traffic.

I tried to push my way through, but a stocky private stepped in front of me. "This area is temporarily closed," she said.

Mac started to say something to her, but before he could speak, someone behind her said, "Let him through."

Parnavic stepped out of the control room and headed straight for me. His presence here indicated that he'd figured things out a little faster than I did, which, given the two-hour head start that he had as I tried to get in the airlock, didn't say as much for him as it might have otherwise. "You're not going to like this."

"There have been quite a few things I haven't liked recently," I said.

He nodded. "Yeah. I'm sure. The suspect escaped through here in a vehicle sixty-seven minutes ago."

I wanted to lash out, but instead I took a second to think. The man—Bingham, if Ganos's information was correct—had gotten from our door to a vehicle and out the airlock in thirteen minutes. That screamed of prior planning. He'd have needed a vehicle on standby and to know exactly which airlock didn't have a line to exit. "Was anyone in the vehicle with him?"

"Yes. A driver. Female, short hair, early thirties."

"Picture?" I asked.

"Nothing we can get a full ID from."

"Send it to my people anyway," I said. I didn't know if Ganos could make more of it than what they already had, but I'd give her the opportunity.

"Sure."

"What about the vehicle? Can we ID that?"

"We don't exactly do license plates here," said Parnavic.

"Fair enough. Do we have a fix yet on where it went once it left?"

"We're working it," said Parnavic.

"Let's get a team after them right now. I'm going with them."

Parnavic hesitated, probably doing the calculus on whether he could get away with telling me no. Apparently he decided that he couldn't, because he nodded and said, "Give me five minutes to get it together. You've got that long to get your kit ready."

Five minutes wasn't enough time to go back to our rooms and get everything I wanted, but Barnes handed me a breather from our previous trip out and that was the only thing I really *had* to have since I was still in my suit. Mac pulled her aside after that and the two of them put their heads together, doubtless talking about how to mitigate the risk of my latest endeavor. I gave them space so they could vent their true feelings to one another, which I'm sure included the fact that I had no purpose in going after this guy. We probably wouldn't find him, and if we did, there were plenty of people better qualified than me to take him into custody. I knew that, even if maybe nobody else on-site believed that I did. And I was okay with them not believing.

It's never good as a leader to be reckless. But sometimes it's okay to *appear* to be reckless. Me wanting this guy so badly that I would stupidly put myself on the line to get him did a couple of things. First, it showed everybody that I would take the same risks they did. You can't put a price on that. Second, it defined in perfectly clear terms the importance of capturing him. With me personally involved, nobody else could quit or turn in a half effort. They had to go full out and do everything they could to apprehend the suspect. With that motivation, they'd probably carry on looking for him even beyond what made tactical sense, just to be sure.

And a small part of me was sick of sitting back and waiting for things to happen. I wanted to make my own action. That part maybe wasn't as well thought out as the first bit. What can I say? Nobody's perfect.

We mounted up into three vehicles: two four-seaters and a troop hauler of unfamiliar design to me that looked like it could hold four or six in the back along with the vehicle crew. I had a back seat in one of the four-seaters with Mac in the back of the other. They originally tried to keep Barnes off the mission, but she talked to someone in the troop carrier, and they dropped someone in favor of her taking a spot there. Another point in Parnavic's favor.

We cleared the airlock quickly, and about three minutes outside the compound, video from a drone appeared on the screen in the front of our vehicle showing the suspect vehicle. It was similar to the one we had rented, apparently abandoned beside a small building and a square cement pad.

"Is that a launch pad?" I asked.

"Looks like it," said Staff Sergeant Jansen from the shotgun seat. His surprise at it being there struck me, though maybe it shouldn't have. Patrolling this area probably didn't fall within his normal duties. This was his squad, and nominally, he was in charge of the operation, though probably nobody believed that, including him.

"How far to that location?"

"Twenty-three minutes," he said. "But they're not there."

"I think you're right." They might be in the flat-roofed square building, but its isolation meant that if they had holed up in there, they'd be trapped. The drone would pick them up if they tried to leave, and we'd have them dead to rights if they stayed. Given the tight planning of the other aspects of his mission, I couldn't see our guy getting himself caught like that. "Can you call in and see if there have been any launches off moon in the past hour?"

"Roger, sir." We waited almost two minutes for a response. He had it on speaker, so I heard it at the same time Jansen did.

"Affirmative. There was a launch twenty-seven minutes ago. Working with orbital traffic control to try to get a fix on the departed vehicle now."

Jansen looked to me.

I shook my head. I didn't have anything for them.

"Roger," he said into the mic.

"See if you can get me Colonel Parnavic," I said.

Jansen spoke into the mic again without hesitation, and twenty seconds later he passed me a handset.

"This is Butler," I said.

"Parnavic here."

"You're up to speed on the vehicle that departed the moon?"

"Roger."

"I want it apprehended."

Silence from the other end that dragged on for several seconds. "I've got no means or authority to do that."

I almost yelled at him, but I held it back. We'll call that growth on my part. If he could get the means or authority, he already would have, so yelling about it would be pointless. "Get whatever you can in the way of description and information about the vehicle and flag it for detainment anywhere it lands in system. And before you tell me you don't have that authority, just do it. I'll get you the authority before he has time to reach any port."

"Roger that. Anything else?"

"We're going to continue to the likely launch site to make sure we haven't missed anything. Butler out."

I regretted putting Parnavic in a bad situation by confronting him over the air. He couldn't really argue without making a public scene that soldiers would talk about. Nobody wanted that. But I wanted Bingham caught, and I didn't have time for niceties. There was *way* more happening on this little moon than anyone suspected, and I needed some sort of break if I hoped to unravel it. I'd apologize to Parnavic later.

The buildings and underground entrances thinned around us, and soon we were on a single rough road headed away from anything civilized and into open moon. We made our way up long, slow inclines and back down. The vehicle in front of us kicked up a thin cloud of brownish dust, but a crosswind took it away just as quickly. The flat hills gave us a decent field of view up close, but they prevented us from seeing too far ahead. Before long, we pulled up on the last rise prior to the scene we'd witnessed already via drone. The road sloped gently down 100, maybe 120 meters to our front and terminated at the launch pad. Jansen dismounted, and I followed. He pulled out a set of high-tech optics, and I called up a private channel to Mac, who had dismounted from his own vehicle.

"What are the chances that something up there explodes?" He said it as a joke, but he also had a point.

"Maybe fifty-fifty?" I patched Jansen into the conversation. "There's no way for anybody to run from here without us seeing them. Take the approach very cautiously. Anticipate the possibility of booby traps."

"Roger, sir." He turned and pointed to the troop carrier, and the vehicle commander dismounted and hustled over to us. Jansen spoke over the team net. "Get the bomb drone. Let's do a full scan before we advance."

"Roger that," said the corporal before trotting back to the troop carrier and around to the back. A minute or so later, a small six-wheeled remote-controlled vehicle sped away from us and toward the target site. The driver used a handset and a VR helmet, but the rest of us couldn't see imagery from the vehicle, so we stood there and waited while it covered the distance.

"Now that we sent the drone, nothing's going to happen," said Mac. I wasn't quite sure if he was happy about that or disappointed.

"Better that than the other way," I offered. I'd gotten enough people blown up by rushing into things to know better at this point. And yet I still ducked and covered my head with my arm at the flash and subsequent *whump* of the explosion. Even from over a hundred meters the pressure wave hit like a sandbag to the chest. Smoke and floating debris choked the target area, shielding it from view, but the wind started to clear it quickly. The vehicle that had been parked there lay upside down, maybe thirty meters from its previous location, a smoking wreck.

Jansen spoke over the private net. "Good call on that, sir."

"Wish it hadn't been. There may have been evidence in the vehicle."

"Probably not," said Jansen, correctly. People who take the time to set bombs rarely leave easy clues around.

The soldier who had been piloting the drone approached, devoid of the VR rig, but wobbling a little, still disoriented back in the non-virtual world.

"What's your take, Mitchell?" asked Jansen.

"Proximity sensor. Bomb was likely attached underneath the vehicle. I'll know more when I can get up there and take a look, but I'd say eighty percent likely that's what it was."

"Roger," said Jansen. "Do you have another drone? I want to take a look at the building."

"Negative," said Mitchell.

Jansen glanced to me. "Your call," I said. I meant it. I didn't think there'd be any evidence in the building, and with the explosion, I'd lost what little hope I had that we'd find anything useful on the site at all. I certainly wasn't going to order a unit into a potentially explosive situation for no gain.

Jansen didn't think for very long before issuing orders. "We advance on foot. Vehicle crews provide overwatch. All sensors on the building. Watch for traps."

THE BUILDING DIDN'T explode, which was nice, but when the team busted down the door, all we found was a single unoccupied room. It had standard control equipment, from what we could tell. The place was dust-free, as if someone maintained it regularly, which might be a lead, and maybe the right analysts could tell us how recently someone had used it by searching the six workstations that lined three walls. But we didn't have any of those people with us, and I had too much else to do to wait around. We'd get the forensics report from the room and the destroyed vehicle later.

PARNAVIC MET ME when we dismounted our vehicles back inside the airlock. He signaled to get my attention, and part of me wondered if he'd waited there the entire time we'd been out or if he'd gone back to his headquarters and returned. Either way, him being here meant he probably *really* wanted to talk, so much so that he didn't want to risk me not coming to see him in his office. I would have. I wanted to talk, too. I handed my helmet off to Barnes before heading over to him.

"Walk with me?" He phrased it as a question, but barely. He didn't want to talk where we could be overheard, which probably meant he wanted to chew me out. Unfortunately for him, Mac wasn't allowing me out of his sight and Barnes probably wasn't either. I didn't have a problem with him saying whatever he needed to say in front of them, though—I don't embarrass easily. But I also didn't need to make it hard for him, so as soon as we got away from his soldiers I spoke first.

"I'm sorry I put you in a bad spot regarding the mission by telling you my intent over the net. It was poorly done on my part."

"What? No, don't worry about it," he said, but I could tell by the way his shoulders relaxed that it had indeed been bothering him. After a short pause he continued: "Don't forget forcing your way on to a mission you had no business going on."

I stared him down for a second, and he cracked, smiling, at which point I smiled too. "Okay. That too. But in my defense, you knew it would be a pain in the ass having me here."

"Fair," he allowed. "Hopefully you'll keep your sense of humor when I tell you this next bit."

"You didn't get the launch vehicle?" I guessed.

"We didn't."

"That's not unexpected. You flagged it to be detained on landing?"

"I did. That's in place and you don't have to do anything about it. But he—assuming that it *is* Bingham—won't reach anywhere he can land for several days. If he lands at all."

"He has to land *somewhere*."

"Maybe. But maybe not. The radar signature from the vehicle is small enough that it could potentially dock with a larger ship in space."

I considered that for a couple seconds. "The resources that would indicate would be . . . a lot." After all, it's not easy to do a linkup in open space. There's so much of it. The norm for that sort of thing would be around some astronomical body, which would at least present the chance of detection. Maybe. They could meet at a rogue asteroid or something, but the idea of that and the level of conspiracy it would represent boggled the mind. Yet it wouldn't be the biggest one I'd seen, so I guess I couldn't rule it out.

"Carl . . . I need to know what's going on. Why is there an interstellar criminal casing your rooms?"

"I could ask you the same thing. After all, you control the airlocks. How did he get in?"

The look he gave me said, "Fuck off." His tone was a little nicer than that, but not much. "Still working that. Initial take is that he simply didn't register. He had fake credentials and some sort of spoof that kept the video surveillance systems from identifying him. Even after the fact, we can't prove he was there from anything except the video that your man provided. How well do you know him? Alanson."

"Are you suggesting that he might have faked the video?"

"Could he?"

I started to speak but caught myself. How sure was I of the man's allegiances? Of any of my team? They'd all been in a fire-fight, and Alanson had taken a significant hit that could have killed him. He hadn't faked *that*. But it might have been un-intentional. Or there might be multiple factions at work. Could somebody have planted him on my team way back when I first took the job? I'd have to check with Mac. Another question in a situation where I already had way more questions than answers. "I don't actually know."

Parnavic nodded. He couldn't do much else. I had the respon-sibility to police my own team, and I would. "For the record, I'm glad you went on that mission. I'm not sure my team would have gone in as cautiously as they did without your direction."

"Of course," I said. "But the whole thing is troubling. For Bingham to escape a contained area and get off the moon that quickly . . . he shouldn't be able to do that."

"He shouldn't. But we didn't know who he was or that he was even here."

"He had to get here somehow."

"I've told you that we don't have a tight grip here on Taug. Not enough assets, not enough authority. There's smuggling and we can't stop it, even if we could find it. I'm sure that extends to people."

"What about the launch facility he left from. Surely you knew about that, given how close it is?"

"I do. It's ours." That was news. "We don't use it, but we maintain it for emergencies in case the main facility goes down for an extended period of time."

"The guy used a military launch point?" I stared at him. "You see how this looks, right? There's too much going on here for us to dismiss the potential that whoever is doing things here on Taug has inside help."

"And I'm telling you that I'm on it. We're checking that as thoroughly as we can."

"I offered you help and you turned it down," I reminded, perhaps not so gently.

"You offered help that no self-respecting commander could possibly accept," he countered. "As it stands, I suspect that there may be infiltration of my systems. If I let Ganos work on it, I'll *know* there is."

I shook my head, but let it go after that. "So what's next?"

"What's next for you?" he countered once more.

I thought about it for a second or two and decided to lay it out for him honestly. Put the ball in his court. "I'm going to trace every aspect of Bingham being on Taug to see what kind of connections I can dig up. I'm going to troll through all the video and prove that Ramiro was here and where. And then, with you or without you, I'm going to get out to Whiteman's dig site and see exactly what's going on. Too many people are hiding things. It's time to bring them into the light."

Parnavic considered it for a long while before speaking. "I'll see if I can get you an escort out to the site. But if I do, you share whatever you learn."

"Deal," I said without hesitation. If it led to me finding Ramiro, I'd be okay with that kind of transparency.

"I'll let you know when I get approval."

"You're going higher?"

"I think I have to. I already set everybody in the solar system on edge when I called in about Bingham's ship. My boss is going to want an explanation, and blaming you is only going to cover part of it."

"Probably more than you think, considering my reputation." I smiled, and he sort of did. "I'll let you know what I find out about Ramiro. But I can tell you this, now: Both Caliber and Omicron are up to something that's not mining. Omicron as much as told me so. They claimed it was Caliber, but that's probably projection. They're blaming their competition for what they're doing themselves."

"It wouldn't surprise me," he said.

"Good. Because I have a feeling there will be enough surprises coming without that."

CHAPTER 10

GANOS PACED THE limited space in her room, dodging equipment and cases, as agitated as I'd ever seen her. "We're fucked. So fucked."

"It's okay. He's gone."

She stopped, put her hands on her hips, and glared at me. *"Fuhhhh-cked."*

"I'll bite. How are we fucked?"

"So many ways." She held up one finger. "One: This guy showed up soon after I broke into Omicron's network to get that picture. They know about the incursion, and they know it was me. The timing is too on point to be a coincidence."

I didn't know about that, wasn't even sure that Bingham had come for her, but she was fired up and she needed to get everything out.

She held up a second finger. "Two: There is no Ramiro. I've run through almost all of the video and there's no match for him anywhere."

"Wait," I said, unable to contain myself any longer. "He was never here?"

"No. That's why we're fucked. He absolutely *was* here. I tracked him here before we ever came, remember? I thought for sure I'd find him once I ran through the video, but those tracks are now gone, which means someone wiped them." She held up her hand to forestall my next question. "And I told you how hard that would be—the kinds of resources it would take. The type of data we're talking about spans multiple organizations, which is hard enough. But do you know how hard it is to scrub somebody out of random snippets of video in a sea of hundreds of hours of material?"

"How hard?"

"It would take me, I don't know, hundreds of hours to do it. Granted, it's not my specialty, and there are certainly people who are better at it than me. But those people aren't cheap, and the equipment isn't either."

"Is that it?" I asked, when she paused for a few seconds.

"Not remotely. I found it so odd that no video captured him that I started to doubt myself. Me! I started to think maybe I didn't see what I thought I did when I looked for him from back home. Maybe I had the wrong guy. So I checked." She put her hands on her head and stretched her lower back. "There's no video of him getting off a ship here, right?"

"If you say so."

"I do. There isn't. And he's not on any manifest. So on a hunch, I accessed video from the departures of four ships that fit the time-line of his most likely arrival." She walked over to her system and punched a few keys. "And boom. There he is, boarding a ship to Taug."

I moved closer to get a better look, and there was no doubt that I was looking at Ramiro.

"Don't ask how I got that. You don't want to know."

"Right." Because I already did know, unfortunately. "So what's it mean?"

"It means that whoever scrubbed the manifest and the video feeds here on Taug didn't think to scrub video—or couldn't get access to it—at his departure."

"Okay. So that's a break for us."

She didn't acknowledge that, just kept on with her rant, saying, "Add to that the case of Bingham. This isn't a guy you reach out and hire. He's a ghost. You can't blame authorities here for missing him, because to them, he barely exists. I found him because I knew where to look, and that place is not a nice place. But here's the thing—he had to already have been here. Before us."

That brought me up short. "How much before us?"

"There's no way to say for sure, but probably before we even considered coming here. Same for scrubbing the video. Even with the best team working on it, they'd have been hard-pressed to get it done since we got involved."

"But you found other information placing him here back before we left."

She shrugged. "Maybe I triggered them. Maybe me looking around put them on notice and they moved to scrub it. I can't define the timeline for sure."

"But you think the timelines of the hit man and the disappearance of the data are tied together?"

"Yes."

"That seems like the worst possible case scenario."

Ganos stared. "This is a Carl Butler operation. When is it *not* the worst-case scenario?"

I couldn't really refute that.

"Now that I know when his ship got here," she continued, breathing a bit more steadily, "if I keep digging, I can pull up artifacts that will show where he was erased. The AIs won't catch it, but I can do it manually. It will give me a better idea on the exact timing of things. But that's the thing—I don't know that we want to keep digging."

"Why not? You think it's that dangerous?"

"I *know* it's dangerous. Would you go into a fight knowing that the other person was way better than you were?"

I thought about that for longer than she probably intended.

"Never mind," she said. "Of course you would."

"What's the other option?" I asked.

"The smart option? We pack up, go home, and tell the little girl that her dad is gone. Because that much is almost certain. Nobody goes to all this trouble if he's still around."

"Unless he *wanted* to make it look like he was gone."

She rolled her eyes. "He was a low-level assistant to an archaeologist. The people who did this could buy and sell him a thousand times over. This isn't a case of a missing puppy where the mom and dad don't want to tell the kid that the dog got hit by a truck. This is real."

"So you want out?" I asked. I wasn't ready to give up on this, and not because I disagreed with Ganos's assessment about Ramiro. She was probably right, and that probably *was* the smart thing. But the other stuff she said had me engaged. People with money doing bad things. As much as it wasn't my business, now that I knew about it, I couldn't turn my back. But I also wouldn't drag Ganos along if she no longer wanted to be here.

She stayed silent for a time, which might have meant she was considering it. But I felt like she'd have come to an answer before even beginning the conversation. She wouldn't be swayed by words when she had her mind made up. "If we're going to do this, we have to be smart about it."

"Of course," I agreed. "What does that look like in your mind?"

"When the other side has you outgunned, what do you do?"

"It depends on the situation, but the general rule is that you'd defend to maximize your own assets and rebuild your combat power until you've got the ability to go on the offensive."

"Exactly . . . wait . . . what? Really?"

"I mean . . . yeah. That's the book solution, and it holds in most situations."

"Huh," she said.

"Why? What would you do?"

"Well, as a gamer, you'd usually attack before the superior weight of the enemy could grind you down any further. Because if they've got more than you, they can keep building faster than you can as well, and it's only going to get worse."

"So you're saying—"

"I'm saying that we take more risks, not fewer. We act fast, before they're ready for it, and we try to steal a win from under their noses before they know what hit them."

I considered that. As a military strategy, it was horrible. But in a missing person case? It might work. Someone had already sent a hit man after us, but he'd fled. It made sense to act before they could come up with another plan of attack. "You've got a deal. We'll go after them. Again, what's that look like for you?"

"We go all in against one of the corporate networks. Get inside and pull it apart and see what secrets they're hiding."

"Can you do that?"

"I don't know. Probably not without some help. If we could get into their building and physically tap a system, it would give me a big leg up."

"Start brainstorming that with Mac and Alanson. See if they've got any ideas." I had slight misgivings about Alanson from my talk with Parnavic, but not enough to block him from doing the job we'd hired him to do.

She nodded. "Yeah. Okay. What are you going to do?"

"Same thing, but on the human side."

"How do you mean?"

"I'm going to go after one of the corporations, try to get inside, pull it apart, and see what I can find."

—

I had to pick a target from the two corporations, and I settled on Caliber. I'd been to Omicron more recently, and while I felt pretty strongly that Alexander was up to something, I decided to shift focus back in the other direction for now. Something that Ganos said had spoken to me. They had us outgunned. We didn't have the means to reinforce unless I could get the military to weigh in, and Parnavic held that authority, not me. So if I couldn't build my own forces, the next best option was to start a war between the two companies and use them against each other.

Unfortunately, I ran into a wall shaped like a muscular ex-soldier named Mac. It was getting late, and he was adamant that we not leave the compound again that evening. I could have pushed back, and he'd might have given in, but Mac had a point. Being aggressive didn't mean being reckless—at least not right now. But I also didn't want to give anybody working against us another twelve hours to regroup. So I did the next best thing: I called Andrew Toney. He picked up right away.

"Mr. Toney. We should talk. I spent some time over at Omicron this morning, and I've learned some things that might be of interest to you."

"I'm intrigued. Shall we meet tomorrow? Say ten o'clock?"

"This is stuff I don't want to wait on. Any chance you can come here tonight?"

The line went silent for several seconds, and I wasn't sure what he was doing. Maybe he was checking with someone else. "It will be difficult," he said when he came back on. "There aren't any vehicles available, and the tram doesn't run very often this late at night. You sure it can't wait?"

I considered how much to share over the comm. There was a good chance that we weren't alone on the line, so I had to be okay with anything I said being shared with not only all of Caliber, but all of Omicron as well. "They told me that they haven't seen Dr. Whiteman."

"Okay," he said, doubt in his voice.

"They're lying."

"You're sure?"

"I can prove it."

"How?" he asked.

"That I can't tell you over the comm. I have reason to believe I'm being monitored."

The line went silent again, and after thirty seconds or so, I started to wonder if I'd lost him altogether, but he finally came back. "Give me an hour. I'll be there. Where do you want to meet?"

"Military dining facility?" I offered.

"Won't there be ears there?"

"We'll sit away from them, and I'll bring a baffle to protect from electronic surveillance and some friends to keep away any curious bodies."

"Okay. It's your information, and I'll trust that you know what you're doing. See you soon."

I told Mac what I had planned so that he could prepare the area. Because not only was I going to talk to Toney and plant information on him—some true, some false—but we'd have access to a Caliber employee outside of their facility, and I didn't know what we might be able to do with that. I didn't want to know. Not yet. Because what I didn't know, I wouldn't be able to subconsciously give away. My team could tell me later, once we'd finished. I had to wonder how aware Toney would be on all fronts. My gut said very. The delays in our call indicated that he was getting advice or checking in with other sources. I didn't expect him to show up alone. Him showing up at all was good though. It meant he wanted something. I could use that.

Toney arrived in an hour almost on the nose, and if he'd hurried, it didn't show in his demeanor or his dress, as he looked much the same as when I met him in his office in gray pants and a long-sleeved, Omicron blue shirt with three buttons at the neck and a small white logo on one breast. It was the kind of casual wear that businesses favored in these kinds of environments. A woman escorted him, though she hung back far enough when they entered the dining facility to indicate she wouldn't be part of the meeting. She didn't have a visible weapon, and neither did he, but her posture and bearing said that she was some sort of security.

I offered coffee, but Toney passed, and we took seats across from each other at a table made for six in one corner of the facility away from all the serving stations. There were maybe thirty people in there all told, but Mac stood with his back to us in a way that would discourage anyone from coming in our direction. It would do. I slid a printed picture of Whiteman in the Omicron parking facility across the table.

"That's Whiteman," confirmed Toney. "Where was this taken?"

"Omicron parking facility."

"This is your proof?"

"That's the physical proof, yeah. The rest is more my read on my visit there. Gut feeling."

"Right," said Toney, still looking at the picture. "Did you show them the picture?"

"No. That wouldn't have been prudent . . . for . . . reasons."

He nodded. Maybe he understood my reasons, maybe he didn't, but either way, he didn't push it. "They could say that he was there and never came inside."

"And I could say that I'm a fairy princess. We'd both be lying."

"I get why you wouldn't want to share this over the comm or to send me the file, but you didn't call me in here this late just for this."

"I didn't. I talked to Francesca Alexander at Omicron, who, in the course of our somewhat abbreviated conversation, accused me of working with you. They either had surveillance on me, saw me there, and made some reasonable but incorrect guesses, or you or somebody you work with gave them information."

"Why would we do that?"

"I don't know," I said. "Maybe you've got a mole."

"If you're suggesting that we have somebody in our facility who sells information to a competitor . . . yes. We probably do."

I stopped at that, surprised that it occurred but more surprised that Toney would matter-of-factly admit it. "Which means that you have someone in *their* facility who sells *you* information."

He gave me a flat smile that wasn't a confirmation but definitely wasn't a denial.

"So you don't need my picture. You already knew Whiteman went to Omicron."

"Having a secondary confirmation never hurts. Especially since we can't use the other one without burning our source."

"You might also like to know that she blamed you for the attack on me yesterday."

"Of course she did. Did she have any proof?"

"Just that we were headed to Caliber-leased land, so you had the most motive to keep us away from whatever you're doing there."

He snorted. "Okay. That's pretty thin. There's a lot of Caliber-leased land out there. A lot of Omicron-leased land too. Doesn't make it ours and doesn't mean we use it all."

"Well, it wouldn't be the first time that I've found Caliber using illegal drones," I offered, referencing the time back on Eccasis when I found them with an entire bot army. Given the look on Toney's face, I didn't have to explain that to him. If it put him on the defensive, I'd take it. "I suppose you're going to tell me it's them."

He shrugged. "We didn't do it, so the odds are good that it was them. Certainly you don't think they lack similar capabilities to what you've seen from us."

"How sure are you that it wasn't you?"

He frowned. "A hundred percent?"

"So you're saying that there's *no* possibility at all that someone within your organization is doing something that you're not aware of."

He smiled, I think because he knew that I got him. He could admit either that he was in charge of everything or that he wasn't, leaving open the possibility of malfeasance. "I'm saying we didn't do it."

Or he could change it up and do neither. Didn't really see that one coming. I had to admit, the guy was good. Much like his Omicron counterpart, I couldn't bait him into something stupid, which, for the moment, seemed to put a crimp in my plans to get the two corporations at each other's throats. "So they say it's you, you say it's them, and nobody can prove anything."

"You could have saved yourself a lot of time by asking the military commander. He'd have told you that."

"Told me what?"

"That you'd never find any proof." That he admitted that so smugly rankled me, but another part of me appreciated his honesty.

"He's official, so he has to have proof. I don't." It was a bluff, but making him see me as unhinged enough to do something rash might cause him to react.

"Come on, Carl. What are you going to do? Go to the press with your unsupported story of being attacked by a faceless corporation?"

"Wouldn't be the first time," I offered.

"No credible news source is going to run something so easily deniable. Especially about corporations with very aggressive legal departments."

"I don't know. Semi-famous person attacked by stealthed drones on moon run by two corporations has a nice hook. It also has the benefit of being one hundred percent true." There was that truth thing again. It had worked with Alexander. Maybe it would trip up Toney.

He seemed to consider it. "If you were going to do that, you'd have done it already, unless you wanted something from me. What do you want, Carl?"

"Have you ever heard of Kirk Bingham?"

"No. Should I have?"

"I don't know. Probably not. He's a bad dude."

"Bad how?"

"Bad killed people," I said.

"And he's tied to . . ."

"Nobody," I said. "Yet."

"Another empty threat? I have to say, I'm a bit disappointed. I thought that the great Carl Butler would have more to him than this."

"Oh, I'm not half of what people say that I am," I admitted. It was true. Stories have a way of growing out of control, and bigger stories grow the most. A couple of genocides—one real, one not—definitely meant that most people had opinions about me one way or the other. That was their right. I'd learned to live with the disdain. The adulation, not so much. "But in this case, it's not an idle threat. You asked what I want. I want the same thing that I've wanted since I got here. I want to find a little girl's dad, or barring that, I want to find out what happened to him."

"And this ties into somebody who has killed people . . . how?"

"I don't know. Maybe it doesn't. But it seems like an awful co-incidence that the guy is here. He didn't come to Taug on vacation." I gestured around to the very-much-not-a-vacation-spot around us. "Somebody hired him."

"Somebody hired . . . what, a hit man?"

"Something like that," I said.

"To . . . what? Kill a random assistant to an overrated archae-ologist?"

"Maybe."

He shook his head. "Why would anybody believe that?"

"They wouldn't," I said.

"So I'll ask you again: Why are we here? This feels very much like something we could have done tomorrow. Or by email." Yet he didn't make a motion to get up.

"Because I wanted you to be looking in my eyes when I told you this, so you could be absolutely sure that I meant it." I leaned toward him and lowered my voice, forcing him to come in closer as well. "What I wanted was a simple thing. And like you said, I've got no proof. And I don't care. I'm going to find Ramiro or find out what happened to him, and I will burn down everything on this moon to do it. Turn over *every* stone. Call that a threat if you want. But it's only a threat if you're hiding something you shouldn't be. I hope you're as sure of that as you're saying you are."

"And if I am?"

"Well, then you've got nothing to worry about. But you said it yourself. If it's not you, it's probably them. So let me ask you what *you* want. Because I think what you want very much right now is for me to go away so that you can go back to whatever borderline illegal stuff you're doing here in peace." I paused to let that sink in. "So maybe you should consider how you make that happen. Because I feel like there are two ways."

He sat back a bit, creating some space between us. "I'll bite. What are the two ways?"

"You could hire someone to get rid of me."

He smirked. "You think that someone hired a hit man to get rid of you? Well, at least that part of the report on you is accurate. You've got a hell of an ego."

I let his insult slide right past me. He wasn't necessarily wrong. "The second way you get rid of me is to help me find the answer I want. If that answer helps you discredit your competitors in a way that gives you an advantage . . . well, that's a bonus now, isn't it?"

He scrunched up his face and ran his hand through his hair. "So now you're saying you want to team up with us and work against Omicron? Isn't that exactly what Alexander accused you of?"

I chuckled. "Oh, no. No way. There's no world where I ever work with Caliber on anything. I don't trust you any farther than I can throw you. And I mean in full gravity, not here. But it doesn't mean that we can't both work at the same purpose individually."

He shook his head. "That's a weird distinction. But I guess anything that helps you sleep at night."

I didn't respond. It wasn't a moral stance, though I wasn't beyond those. It was a practical one that allowed me to separate the two things. I really *didn't* trust Caliber—or Omicron—to do the right thing. If they saw a baby in the road and a profit on the other side, they'd take the profit and leave the baby there to die.

Or run over the baby to get to the profit. But in that, I had a different kind of trust. I trusted both of them to work for their own benefit, and as competitors, that meant I could trust them to work against each other. Whether that would lead to me finding anything about Ramiro, I couldn't say. Despite what Toney said about my ego, I didn't have enough of that to believe that they really wanted me off of Taug enough to help me. But maybe I could get some collateral assistance. I looked to Mac, who was still facing away from us, but had one of his hands behind his back with two fingers out, which meant that I could stop stalling.

"Are we good?" Toney asked, after the silence became too awkward.

"Probably not," I said, but I smiled when I said it to indicate that I was joking. Mostly. "But yeah, for now. I'm sure we'll see each other again soon, though."

"I'm not sure if that's good or bad." Toney stood.

"Me either," I admitted.

I WAITED FOR verification that they had departed the facility before I gathered with my team. "We got it?" I asked, even though I still wasn't clear on exactly what we were getting.

"We got it," said Ganos. "I wouldn't have thought of it on my own, but when Alanson mentioned that he had the equipment to create a spoofed network, it became obvious. Mr. Toney is now carrying a script on his device that will wait for him to connect to the server back at the Caliber compound. When he does, it will infiltrate and open a hole for me to exploit."

"Don't they have defenses for that?"

"Of course. But no defense is proofed against everything, and the biggest hole in most networks is the stupidity of the humans who use it. And that goes about triple for executives like Toney. I'm sure someone has briefed him at some point about connecting to a network where he didn't know who controlled it, but he doesn't even think about it."

"Granted, he probably thought the military network was safe," I offered in his defense.

"He didn't think about it at all. He probably doesn't even know that someone like me can spoof a network and have him connect directly to me. Which is why he should listen to the people who know things. But hey, it worked out for us."

"What are we going to be able to do?"

"That's where it gets tricky," said Ganos. "I can make a hole that will let me exploit their network at a place and time of my choosing. But as soon as I trigger it, their defenses *will* kick in. I'm going to get one shot at this."

"So how's that affect us?"

"Put it this way. We can do pretty much anything. But we can't do everything. I'm going to get off one good action and then we're going to get booted. So be thinking about exactly what you want."

CHAPTER 11

I **DIDN'T HAVE TO** make a choice right away, so I didn't. Ganos assured me that I could wait without much risk of her losing her window to act, and I wanted to keep that advantage in my pocket. Who knew what I'd learn before I needed it? I might be going in an entirely different direction by then. But to do that, I had to keep pursuing information and that had me heading in to visit Parnavic's satellite imagery analysts right after breakfast. Castellano drew escort duty, and we walked side by side, him sliding in front of me when anybody approached from the other direction. Unlike Barnes, who spoke only when she absolutely needed to communicate something, C would probably have kept up a nonstop wall of talk if he could have. I didn't mind. Sometimes talking about stuff could break an idea free.

"So what's the plan, sir? Why imagery?"

I found that question tougher than it should have been. Why do people always think I have a plan? I mean, I get it. He was a soldier and officers had plans, so he assumed that I had one now. When I ran military operations, I did have plans, though not as meticulous as some people's. In this case, I didn't, and part of me feared that if I told him the truth, it would dishearten him. But I'm also not going to lie to someone who is in line to throw himself in the way of a bullet for me. "I'm going to level with you, Castellano. I don't really know. Right now I'm kind of randomly ingesting information and talking to people and expecting that at some point, everything is going to come together and I'll know what to do."

"Does that work?" he asked.

"More often than you'd think—for me, at least. I don't always know what I'm looking for, but I find that I often recognize it when it appears."

"Fair enough," he said. "Whatever works. Anything I can do to help?"

"Watch the people."

"I always do. It's kind of part of the job with security."

"Sure. But don't just watch for people who might be dangerous in the moment. Watch for what people are thinking."

"I don't get it, sir."

"Say I'm talking to one analyst, but others can hear what we're saying. Maybe the person I'm talking to doesn't have an answer, or they do have an answer and someone else thinks it's wrong. They might not come out and say anything. Senior officers—even retired ones—might be intimidating. Or maybe there are office politics at play, and they don't want to challenge their coworker, or their boss has told them not to talk. If you're watching, you can pick that up sometimes in their facial expressions or body language. Did they roll their eyes? Nod their head? Scowl? Seem eager? If you pick up on stuff like that, often it'll lead to the person we should be talking to next."

"You want me to do that?" He seemed excited at the prospect, almost bouncing with energy, which was easy to do in the low gravity.

"Absolutely. Everybody is going to be naturally focused on me. They'll often forget that you're even there, which allows you to observe the truth of things. I'll look to you from time to time for a signal, and you guide me to the right person."

"I can do that."

A tall, dark-skinned captain met us at the door to headquarters. It didn't surprise me that Parnavic had chosen not to meet me himself. I was becoming a bit of a nuisance, for sure.

"Good morning, sir. I'm Captain Janelle Nixon. I'm the intel fusion officer."

"Good to meet you, Nixon. Lead the way."

She turned and headed down the corridor, slowing enough for me to come alongside her. "It's an honor to have you visit our operation, sir."

I didn't know about that, but I'd learned enough grace not to rebuff such sentiments. "Thanks. I've always enjoyed spending time with analysts." That much, at least, was true. I always had. They were their own brand of nerd in the best possible way.

Nixon palmed us through an outer security door, and then we waited at an interior one for someone on the other side to let us in. I didn't have the appropriate clearance for this anymore—shit, I probably had no clearance at all—but Parnavic had approved it, and as the senior commander on the moon, he probably had that authority. Honestly, I didn't care much, as long as I got to see what I wanted. I'd never been much of a rule follower. They'd hide what they thought they needed to, and they'd had plenty of notice. They did relegate Castellano to the outer office, which somewhat negated the lesson that I'd presented to him on the way over about watching people.

Inside, the whir of air circulation mixed with sound baffling in the walls created a white noise that drowned out most of the conversation in the room. An analyst sat at each of the four over-sized terminals, half-meter screens in front of them, while a staff sergeant and a lieutenant diligently walked among them, checking their work. I almost laughed. The scene was so staged it could have been out of a training video. No way did they work like this on a daily basis. They had an important guest and wanted to look good. I couldn't blame them. If I made a negative report to their commander, they'd probably get in trouble. I wouldn't do that, of course, but they couldn't know that. Plenty of former officers would. Assholes.

Because of the setup, when they introduced me to a corporal named Sevilla, I knew that she was the best analyst they had. Or at least she presented the best. Sometimes those two things didn't go together, sometimes they did. Either way, I'd let them guide the tour for a bit since I didn't have a specific destination in mind. I'd find a way to steer it when I needed to.

"Good to meet you, Sevilla. What have you got for me?"

"Sir, this is the T4460 intelligence analyst's workstation." She gestured to the standard piece of equipment with a perfectly flat knife edge of a hand.

Okay. I lied. They didn't get to guide the tour. Not if they planned on treating me like some senator who had never been in a military headquarters before. "You can skip the orientation and assume that I've got a handle on how stuff works. Let's look at some data."

Sevilla cut her big, dark eyes to her boss, but Nixon was looking away. The staff sergeant and lieutenant who had been hovering had also managed to not be paying attention, further throwing Corporal

Sevilla under the tram. Wow, this was dysfunctional. Okay. I had to step in.

"Sevilla." I waited until she met my eyes and focused. "Don't worry about anything. You do this every day. You know how to do it. Don't worry about explaining what you're doing, just have a seat and do your job, and I'll chime in if I have any questions."

She hesitated, glanced around again, unbelieving. As a guest, I'd eventually leave, and she still had to work there. Her boss controlled her life, and I didn't. I'd protect her from repercussions, but I couldn't explain to her in that moment how I'd do that, and she didn't know me well enough to trust me. It was sad that they'd done this to what, on the surface, seemed like a squared-away soldier. Which was stupid, because everybody has value. Sometimes they're in situations that make them believe that they don't, but in those cases, they could often be especially helpful if you showed that you recognized that value. I couldn't fix her work environment—not my unit, not my business. But I could at least model for them a better way. I patted her chair and smiled.

"Roger, sir." She took her seat and spent about fifteen seconds inputting commands, her fingers flying in the practiced ease of someone who knows their equipment. A high-definition image of a mountain appeared on the screen, and I recognized it as our destination from the day of the firefight. She had it zoomed out to encompass several kilometers around the area. "This is the area that you were interested in, sir."

"That's correct," I said, even though she hadn't asked it as a question.

She zoomed in once and left the image there for a few seconds for me to look it over, and when I didn't say anything, she zoomed in again. "I picked this image from seventeen weeks ago, because anything further back than that showed no significant difference from this one. So I established this as our baseline."

"That's perfect. Good work. Thank you."

She nodded, perhaps without realizing it. "This image is from two weeks later." I didn't immediately notice any difference, with the exception of some sort of metallic object located about a quarter of the way up the hill that definitely hadn't been in the original picture. After letting me look at it on my own, she hit a button and an overlay superimposed on the picture. There was a circle around the piece of equipment that I'd seen, as well as several other circles and arrows indicating other, smaller changes that I'd missed. The piece of equipment had measurements on it: 4.3 meters by 2.9 meters.

"Nice. What am I looking at? Can we start here?" I pointed with my finger at the thing that had first caught my attention. I noticed that the staff sergeant and the lieutenant had come closer as we talked.

"Yes, sir. This isn't military equipment, so we don't have a firm confirmation of what it is." Sevilla looked up at me over her shoulder.

"But you have a guess."

She hesitated, but then said, "Yes, sir."

"Sevilla," said the staff sergeant behind me in a gruff voice.

I held my hand up. "It's okay. I'm interested in any theories, and I can guarantee you that her guess is better than mine. I'm not going to hold you to it if we later find out that it's something else."

He wanted to say something, was struggling to hold it back.

"Go ahead," I said. "Say what's on your mind."

He hesitated before speaking but looked me direct in the eyes. "Sir. Respectfully. We train our analysts not to guess."

"Understood. She can caveat her unconfirmed information with a level of confidence, though, right?" It wasn't a real question. Of course she could, and doctrinally, she should.

"Yes, sir. But that's beyond her skill level."

"Well, I guess it's a good thing that this isn't an official exercise. What better chance for her to stretch than on a goose hunt for a self-important civilian?" I smiled to take some of the bite out of the rebuke.

"Sir—" he started, still not ready to let it go.

"Sergeant Josephs. Please. This would help me out a lot." It wasn't like we were breaking an actual rule. Finally he nodded, and I turned back to Sevilla.

"We enhanced the picture and ran it through an image search, and I think that it's a civilian ground-penetrating radar. Eighty percent confidence." She didn't even look back at her boss when she said that and kept all inflection out of her voice. She knew how to play the game.

"Interesting," I said. "Like they use to find minerals?"

"That I don't know, sir."

"What are the other things you have highlighted?"

She moved to one of the arrows pointing to a circle. "Here we have vehicle tracks. No determination about the type or number of vehicles, but they'd have to be reasonably fresh based on wind patterns and blowing detritus." Another arrow lit up. "Same thing here, going up the hill. Reasonable assumption is this is how they moved the potential ground-penetrating radar."

"Excellent work. What else?"

She highlighted the biggest circle, which was only a few meters up the side of the rocky hill. "This here was the hardest to figure out.

The ground has definitely been disturbed over a large area, but there's no recognizable pattern. That is, until we jump forward in time another four weeks, when we see this."

The disturbance turned into a large hole, and the number of vehicle tracks grew exponentially. Six vehicles were parked side by side to the left of the opening and down the hill. "This is the start of the excavation."

"Looks like it, yes, sir."

"And this is from how long ago?"

"Right around eleven weeks, sir."

I nodded. "The vehicles here . . . do we think that's consistent with a team that has come in, done work, secured equipment, and left?"

"Hard to say, sir."

I thought about it. Eleven weeks ago would be about eight or nine weeks before our man disappeared. "Anything more recent?"

"Yes, sir. From two and a half weeks ago." She pulled up the image. The hole had grown, and scaffolding rimmed three sides of it. Only a couple of vehicles remained, not parked as neatly as before. Some small dots around the opening might have been people.

"What's this over here?" I pointed to an area away from the dig site on flat ground that seemed to be discolored.

"Not sure, sir," said Sevilla.

I looked around the room. We had everyone's attention now, and I studied faces, seeing if there might be another source of information. Staff Sergeant Josephs was glaring at me, and the lieutenant showed nothing in his demeanor at all. One of the other analysts seemed extra interested, though, turned fully around in his seat. "You have a thought?" I asked.

He stood. He was pasty skinned and a little on the heavy side for a soldier, but not so much as to be out of regulations, and he wore a uniform that looked like he might have slept in it. Unlike Sevilla, he didn't even glance at his leadership before speaking. "Private Torrens, sir."

"Torrens." I nodded. "What do you think?"

"Scorch marks, sir. Like from a vertical landing craft."

I looked back at the picture. Interesting. The theory fit, as a craft like that would prefer flat ground. Perhaps someone was using the area as a makeshift landing pad without officially marking it. "How confident are you?"

"Not confident at all, sir. Just a wag." Wag. Short for "wild ass guess." But a wild guess beat no guess, in my mind.

"Thanks," I said.

"Roger, sir." Torrens hesitated, as if unsure what to do next, and spent an awkward couple of seconds before taking his seat.

I looked to the lieutenant, and then found Captain Nixon, against the back wall. Unsure which of them to direct my question to, I asked it to the room. "How hard would it be to get a current shot?"

"It wouldn't show us anything, sir," said Sevilla, apparently having found her confidence. "That area is darkside right now, so we could only get IR or thermal, depending on the satellite tasked. I've looked through what IR imagery that we do have, and there's nothing that stands out as significant beyond what we've already seen."

"Thanks," I said, even though I didn't like the answer. No new pictures put me right back where I started. I needed to get out there. The possible scorch marks presented another potential option. We could fly out there. It seemed likely that somebody already had. But if they did, why hadn't we seen those marks from the start? Either way, I'd gotten everything I could from the visit. I couldn't ask more without putting the analysts in an even worse spot, but hopefully the leaders had learned something. Probably not. I'd need to be more direct, which I couldn't do here, so I said my good-byes and let Nixon walk me to the front of the headquarters.

I headed to the command group to talk to Parnavic and see if he could fly us out to the site, but the sergeant major told me that his boss had stepped out, and I decided not to leave a message. I'd find him in person later and make my request, as he'd have a harder time saying no to my face.

I GATHERED MY team together in my room to give them an update and hear what they'd learned today. Part of me also wanted to watch the new people, see how they reacted to information. Every interaction created an opportunity to learn more about the people on the team so I could continue to revise how much I trusted them.

Ganos and Mac sat on my bunk and the other three leaned against the wall, taking up almost all the usable space. Alanson had his arm in a soft cast but seemed to be in decent spirits about it.

"I want to share information, so we all know where we stand and we're on the same screen." I took time to make eye contact with everyone individually. "I don't have a lot of leads. So far, what we *don't* see is almost more significant than what we do. Someone has hidden Ramiro's presence here, scraping him from surveillance video, and they'd need a reason to do that. What did you find out with that today?"

"Not much," said Mac. "Barnes and I took pictures of Ramiro down to the landing facility and showed them around, asked if anybody remembered seeing him. No firm hits. A couple people said maybe they saw him, but the thing is, there's nothing super memorable about him and it's been a while. Unless someone had a significant interaction with him, it would be easy to forget. It's a transient facility. People come and go all the time."

"Thanks," I said. "Alanson, anything back from forensics about the vehicle that blew up or the building?"

"We heard back, but nothing useful," he said. "Looks like they dumped bleach in the vehicle, and between that and the high-temperature explosion, there's not even usable DNA. The building was clean. No indications that anybody accessed it that shouldn't have. Cameras were intact and apparently untampered with."

"Pfft," said Ganos. "Like they'd know."

"Okay. So that's a dead end," I said, moving past her skepticism. I understood it, but it didn't help. "That only leaves open issues. We saw some indications of flights out to Whiteman's excavation site. When I met with Omicron, they were potentially open to helping us get out there." Mac frowned, but I kept going, not letting him interject. "But I'm not inclined to do that at this time. Too much risk, and I still want to pursue getting the military to take us."

"So we're dead-ended?" asked Castellano.

"Not necessarily. Last night I planted some seeds within Caliber, trying to fuel their natural distrust of Omicron. They're at odds over Whiteman already, and there's a chance I can get them to go after each other. But the military is a wild card in that."

"How do you figure?" asked Mac, curious now, rather than mad.

"It's like a three-body problem," I said. "Left alone, the two would act on each other in potentially predictable ways. Direct conflict. But with the military here—theoretically with a job to prevent that kind of open hostility—it changes how everybody acts. Each of the three has an effect on both of the others, and when one changes, others change as well. It's way less predictable."

"So we wait and see?" asked Mac. "Doesn't seem like our style."

"It's not. But I don't think we have a deadline—if Ramiro is truly gone, we can afford to wait a bit and see what happens. Maybe we'll get a hit on Bingham's ship. Maybe Whiteman will turn up. He's got to be somewhere." I looked around the room, trying to gauge interest from the new members of the team, but nothing in their demeanor jumped out at me as unusual. "If there's nothing else, I'm going to turn in early so that you can all get some extra rest tonight."

Nobody had anything to say, so they filed out of the room. Mac hung back.

"We could go home," he said. "Say we looked but that we couldn't find him. Nobody would know."

"We'd know," I said.

He nodded. "Yeah. That's true. I appreciate what you're doing here. Being safe. Just wanted to say that I see it. You not running off on your own, putting yourself at risk. I know it's hard on you."

"It's good," I said. "There's nothing so far that's worth the risk. We'll stay here on Taug for now, but we'll keep things under control."

When I said it, I almost believed it.

CHAPTER 12

WE COULDN'T SEE the enemy through the fog. Or maybe it was smoke. Gray and swirling, it hemmed us into our defensive positions. There were eight or ten of us, so we had wide sectors of fire in our 360-degree base. The ground was wet dirt, but not mud. We had good drainage, and whatever storm had dropped the precipitation had moved on. We had sandbags, though. Those would help against whatever was coming.

That they were out there was obvious, though at the moment it was more of a feeling than any sort of real evidence. Sounds echoed all around, but nothing specific, and this type of terrain made sounds unreliable.

The first thing—not really something tangible as much as a dark shape, dancing in the mist—came and went quickly. Part of the problem was not knowing. There were bad things out there, sure, but we couldn't definitively say that everything outside our perimeter meant us harm.

Another shape appeared, longer this time, before once again backing off or being covered by the gray.

Someone fired.

Shit.

Like the beginning of a dam bursting, that one shot became

two, and then five, and then everyone was shooting. Tracers disappeared into the darkness without any defined targets.

"What are you doing?" I yelled, though whether they could hear me over the cacophony of gunfire, who could say? They didn't stop, but the scene dissolved away, and I lay sweating in my bed.

PARNAVIC'S OFFICE CALLED early, which was almost a blessing. He wanted me to get over there right away. I hadn't even gotten coffee, but enough urgency came through in the voice of the caller that I collected Mac and moved out.

"What did you do?" he asked.

"Nothing," I said.

Mac looked at me.

"*What?* I really didn't." At least if I had, I couldn't think of what it was. Ganos hadn't used her hole in Caliber's network yet—unless they'd found her backdoor program. That seemed unlikely, as she'd been pretty confident that they wouldn't until she used it, but also because even if they *had* discovered it, they wouldn't tell Parnavic on me. That would mean admitting that they got hacked, which they'd want to hide. "I was a bit of an unfriendly guest in the intel shop yesterday, but no way does he call me in for that. He'd just mention it when I saw him again. And I wasn't even that bad."

Three soldiers rushed past us, heading in the same direction as us. "Think they're going the same place we are?" asked Mac.

I didn't see where else they could be headed, given our position on the base. "Have to be, right?"

"You want to run?"

"I don't. But maybe let's walk faster." It took a lot for me to run.

A good exercise regimen meant that my robot foot didn't hurt much, but I liked to save running for true emergencies. And while this might be one, nobody was shooting at me, so it wasn't *my* emergency. Another soldier hurried past us at a run.

The sergeant major met us at the entry, another indicator that something big was happening. "This way, sir." That we didn't head for the command group offices meant something as well, but I didn't know what. Several soldiers walked the halls, hurrying from one place to another. More people scurried about than on my previous visits.

"Where are we headed?"

"The commander asked me to bring you to Ops," said the sergeant major.

The Operations shop was not a big place in this out-of-the-way headquarters, maybe twenty meters by thirty meters, with several big screens up front on the wall and several rectangular tables throughout the room holding different types of terminals.

"Colonel Parnavic," barked the sergeant major, alerting his boss to our presence.

I tried to take in as much as I could before he got to us, but there was too much too fast, and it mostly washed by me.

Parnavic put his hand on my arm and guided me to the corner, as far away from the fifteen or so other people in the room as we could get without leaving. When he spoke, he used an exaggerated whisper, as if trying to yell at me and keep quiet at the same time. "Did you foment a shooting war?"

I stared at him for several seconds, trying to process the question before finally responding. "Huh?"

He assessed me, possibly trying to find guile where there wasn't any, before speaking again. He pointed to the front of the room. "Second screen."

At first, it appeared dark, as if the screen might not even be on. Then a flash lit one side of it for a second before fading. Someone unfamiliar with it might not have recognized it, but I knew an explosion when I saw one. A second later, a line of tracers cut across the screen, a few of the rounds bouncing up in various directions. Ricochets. "Shit. Where is this?" I asked.

"Guess."

It had to be the excavation site. "Really?"

"We sent a satellite over to get IR pictures of Whiteman's dig, but this is in the visible spectrum."

"What'd IR pick up?"

"Multiple heat sources, but it's not really sensitive enough to count human bodies when they're close together and moving. Current estimate is ninety to a hundred and twenty combatants. Several unidentified vehicles. At least one heavy pulse weapon, and an unknown number of armed drones."

"You getting a drone up?" It was a dumb question. Of course he was.

"On station in"—he checked the time—"seven minutes, give or take."

"Does it have thermals or just IR?" The IR from the drone would give a lot more fidelity than the satellite, so even with just that we'd get a lot more information.

"Full suite," he said.

I nodded. "Any idea who's fighting?"

"That's why *you're* here—I was hoping you knew. I know you've been stirring things up with the corporations."

"Inter-company espionage at most—I didn't know it would come to *this*. If it's even them." That I had sort of hoped they *would* fight wasn't something to share right then. Besides, even when I hoped for that, I had thought about boardrooms and strongly worded missives, not armed conflict.

"Who else could it be?"

"Good question," I said. But it seemed too clean to expect to find Caliber and Omicron slugging it out over a dig site. "Another good question is why."

"Has to be what's in that hole, right?"

"It's Caliber-leased land, assuming that I got accurate information," I said. Although that didn't tell us anything, really. If it *was* two companies shooting at each other, I also wondered if this was the first time. If not, maybe Ramiro got caught up in it before. That wouldn't explain the cover-up, but it might explain the cause of death. And we still didn't know Whiteman's location. Though *someone* knew that.

We watched the battle unfold—or what we could see of it in the intermittent flashes—for a few minutes. I was itching to walk around, check on each of the operators, give them a piece of encouragement or guidance, but it wasn't my place. I didn't miss being in the military often, but the moments in an Ops center when something big is happening are electric, and it's hard not to get sucked in.

"Drone on station in ninety seconds," announced a faceless voice over an unseen speaker.

"Put it up on screen three," said Parnavic. A couple seconds later an IR feed appeared on the third screen from the left, recognizable by its gray tint. Warm objects would show up black, but none had shown up yet, which meant that the search area of the drone hadn't reached the battle shown on the satellite monitor. We'd learn a lot more in a hurry once it did.

"Sir." The voice came over the speaker again, and a chill ran down my spine. The drone operator had only said one word, but I knew that tone. Parnavic did too, given the look I got from him when I glanced his way.

"Go ahead."

"Sir . . . we've lost contact with the drone." He almost seemed apologetic, though it wasn't at all his fault. As professionals, we had to consider all the possibilities and weigh each one before reaching a conclusion, but in my gut, I already knew. Someone had shot it down.

"Any indications from the connection as to what happened?" asked Parnavic, doing exactly what he should.

"No, sir. It was there one minute, gone the next."

"No flash or streaks on the video?"

"No, sir." That question impressed me, as it was a key piece of information a lot of commanders might not have asked for. If someone shot the drone down from below, sometimes it would show up for a split second before the feed cut out. This drone had been attacked from outside its camera fan—meaning probably from above—or someone had used something that didn't leave a signature the drone could detect. I'll say this for Parnavic: He was calm in a crisis.

He turned to me. "It could be that we lost the connection. That happens, right?"

"Pretty big coincidence," I said, confirming what he already knew. But hearing it from me couldn't hurt.

"Could be they jammed it. Maybe not even intentionally."

"Could be," I allowed, though neither of us believed it.

"But . . . most likely, they took it down, either kinetically or via other means," he said.

"Agreed."

He shook his head. "There's no way they think they can get away with a direct attack on the military. They had to have mistaken our drone for a civilian."

I didn't answer for a few seconds, allowing him to work it through on his own. When he didn't continue, I had to put voice to it. "They absolutely *do* think that. They're going to deny they did it, of course. And if that denial doesn't work, they're going to blame someone else. Or they're going to call it a mistake. They're going to obfuscate and do everything they can to bury it, and back in the real world, they're going to lobby every politician who will take a payment to make sure it *stays* buried out here in the middle of nowhere where nobody can see it."

Parnavic considered that for a time, taking a few paces in a circle as he did, his head down toward the floor. While he did, I looked back up at the screens in the front of the room, and I happened to be looking that way when the satellite feed went black. I put my hand on Parnavic's forearm to get his attention, and he followed the path of my eyes to the now black screen. He nodded ever so slightly. "I guess if I had any doubt, that's the end of it."

"Yeah," I agreed, but I was thinking beyond that. Taking down a drone was one thing. It wasn't easy, but it used readily available technology that we'd already seen employed on Taug. Taking down a satellite was an escalation by an order of magnitude—not something one could write off as a potential mistake. That bore examination, but we had more pressing matters. We'd lost our ability to monitor the ongoing fight. "We need to get out there."

"With what?" asked Parnavic. "I've got one troop transport that holds twelve soldiers. It's unarmed. I can't throw twelve soldiers into a situation like this with this little information."

"How many combat effectives can you manage from your detachment?"

"Thirty-five. Maybe forty."

"Add me and my team to that," I said.

Parnavic paused, and for a second I thought he might reject that, but finally he said, "Yeah. Okay. But it doesn't change the fact that I've got the single transport."

"What else have you got that flies?"

"A couple of supply ships, but they're bulky and slow and definitely not combat ships."

"Right. So we set it down a couple klicks out and hump it in. Better than landing right in the firefight anyway. We'll go in slow, gain information, and then call it in to you for a decision before we engage." He could easily cut me out of the whole thing if he wanted, so by explicitly acknowledging his command, I hoped that I made it easier for him to accept.

He thought for several more long seconds before responding. He was in a shitty spot, regardless of which decision he made. "Let's do it." He raised his voice, "Ops, call a muster of everyone who can fight. Full battle load at the launch pad in twenty minutes. That means you've got ten minutes to come up with an assault plan using the troop transport and one of the supply ships."

"Roger," said the Ops officer with no hint of emotion in her voice. These were professionals. When they had ten minutes, they didn't ask questions. They got to work.

So did I.

CHAPTER 13

WALKED WITH MAC to the staging area. He'd want to talk, and I owed him that. I'd promised him that I wouldn't fling myself at danger, and this definitely constituted danger. Hard to look at combat any other way.

"You good with this?" I asked.

Mac grunted. "Not really our place to be in it, but they need help and we're here. You just stay close to the team. No heroics."

"Roger. I'll hang back. Hopefully we all can. Maybe we'll get out there in force and the two sides won't want to directly engage the military. Just our presence could end it."

Mac rolled his eyes. "You believe that?"

"No," I said. "But you gotta have hope."

The crew that received the briefing in the underground launch facility didn't fit the standard mold for a military operation. We had a platoon of security soldiers, understrength because they had a round-the-clock mission here on the base that they couldn't abandon completely, along with whatever other pieces the unit could pull together in short order. Individually, the soldiers looked fine, but as a group we left a bit to be desired in terms of organization and cohesion. But in true military fashion, a senior non-com took charge and put us in four squads: one of twelve, who would go on the transport, and three of nine each that would fly on the supply ship. Mac led one of the latter, with me, Barnes, Castellano, and Alanson along with four auxiliaries. I'd tried to talk Alanson out of coming, given that he still had a soft cast on his arm, but he had his bag of tricks slung over his shoulder and wouldn't be denied. Honestly, I appreciated having him and whatever surveillance devices he had along. Going in blind, we'd need every bit of help we could get.

We had a simple plan, which fit the ad hoc nature of our formation. The twelve would land first in the more capable ship and establish a landing zone behind an intervisibility line. Our slower ship would come in after that. From there, we'd form up as a platoon, start a reconnaissance effort, and develop the situation. Our kit was basic but effective. Our helmets had built-in comms with four channels: one for squad, one for platoon, one private, and one spare. I tuned my spare to the command net. I might lose connectivity with it once we deployed forward, but for now, it allowed me to keep situational awareness of the bigger picture. I had borrowed standard-issue body armor but held on to my own civilian version of the Bitch. I had plenty of ammunition, and nothing could replace having a weapon set up to your own specs.

We loaded the supply ship in two files. It had no seats, so we lined up on each wall, clipped in, and crouched down. A few people sat, but others quickly corrected them. Even crouching, I really hoped that we didn't have too bumpy of a ride. Something about being inside a ship made reality kick in: I wasn't as young as I used to be, and for the first time since seeing the action while standing in headquarters, I started to question the wisdom of my going along. I quickly put that out of my mind. Sure, I could stand back and let the young folk do their jobs. But if something went wrong—and something *always* went wrong—I'd be there to help put it back on track. Besides, I still didn't know exactly what we would find—or even what we were looking for—and I could only remedy that on site.

I flipped my private net over to monitor the flight channel, and soon I had the pilots' chattering mixed with the steady flow of information across the command net. It took me a few seconds to readjust to hearing multiple streams at the same time, but you never really forget the skill. With our thirty-one-minute flight, by the time we got to the LZ, almost an hour would have passed since the drone went offline. That created so many potential situations that I couldn't parse them all. The firefight could still be going, or it could be over with the victor having incapacitated the other or forced them to withdraw.

They probably knew we were coming—it would be hard to keep it quiet. Like I'd told Mac, there was a chance that they'd both have withdrawn, not wanting to clash directly with the legal authority of the military. I rated that one as a *pretty low* chance. What I *hoped*—the best possible situation—was that the two sides had continued to slug it out for an hour and had worn each other down to the nub, so that we could come in and clean up the leftovers. Hey, a guy can dream. If that happened, we'd gain control of the area and also be able to take prisoners whom we could question. That would be priceless. Soldiers weren't spies. They'd talk. And knowing *why* they were fighting mattered almost as much as stopping them. Though what I really wanted to know was a lot simpler:

What was in that fucking hole that was so important that corporations would risk all-out war to get at it?

And: What did it have to do with Ramiro?

I flipped my private channel to check back in with Mac now that we were beyond the point of no return. "How are you feeling?"

"I don't love it," he said. "If we bog down or lose momentum, I can't say how these troops will react. Best if we don't find out. And I'm worried about the heavy weapons."

"How so?"

"They've got 'em, we don't."

"They did an hour ago. They might not now."

"I'm going in expecting them to have them," he said, and I had to agree. Best to plan for the worst.

We mostly flew in silence from there. We didn't have any new information, so we had nothing to say. I kept monitoring command, hoping that they'd get some kind of sensor back over the area, but they'd run out of assets. Then the command net went dead. I checked my helmet comm, but after a few seconds it became clear that the pilots had lost contact with base as well.

Shit. Not good.

We still had internal communications, so that probably ruled out being jammed at our end. No telling what was happening back at base. They'd have to work through it on their side, and we'd focus on what we could control on our end.

My mind drifted for a few minutes, but something in the pilots' voices snapped me back to attention. I didn't know what they'd said, but the tone screamed, "Something's wrong." You ignore that instinct at your own peril. I listened intently, trying to piece things together.

"—ground fire," finished one of the pilots, a feminine voice.

"Is it *at* us?" asked the other pilot, this one masculine.

"Not sure. It's closer than I'd like."

"Fuck yeah it is."

The ship jerked, and I pulled hard at the handhold to keep from falling.

"Shit!" The feminine voice. "It's definitely at us."

"Roger. Beginning evasive maneuvers." The masculine voice was the pilot, the other the copilot—I had that now. The ship pulled one way and then another, each shift adding strain to my grip as I fought to hold on.

"We're taking fire," said Mac, over the platoon net, keeping the rest of the team informed. "Hold tight."

Silence took over the net for what seemed like minutes, but was probably seconds, each of us in our own thoughts.

"Missile launch," said the copilot, remarkably steady, given the situation. "Deploying chaff. Roll right."

"Rolling right," responded the pilot. We immediately slammed hard in that direction, leaving me hanging from my handhold and belt clip as the ship rolled into a ninety-degree angle for several seconds before flattening out again. The craft wasn't made for this.

"Lost it! Good job!" shouted the copilot. "Shit. Another launch."

"I've got visual," said the pilot. "Deploy chaff."

"Deploying." We rolled the other way this time, shoving me hard into the wall.

"It's still on us! Fuck!"

"Brace for impact!" yelled the pilot.

The plane slammed into something—it felt like hitting a brick wall. I was on my ass, the world black, my hearing gone. A second later, my sight and hearing came back, and I realized my helmet had temporarily dampened flash and sound to protect my senses.

Black smoke roiled like fog in front of a fan throughout the passenger compartment, making it hard to see. It cleared for a moment, at least in a spot, and I realized I was looking out a hole in the other side of the ship where the wing used to be.

That seemed somewhat less than ideal.

There are these moments in combat where things slow down. I don't know the physiological cause of it, but something in my brain kicks in and I process more than rationally possible in a split second. We were missing a wing. Theoretically, this class of ship could fly without them, using vertical takeoff and landing thrusters, but who knew how much of the ship was still functional or even intact? I needed information, and as much as I didn't want to bother the pilot, he was the only one who had it.

"Pilot. Status," I barked into the net.

"Pilot's out." The strain in the copilot's voice bled through the net. "Little busy."

"Can you hold it?" I asked.

"Negative. We're going down."

"Call altitude and speed. Slow us as much as you can. We've got to jump." Without waiting for a response, I flipped to the platoon net while trying to crunch numbers in my head. We couldn't stay in the ship for a crash landing. Without proper seats, we'd bounce around like pinballs and die. Taug's 15 percent standard gravity meant we could survive a fall from . . . what? Thirty meters? Forty? The limited atmosphere would help slow us some. Body armor and helmets would help absorb impact. We might lose people, but getting out gave us a better chance than staying in. "Prepare to abandon ship. We've got to jump. Feet and knees together, roll to your hip and lat on landing."

"Altitude three hundred meters and falling," said the now pilot. "Forward velocity two hundred KPH."

Shit.

I forgot about forward velocity. Falling slowly didn't matter if momentum launched us forward at fifty or sixty meters per second. And there it was. I was going to die here, doing math. That would suck. "We need to brake."

"No shit," she yelled. She understood the mission.

I left the net in silence and unclipped from the ship, only the handhold now keeping me in place.

"Altitude two hundred. Airspeed one thirty."

"Everybody unclip," I said. 130 divided by 3.6 . . . 35 meters per second, or something close to it. Still too fast, but getting better. All of this assumed that another missile didn't slam into us and finish the job. The smoke had cleared and the hole on the far side gaped at something close to two meters. We'd already lost people, but I didn't have time for a head count. Hopefully squad leaders had done that on their own. If we still had squad leaders. The back ramp lowered. Thank goodness for that still working.

"One hundred meters. Airspeed sixty."

Holy shit. We might actually make it. What a stupid thought for someone about to jump out of a failing aircraft onto an unknown surface in the dark in an area where, if we survived the landing, one or multiple groups might want to kill us.

One problem at a time.

We couldn't know the enemy's numbers or their position in relation to us. It wouldn't matter if we didn't survive the landing.

I stopped doing math. When our altitude hit forty meters, we'd jump. I'd know if my calculations were right when I hit the ground. Granted, I might only know for a second. "Abandon ship on my call," I announced.

"Forty meters—"

"Go! Go! Go!" I shouted, not waiting for the rest of the pilot's call.

Soldiers leapt into action around me, most heading for the back, at least some for the ad hoc hole in the side. I waited maybe one second to assess, realized the futility, and ran for the back ramp myself, turning to the side at the last second so I would hopefully land at that orientation.

In the dark, it's impossible to tell how fast you're falling.

With your mind racing at a thousand thoughts per second, it's impossible to tell how much time has passed.

It felt like forever.

I focused on keeping my feet and knees together. That much I could do. Let one get away from the other and you'd break an ankle or leg or rip your hip out of its socket or some other horrible thing.

When my feet struck the ground, instinct took over and I half slumped, half rolled, and a split second later there were spots in my eyes as my helmeted head slammed into the ground. I rolled onto my back, staring upward, waiting. Waiting for the explosion of pain that would tell me how bad I was hurt.

It didn't come.

I had the full-body ache of someone who had experienced explosive deceleration, a dull ringing in my ears, but that wasn't much more than being old and trying to get out of bed in the morning. I lay there a couple more seconds, just in case. I moved one foot, and then the other. Even my robot foot seemed none the worse for wear. I wiggled my fingers.

Everything worked.

The ground shook and sound disappeared as my helmet worked to protect against the thunder that had to be the ship hitting the moon's surface not far away. I hoped that the copilot and pilot had made it out. Probably not. At least they had crash seats. Maybe they'd survive. Anyone who didn't get out of the makeshift passenger compartment . . . I couldn't dwell on it. We had too much still to do.

I flipped my net to the private channel I had with Mac.

"Mac."

"Yeah," he said, after a long second.

"You okay?"

"Yeah. You?"

"Yeah. You know where we are?"

"Working on it," he said.

I pushed myself up into a sitting position, assessed again to make sure I could still function, and then got my feet under me and stood. I toggled my visor to night sight, and the black turned to green and brought light to the world. A glow to my right threatened to white everything out. That would be the ship, burning, probably. I headed that way at a quick walk. If people remained inside, we had to try to get them out. I could do that. I'd let Mac get started consolidating the force and figuring our course of action.

It was maybe three hundred meters away, but I hadn't gone even 10 percent of that when I spotted two forms to my left, so I hurried over to find one soldier crouched over another who was on their back, propped up on their elbows. I found the private channel of the crouching soldier—my heads-up display named them as PFC Ezekiel—and asked, "Are they all right?"

"Ankle," said Ezekiel. He turned to look at me and added, "Sir."

"How bad?"

"Can't tell if it's broken or just sprained. Can't raise the medic and probably couldn't tell anyway without an X-ray. Either way, she's fucked for now. Uh . . . sorry, sir."

"Don't worry about it. Patch me into your conversation." A second later, I connected with both Ezekiel and another PFC named Jonas. "Whatever you do, Jonas, don't take your boot off."

She looked at me, though I don't know how much she could see given the dark and the limitations of our sights. "Roger that, sir."

"Can you go?" I asked.

"Tighten the laces. I'll fucking go."

"Roger that. Help her out, Ezekiel." Normally I might try to protect a soldier from herself, keep her from doing further damage. But we didn't know our situation, and we didn't currently have a way home. Either she got up and fought through the pain, or she died here. That's an easy choice.

Ezekiel helped her to her feet, and she stumbled a little before finding her footing, testing the damaged extremity, slowly putting weight on it. Low gravity would help that part, at least. I dropped off their net and found Mac's again. I started at a slower pace toward the downed ship. It took us four or five minutes to reach it, as Jonas did her best to keep up. We really could have used a shot of painkillers for her, but only medics carried those, and I didn't know where ours was. We collected two other soldiers along the way, a sergeant named Walthes and a corporal with a long name that everybody shortened to Bootch. We stood in a loose wedge, surveying the wreckage of what used to be a ship but now was a mound of mangled metal and polymer, burning in at least two places, though the fires seemed contained.

"Nothing for it but to try to get inside," said Walthes.

"Roger. You and Bootch try to find a hole. Ezekiel and I will circle to the other side and try to get to the cockpit. Jonas, you take up a prone position here on the high ground and keep overwatch. Tight ID on friend or foe. If you can bring the good guys to us, do it. But don't expose yourself until you're sure."

I got a chorus of "Rogers" in return, and Ezekiel and I trotted around the craft, giving it a wide berth because of the popping and crackling coming from the ship. I didn't know what might cook off in the fires and didn't want to take any more chances than I had to.

"Sir, this is Mac." His familiar voice came over the net as we moved.

"What've you got?"

"The troopship made it down. That's the good news."

"What's the bad?"

"They're pinned down by enemy fire about five klicks from here. Our group is down to twenty-one including your five. Sixteen effectives, two litter, three walking wounded."

Almost a third of our group, dead or MIA.

Ezekiel put a hand on my forearm, stopping me and drawing my attention. He pointed with his other arm, and I followed with my eyes. "Give me a minute, Mac."

Ezekiel had found the cockpit, but more important he'd found the body sticking halfway out of it headfirst, unmoving, hanging maybe a meter and a half from the ground.

"Let's go." I broke into a run, covering the last thirty meters or so, potentially exploding ship be damned.

She *was* moving. Barely. It only became apparent as we drew up close. She seemed to be inextricably stuck in the cockpit window, unable to get out. Blood leaked down the front of the ship in a wide rivulet. Never a good sign. With her inverted, our heads were at the same level, but I couldn't look into her eyes since she was facing the ship. I scanned her for a potential frequency that I could use to communicate but came up empty, so I switched to external speaker and turned it up to max volume. It wasn't wise from a combat perspective, as it would alert anybody nearby to our presence, but given the giant burning ship, we weren't exactly being subtle anyway.

"Can you hear me?"

Her body flinched at the sound, but if she responded other than that, I couldn't hear her. Her comms were probably tied to the ship's systems and thus useless. We needed to get her out of there, but half her body was still inside, and the blood might mean that some part of her was caught on something sharp. If we tried to pull her out, we could rip something. She might bleed out before we even got her to the ground.

"What do you think?" I asked Ezekiel, after flipping back to his channel. In theory, it was my call, but in a situation like this, the right decision doesn't give a shit about your rank. It could come from anybody.

"I'll put you on my shoulders," he said. "I'm probably stronger than you."

It seemed dicey at first, as we'd be fighting balance, but after a second I realized I'd failed to account for the conditions. In 15 percent gravity, he'd be able to hold me easily and give me the support that I needed to try to work the copilot out of her predicament. It took us a few seconds to figure out the logistics, but soon enough I was standing on his shoulders and staring at the jagged opening of the cockpit, trying to figure out how to pry it open enough to free her trapped limb.

I grasped at the cockpit screen with both gloved hands and lifted up. I had very little leverage, and it took everything I could to move it a few centimeters. Her left leg—the trapped one— moved. A stain soaked the pants of her suit around the wound, but I couldn't do anything about that yet. I released my hold on the screen to try to move her, but as soon as I did, it slammed back down onto her leg. She screamed.

Shit.

My mind raced. I didn't know how long she had, and beyond that, the ticking time bomb of the burning ship still loomed large. I couldn't figure out how to lift the cockpit screen off her leg and still pull her free. Then I did. "Ezekiel, when I tell you, I want you to let go of me and pull the copilot out of the cockpit. Don't hesitate. I'm not sure how long I'll be able to hold it open."

"Roger, sir."

I worked to lever the polymer screen off her leg again, and from there, I slowly worked one of my hands directly over where it would reenter her leg. It bit into my hand, and I didn't look to see if it had penetrated my glove. We had enough atmosphere where I could survive that. But shit did it hurt. I took a deep breath and blew it out, and then I wedged my elbows against the bottom of the cockpit opening, holding myself in place. I hoped my forearms were long enough to give room for the escape. "Now!"

Nothing happened.

Shit.

And then she was moving, sliding away behind me, and she was gone. I couldn't look back, as I was now trapped myself. Warm liquid ran down my forearm. That answered the question about whether it had penetrated my glove. I worked my arm back and forth, each motion sending a searing pain through my hand.

I fell.

I hit on my heels and rolled backward onto my ass. The back of my head smacked the ground, stunning me. A second later, I rolled over to push to my feet. When my bloody hand hit the ground, that arm gave out and I suppressed a yell. I fought to my knees and got my good hand over to my bad to put pressure on it and stop the bleeding. I hurried to help Ezekiel, but he was tightening a tourniquet onto the copilot's leg already and didn't need me right away. He finished and looked up, saw me holding my hand and probably the blood, and stood.

"Let me see, sir."

I removed my good hand, revealing about a three-centimeter hole in my glove and a growing bloodstain there and down my arm. He took me by the wrist and turned my hand over. No wound on the other side. Thank goodness for small bits of luck. Ezekiel fished in a pouch on his hip and came out with a roll of duct tape. He pulled a generous strip of it and began to wrap it tightly around my palm between the thumb and forefinger. Round and round he went, five or six times, and then he stopped and studied his handiwork.

"Not the best solution," he admitted, "but it should at least slow the bleeding and should help your suit retain air. "

I tested my hand—it was throbbing, but the sharpest of the pain had gone. You really *can* fix anything with duct tape. I nodded. "Let's get her away from the wreckage and then reassess."

Ezekiel got her up onto his shoulders in a fireman's carry, and we headed back the way we'd come, and I called Jonas to let her know we were headed to her.

"Roger," she responded. "I've got visual on you. Heads up, we've got troops in the opposite direction, four to five hundred meters, neither approaching nor withdrawing."

We reached her a couple minutes later and I dropped down next to her in the prone position to get a read on the situation. I maxed out my helmet visor's night vision setting at three times magnification and scanned 360 degrees. For the moment, we were in the clear.

"Walthes, status," I said.

"We're clear. We pulled one body from the wreck. Nobody living to be found."

"Roger. Link up with us ASAP."

"Roger. You want us to bring the body or leave it?"

I considered it. We'd want to evac the dead if we could, but without the assets for it and with no idea what else lay in front of us, the landmark of the wreck gave us our best chance of finding it again. "Leave it."

"Roger. With you in two."

The copilot—Lieutenant Potter, I learned—stirred. Ezekiel, who was crouching over her, and thus close enough to hear her, said, "She's asking where she is."

"That's a good sign," I said. "Fill her in and try to get an assessment of how bad her injury is. We're going to have to decide whether to move her or stay with her, and my gut is saying move her. The burning ship is a beacon that's only going to bring trouble."

"Roger."

I flipped to Mac's channel. "Status?"

"We've got everybody consolidated. Is that you by the wreck?"

"Roger. Six of us, two injured, one serious." I didn't include myself in the wounded. I wasn't thinking of myself that way right then. Too much adrenaline, maybe.

"Start heading our way. I'm leaving three here, but we've got to hightail it to help our other team. They're in a bad way. We're heading out from here at eighty-eight degrees. We're going to approach the enemy from another side and try to put them into a cross fire. Have your effectives catch up as soon as you can."

"Roger."

CHAPTER 14

WHEN SERGEANT WALTHES and Corporal Bootch reached us, it took just a second to get us all on the same channel, and not much more for me to issue instructions.

"Bootch, you take the lieutenant. Jonas, you stay with them. Go as slow as you need to. Consolidate with the rest of the team, 121 degrees, about 450 meters. Walthes, Ezekiel, you're with me. We're at double time."

"I can go with you," said Jonas, getting to her feet.

She had a bad ankle, but in low gravity, maybe it would work, and we didn't lose anything if she tried but couldn't make it. "Fine. But keep up. We can't slow down."

Jogging in low gravity is weird. You don't speed up much faster than you do in full gravity initially, but after a few seconds you keep getting faster. The stride is different, too—much longer—so you took a lot fewer steps. But for that reason, you really had to watch where you came down, because you usually couldn't see your landing spot when you launched the way you would in normal g. The higher speed made turning harder, and slowing down took longer. We closed the distance to Mac's previous location in just over seventy seconds, slowing at the end. Jonas trailed behind us, but only by a few seconds.

I reoriented us to eighty-eight degrees and we took off again, about four hundred meters behind Mac and his team, who dipped in and out of view with the terrain. He'd said the distance was five klicks, so I set a more sustainable pace.

We didn't speak. The slower pace didn't mean we had air to waste on chatter. I found Mac's group talking on the platoon net as they approached their target. Mac had taken charge, which meant the actual platoon sergeant was incapacitated or they'd made a joint call to switch command based on Mac's experience.

A rocket streaked away from Mac's position, announcing their entry into a battle that was little more than a few tracers before that. A couple seconds later, a bright flash lit the darkness a klick or so out from the launch point. Mac had probably targeted the heavy weapon position of the enemy. He'd mentioned it before and would want to take that out quickly. We didn't have a read on enemy assets or their ability to replenish, but that surprise attack would help even whatever odds we faced.

I caught bits of the battle—a flash here, an explosion there—as running took most of my focus. Tracers whipped up into the air from three or four shooters, but I couldn't look up long enough to see their target. Probably a drone. Wasted fire since hitting a moving object with projectile weapons in the dark is almost impossible.

A rocket streaked from the air and lit the night as it slammed into Mac's position. I held my team up about a hundred meters short of that to see if the drone attack continued. No sense running straight into it. I hadn't noticed my lungs burning during our run, but now it hit me hard. We all went to a knee, and I used the time to take a better look at my heads-up to assess our remaining effectives.

Fourteen names came up for Mac's team, which made eighteen with my four. As I studied it, one of his grayed out. Kaska. Dead. The drone probably got him. Mac had left some wounded behind, and I had too, but the toll was rising. Another mark against me in a career of leading people to their deaths.

I scanned down the list looking for specific names and found them. Alanson. Barnes. Castellano. Still alive, still fighting. It was horrible that I put certain lives above others in this kind of situation, but here we were. It's hard to control what you think about in those kinds of moments. But wherever your mind ends up, you can rest assured that it's probably your true self, like it or not. A mirror is a fucking mirror.

Things went quiet.

That sounds like a good thing, but in truth, it's pretty disconcerting. One minute, you're shooting at them and they're shooting at you, and then . . . nothing. But it wasn't nothing. We were still here, and they probably were too. Maybe we'd both run out of rockets. We had a limited supply, and one disadvantage of drones was that most of them could carry only a light load of ordnance. I stood and moved my team forward to join Mac.

"We're coming in," I said.

"Watch for drone fire," he warned.

"On it," I assured him. "What's our situation?"

"Enemy is to our direct front, about nine hundred meters. Pretty sure we took out their heavy weapon, but they've got fifteen to twenty soldiers. We're out of range of small arms stuff. Got their attention, though, which took some pressure off our squad on the other side. I can't raise them, which means they're either jammed or some of them are dead, and the others haven't reestablished comms."

"We won't figure that out from here," I said.

"Nope. But what the enemy does next should tell us a lot. If they come for us, we'll give better than we take being up on this rise with good fields of fire."

We reached Mac's team, and I waved my crew to take up positions within their formation and form one unit. I took a knee again, both to drop my silhouette and to keep recovering from the physical exertion. Mac's plan was a solid one, but perhaps too simple. The enemy could see the terrain too and probably wouldn't charge over open ground with us here. Even if they had greater numbers, that was suicide. By waiting, we kept an advantage in that regard, but we ceded initiative to the enemy.

We didn't have the range to engage them from here. If we charged at them, they'd have the same advantage that Mac was trying to gain for us by holding our position.

Mac figured it out the same time I did. "They're not coming. We're going to have to move."

"What've they got for range?" I asked.

"If they don't have more heavy weapons, we can probably get halfway there before they start to make us uncomfortable. Almost two-thirds before they really fuck us up."

"And if they do have one?"

"I think we'd know that by now," he said. I agreed. If they could reach out and touch us here, they'd be doing it.

"Base of fire and flank left?" I asked.

"Best terrain," he agreed. To the left lay the hill, which was theoretically the goal of the initial fight. It also had a lot of large rocks along the way, which would make the going slower but at least provide some cover. "Which one do you want?"

"Flanking. Always."

He snorted. "Figures. Okay. You take Barnes and Castellano and six others. I'll take the rest and move first."

"Roger." Eight names slid to me in my heads-up, forming a second squad, and I took a few seconds to get them organized on one channel. "We'll give the other team thirty seconds and then we move out on the left flank. Keep to cover where you can. Short runs. Once we get closer, pair up and we'll shoot and move until we're close enough to assault through." We'd never get that far in the plan. Something would change by then. It always did. But we still had to have one.

Ten seconds later a flash dimmed my sights, and a crunch shook the ground, flinging dirt and detritus into the air around us.

Fucking mortar.

"Move now," I said, changing the plan earlier than I'd anticipated. They had our range; we needed to change that. We'd be vulnerable moving, but harder to target, too. I'd take that tradeoff.

I sprinted for about twenty seconds, covering maybe a hundred meters, and then called a quick halt to reassess. I still had everybody. Another mortar crunched behind us, but they hadn't reoriented yet, so it was all bark, no bite. I took off again, at a slower pace this time, picking my way through the increasing number of head-sized rocks now littering the ground. We'd reach bigger ones in a minute, which would give cover, but for now they were a nuisance.

Another mortar crunched behind me somewhere, too far back to cause damage. Barnes was to my left and slightly ahead, Castellano in the same position to my right. If I had planned to lead the charge, they had other ideas. They'd probably gotten their orders direct from Mac, and only part of those orders involved the enemy. I'd have to make sure I didn't put them into bad positions with my own choices. That wasn't a great way to think about a battle, but it was too late to do anything other than deal with it.

"Let's keep moving so that mortar doesn't catch up," I broadcast. I paused three seconds and then headed out again.

"Contact, front. Vehicle." Barnes.

I searched for about half a second before a line of tracers from an automatic weapon ripped into the ground to my right front, announcing the vehicle's location, about three hundred meters to our front and closing.

Shit. So much for them not having a heavy weapon. Where had that come from? Obviously they'd held it back. I dropped prone, sighted in on it, and fired a three-round burst of guided bullets into where I expected the front window to be. At least one of my shots hit it, shooting straight up into the air afterward in a burning ricochet. Shit. Probably armored. I fired again, then rolled, got to a crouch, and moved for three seconds before hitting prone again. I didn't want them to get a bead on me. Two smaller weapons joined the automatic from the vehicle, scattering shots all around me. I didn't have time to check my heads-up to get the exact positions of my team, but they were the targets.

We couldn't match their firepower, but our own tracers whipped back at the vehicle. It kept coming, still raking us with intense fire. I needed to stop trying to fight this as an individual and take control of the battle. That's harder than it sounds when bullets are flying. I took a couple seconds to study my HUD and devise a plan.

"Castellano, Walthes, Yarbo, Flair. You're team one. Lay fire on the vehicle to keep it occupied. Barnes, Ezekiel, Macic, Horatio, get further left. Flank it and take it out." I had no idea what the side of that vehicle looked like or if we had anything that *could* take it out, but standing still and letting it drive right into us or letting that mortar catch us were sure losers.

Our fire dropped off as half my people started to move, but the four still shooting kept enough pressure on to keep a shower of sparks on the front of the vehicle. If nothing else, it would be distracting.

"Fuck! I'm hit." It was Yarbo. The four streams of fire became three.

"Shoot and move," said Castellano over the squad net. He hadn't had time to gather his smaller team on their own channel.

The vehicle had closed inside a hundred meters now, still firing, and I'd been so caught up in directing the team that I hadn't re-alized it was headed straight for me. I took a second to assess. It was some sort of armored vehicle with an open top with wheels in the front and caterpillar treads in the back. The automatic weaponeer and the two other shooters stood, firing over the top of the armored area. It seemed like an impractical vehicle, but it worked here. I aimed, but at the last second, didn't fire. While it was headed for me, it wasn't shooting at me. Castellano and company had held the attention of two shooters, and the third targeted well to my left.

Shooting up from the ground, my bullets would glance off the armor unless I made a perfect shot, which I wouldn't. I pushed myself into a crouch, and as the vehicle continued to come at me, I launched myself into the air. I hit my apex maybe three meters off the ground, and only then did I start firing. From my new angle, my shots ripped into the exposed top of the vehicle, slamming into equipment and body armor.

The automatic weapon swiveled toward me. From forty meters, it wouldn't miss.

Something moved to the left of the vehicle. Not something. Someone. Barnes. She launched herself forward and into the air, up and over the vehicle. One of the shooters started to raise their weapon, but I drilled them in the chest with a shot and they stumbled back.

I hit the ground just as the vehicle exploded. Without hesitating, I sprinted four steps to the left and launched myself as far out of the path of the oncoming destruction as I could.

By the time I picked myself up from the dirt and adjusted my kit from scraping along the ground, my troops had swarmed the vehicle. Two distinct shots announced the end of the threat.

I didn't have time to think about it. We needed to get moving again, and before that, I needed to assess my situation. My HUD showed Flair offline, but you can't always rely on that. "Can anybody see Flair?" I asked.

"He's hit," said Walthes. "Hold on." After several long seconds he came back on the net. "Dead."

"Anybody else hit?"

"Yeah," said Yarbo, her voice thick with pain. "Leg. I think it's broken. I can't put weight on it even at this gravity. I'm done."

"Bleeding?" I asked.

"I don't think so. The armor stopped the round from penetrating."

"Roger." I flipped to talk to Mac. "We ran into some trouble. Resuming our move now. One KIA, one WIA out of the fight. Seven moving."

"Roger. We're moving forward slowly. We'll be engaged in about ninety seconds. Assault through as quick as you can get there."

"Roger." Flipping to my team net, I said, "Let's move."

For the next couple of minutes, we ran. We couldn't quite sprint—the terrain and our lungs didn't allow for that—but we moved fast. I pulled us up three hundred meters short of our target, because taking a few seconds to assess the situation would be worth it. Based on muzzle flashes, the occasional pulse weapon burst, and what my HUD could put together, the enemy had about fifteen fighters left. But we had them engaged on two sides already by Mac's team and the troopship contingent, so they had about half their force facing one way and half facing the other. No wonder they hadn't engaged us as we came down the slope on their flank.

We weren't in great tactical shape, either. For my team to assault through, both Mac's element and the troopship squad would have to lift and shift fires to avoid hitting us, and we'd be running straight into a superior force.

"Holding on the assault. I've got an idea," I told Mac. "Castellano. Pick a target and take it out."

"Roger." He took up a prone position behind a flat rock. I'd seen him engage a vehicle at long distance. Three hundred meters wouldn't even challenge him. It would give away our position, but I had a hunch. These were mercenaries, not people defending their homes. We didn't have to beat them to a soldier. We could make them quit. When they realized that we had them from three sides, hopefully they'd tap out. Castellano's weapon coughed and a second later an enemy soldier dropped.

"Reposition. Hit 'em again."

He crawled quickly to his right about ten meters and took up another position. They'd be looking for him now. Maybe. If they could focus on us with two fights already underway. His weapon spoke again, and another shooter on the objective went silent. I watched on, seeing what the enemy wanted to do. Slowly, their outgoing fire dropped off, like a spigot shutting down. It would take the cease-fire call some time to permeate through their formation. We didn't have comms with them, so they couldn't call us to surrender.

"Cease fire," I said to Mac. He must have relayed it to the troopship contingent because their fire cut out a couple seconds after Mac's, and all of a sudden everything went quiet. It was less disconcerting this time. "Cover me," I said on my team's net.

"What are you doing, sir?" asked Barnes. That was a fine question.

"Accepting their surrender."

"Is that wise? Exposing yourself?"

"Probably not. But enough people have died for this bullshit. I'm ending it." I stood and walked toward the enemy position as Barnes hurried to join me. I didn't want her with me, but I had exactly zero chance of stopping her, so I let her come.

I moved in a way to keep rocks between me and a clear line of sight. Yeah, I was making myself a target, but that didn't mean I needed to be stupid about it. A trained soldier would still have dropped me easily, but it did give me some comfort, regardless.

I activated my external speaker when I reached about two hundred meters out from their closest fighter and broadcast, "You done?"

A couple seconds later, a speaker from their position announced, "Yeah. We give."

"Toss out your weapons and put your hands on your heads. We're coming in. Don't do anything stupid."

Several weapons clattered on the ground over the next few seconds, and I signaled the rest of my team forward. My mind raced ahead as we covered the last bit of ground. These mercs had been fighting with somebody else before we got there. Where was that other force now? It didn't seem likely that they'd have combined forces to fight against us. Not unless the firing at the start was the bait in a trap to draw us out to fight. But why? That didn't make any sense. "When we get up there, after you check for more weapons, separate everybody and disable their private channels," I told my team. I didn't want the prisoners collaborating on their stories.

Ten minutes later, we had the enemy sitting in a line with a meter between each of the fourteen of them. Two at the end were wounded, and two of Mac's soldiers tended to them as I paced in front of the rest, putting on a show. They'd given me access to their comms net, so I didn't have to rely on speaker. Staff Sergeant Peña led the eight remaining effectives of the troopship crew now as they collected the enemy weapons and deposited them in a hole. We could guard them there or bury them.

"Who's in charge?" I asked, after letting the prisoners stew for a bit.

No answer. Really? Come on. Don't tell me that corporate hires were going to go all *we've got a code* on me.

"Look. It's over. I just want some answers."

More silence. But this time, a few of the soldiers glanced at each other. Enough of them glanced at one broad-shouldered man that I got a good idea of who had command without them saying so. I walked over and stood directly in front of him. "Stand up," I said.

He unwound himself from his spot on the ground and complied. I immediately regretted it, as he stood a solid ten centimeters taller than me, and I had to look up to meet his eyes through our visors. I took a step back to mitigate that.

"You in charge?"

"Fuck you," he said.

"There's no point in keeping quiet," I offered.

"Says you. We talk, we don't get hired again."

"Oh bullshit. You're not getting hired again regardless. You'll be lucky not to go to prison." I wasn't bluffing. They'd killed government troops. There would be a reckoning for that in some court somewhere, and while the corporations would fight to protect themselves, that didn't extend to these poor saps. We had them dead to rights with all the evidence we needed. "You talk, I'll put in a good word."

He didn't speak, but he did waver. Before he could get up the nerve, one of the seated people spoke up. "I'm not in charge, but I'll talk."

The guy turned to glare at her.

"What?" she asked. "This is the fucking *military*. Ain't none of us sign up for fighting against the government." Smart woman.

"Deal. You, sit," I said to the big guy in front of me. "You. Come with me."

The woman got up from the group and followed me as I started to walk away. Barnes intercepted her and checked her again for a weapon.

"You can come too, Barnes."

She did.

"What the fuck happened here?" I asked, after establishing a private channel for the three of us, which took a minute since the prisoner ran different software. I wanted to keep the question open-ended, because I didn't want to miss something because I didn't think of it.

"They sent us here to seize that hole up there and hold it," she said.

"*Who* sent you here?"

"No clue. We've got a contract guy who relays instructions from the client. He also pays us. Everything else is cut out." After I didn't respond for a couple of seconds, she added, "Honest. I swear. None of us know."

"When were you hired? Where'd you come from?"

"We're from out of system. We got the word maybe ten, fifteen days ago. Boarded a ship, they put us in stasis, we woke up, and here we are. Been on Taug a day, maybe a little more."

That was good to know, if not entirely unexpected. I decided to focus on the here and now. Somebody else could dig through the big-picture stuff later. "Okay. What happened when you got to this location?"

"We landed right about here, which is the closest you can really land a ship. We were getting ready to move out and secure the objective when someone else showed up. Next thing I know, there's shooting."

"Where's that group now?" I asked, jumping to the most important question. If we had another armed group out here, we needed to know it.

"They tried to get to the hill—same place we were heading— but we had them outgunned. Eventually they pulled back and evacked. But we fucked 'em up. There are probably some bodies over there, unless they dragged them all out."

"What's in the hole in the hill?"

"No idea. But it has to be pretty fucking important, don't it?"

Yeah. It did. "How many did you start with?"

"Thirty," she said.

Shit. Fourteen left. "What happened to the rest?"

"Casualty point is about a hundred and fifty meters that way." She pointed the opposite way from the direction I'd approached. "None of us got out. We're either here, there, or still out there somewhere. But anybody still out there is either dead, incapacitated, or a fucking coward."

I hoped for coward. It beat the alternatives. But regardless, we'd need to do a search at some point soon to try to find any wounded and collect the dead for processing. We'd need more troops, though I didn't know where we'd get them from or when, as we still didn't have comms with headquarters. "Did you know we were military?"

"No way," she said without hesitating. "Nobody even mentioned that as a possibility. They said the military never comes off their base, so we had no reason to suspect. I swear, I thought you were those other mercs coming back. Or new ones. This whole thing is fucked."

That we could agree on.

"Thanks for your cooperation," I said.

"You said you'd put in a good word," she said.

"I will. What's your name?"

"Onyango."

"Got it. Count on it." And I meant it; I made a note so I wouldn't forget.

I gathered up with Mac and Peña, the two leaders—at least as far as anybody had control in this mess. Barnes didn't join us in the circle, but she didn't let me get too far away from her either. "Thoughts?" I asked.

"We're going to need a ride out of here," said Mac. "I tried one of their comms, but theirs don't work any better than ours. It's like someone cut the link to the other side of the moon."

That was possible. Knock out the comms satellites and it put us all in the same dead ship. Given that we'd had a gunfight with a bunch of mercs, it didn't stretch the imagination to assume they'd done that.

"Parnavic will be trying to get to us," I said. "He's got the troop carrier still." Assuming it made it back and hadn't been shot down like we had.

"Not much to do but sit here and wait," said Peña.

"I don't know about that," I said.

Mac looked at me. "You want to go in that hole." That he didn't ask it as a question showed how well he knew me.

Of course I wanted to go in that fucking hole.

CHAPTER 15

WE TOOK ABOUT five minutes to reorganize into two squads. One would stay here with the responsibility of guarding the prisoners, tending to the casualties, and consolidating with the additional wounded that we'd left in spots along the way. After that, they'd follow on up toward the hole and improve our position against a potential counterattack. None of the prisoners could tell us which corporation had hired them, but they all agreed that they'd all been hired by the *same* outfit. That left another side still out there, and we couldn't be sure that they'd given up. On the contrary. If this site was so important that people would physically go to war over it, they probably *hadn't* given up. But the isolated nature of Taug helped. We all had the resources we had and couldn't easily get more. That included soldiers.

Still. Better to be safe and dig in. You always improve your position when you've got time, because when time runs out, you'll be glad you did.

I headed up the hill with Mac and my three original team members along with three more, including Ezekiel. Alanson still had the bad arm, and Mac was clearly hurting in some way but lying about it and saying he was fine. I was intact but worn down—my hand was throbbing, but when I checked it, the blood had dried. It would have to hold. Fatigue worried me more. I wouldn't be ready for another run anytime soon. Hopefully it wouldn't come to that.

We approached the entrance to the excavation site, halting among some larger rocks about three hundred meters out to observe. From here, it looked like a natural cave, though I knew it wasn't. We used every optic we had to look for anything out of the ordinary. We didn't have unlimited time, but enough bad things had happened to me in my life to be wary. Something felt off, and I wasn't sure whether that was paranoia or something I should trust. We advanced, two at a time, with the others providing cover, until we reached a relatively flat area a hundred meters away from the entrance.

After a minute of observation, Alanson fished in his pack and brought out a disc-shaped drone a little bigger than his fist, pushed a few buttons, and flung it skyward. It wobbled in the air for a few seconds before righting itself and zipping away toward the entrance. I moved closer to him so I could see the video feed on his flexible tablet. I know better than that, of course. As a commander, or even as a team leader, you have to avoid the temptation to get focused on a single source. You let the technician work their system and report, so that you can stay aware of all possible inputs. But right then, I couldn't help myself.

The smallish drone didn't have much in the way of night vision—just a cheap starlight lens—and it was moving, which led to a grainy, green-tinged video. On a positive note, it reached the entrance unmolested, which put it well ahead of most of the drones we'd tried to use lately. Alanson looked at me, an unspoken question of whether to push inside. I nodded.

The feed dimmed even more inside the cave without the ambient light from the sky, and Alanson piloted the drone slowly, not wanting to slam into a wall or the roof and lose it. "I'm going to activate its light," he said. A moment later, the picture changed, black now except for a single cone of light. "It's hard to fly this way, but we're not going to get anything from the night vision camera in here."

"Roger," I said, more confirming than approving. He knew his job better than I did. Even watching the screen, I couldn't figure out what I was seeing, and I began to get bored with it until Alanson spoke.

"Sir." The tone of it grabbed my attention. "You're going to want to see this."

I looked at the screen, which now featured a stable if wobbly image from a mostly stationary drone. The object on the screen was an oval with a circular apparatus in the center that looked like something one might rotate. "Is that . . . ?"

"It looks like a door," said Alanson.

My mind flipped through the possibilities. Had someone on an archaeological dig installed a door at the back of their excavated cave? It didn't seem likely. But if they didn't, that meant that they found it there, which seemed equally unlikely.

Mac must have sensed something, because he joined us, looking over Alanson's other shoulder. "Well shit." As usual, Mac had summed it up well.

"Let's go in," I said. Neither of the other two protested, and we resumed our slow march toward the opening. As we got close,

Mac assigned three people to stay outside the entrance to guard our backs. I didn't expect anybody to come up behind us, but I also didn't want any surprises.

Inside the cave, we all flipped on our helmet lights, and the crisscrossing beams lit the room well enough where we could make out most of the place. The walls were rough stone, unfinished, and a mix of rock and scree shifted a bit under my feet when I scuffed them. It all looked like what I'd expect from an excavated hole. All except for the door set in the back wall, which resembled something like an internal hatch on a bulkhead on a spaceship. Or an airlock, but slightly bigger than a standard personnel lock that one would expect on a ship.

"Cover me," said Mac, though there wasn't much need for that inside. Instinct, I guess. He moved to the door, where he slapped at the handle first, maybe in case it was electrified or something. After a couple of seconds, he touched it longer, as if testing whether it was hot. Finally, he grasped it fully with one hand and then both. He twisted. The handle turned easily with a slight metal-on-metal sound. The door made a soft *thunk* when he'd turned the mechanism as far as it would go. "Ready?" he asked.

"Do it," I said.

He pulled the door open, exerting a bit against the heavy weight of it even in the reduced gravity. There was no catch to hold it open, but he tested letting go of it and it didn't slam shut. "Alanson, Castellano, you stay here. One of you hold the door to make sure it doesn't close behind us."

That was good thinking. I wanted to see inside there more than just about anything I could remember wanting, but I also didn't want to be trapped in the bowels of the moon with no way out.

Mac pushed through first, and I followed him, with Barnes coming in behind me. We entered into a corridor that went both right and left, with a wall of some sort of manufactured material to our direct front. I reached out to touch it but couldn't tell its composition through my glove. One thing I did know: This wasn't a natural occurrence.

To our left, the beam of my light hit a wall after about ten meters. To our right, it seemed to go on farther, so I gestured in that direction and Mac moved out, weapon at the ready. I had mine still gripped in two hands, but I kept it pointed down and away. Nobody needed me firing in here.

The corridor turned sharply to the right and Mac pied the corner, keeping his weapon at the high ready. When he relaxed that, I moved around behind him, knowing it was clear. We went another three meters and turned back to the left using the same technique. This corridor ended in another door, similar to the one we'd entered through, but a bit smaller. Barnes covered behind us while Mac moved forward, testing the handle much as he did the other one, before determining it was safe.

"You pull it open, I'll go through," I said.

He wanted to argue. I could tell by his posture, the tension in his shoulders, but he relented. If there was something behind the door, opening it would warn who or whatever it was, so we had to do it all at once. I gave him a sign with my fingers. *One. Two. Three.*

Mac yanked the door open, and I started to go through, but light poured from the opening, stopping me in my tracks. It wasn't bright enough to be painful or blinding. Just unexpected. After a second, I gathered myself, but we'd lost any opportunity of surprise, so I edged around the door slowly, my weapon tucked to my shoulder and ready in case I needed it. Even through my suit I could feel air rushing out, almost pushing me backward. Inside, a body lay in a pool of blood in the middle of the floor. I stared for a minute, taking it in. The dead body was a soldier—or more likely, a mercenary—in body armor and a helmet, their face turned away.

After a few seconds, I got the sense that I was being watched and looked up to see a light-skinned man leaning against the far wall with no helmet on. He held a pistol in his hand, and while he didn't have it pointed at me, he wasn't exactly *not* pointing it at me. Given the low oxygen, without his helmet, he'd likely suffer from hypoxia in a matter of minutes if he wasn't already.

"This isn't what it looks like," he said, calm, given the situation. "If you come in and close the door, the room will re-oxygenate and you won't need your breather."

The matter-of-fact nature of his statement struck me. "Mac, come through," I whispered into my comm. I moved in to make room for him and flipped my speaker on. "Toss down your weapon."

The man rolled his eyes, but bent down, put his weapon on the floor, and pushed it away from himself. He looked very familiar. "As I said, this isn't what it looks like."

"We're going to close the hatch," I said on the net. "Barnes, you stay there, warn us if anything is coming."

"Roger."

On cue, Mac pulled the door behind him. As he did, it clicked as to where I had seen this man before. "Dr. Whiteman," I said.

The man inclined his head slightly, acknowledging the name.

"Why don't you tell us what's going on."

"Take off your helmet," he said. "It's going to take a minute."

CHAPTER 16

I **THOUGHT ABOUT IT** for a good long time before I took off my helmet. I had no idea how he could breathe without his, but the evidence was right there in front of me. Except I couldn't focus on that as I stood face-to-face with the person I'd been trying to find for several days. That came with a lot of thoughts of its own. Whiteman was the key to finding the person I'd set out to find weeks prior. And he was just . . . there. And then there was the dead body in the middle of the room. You know you've got a fucked-up situation when the dead body isn't at the top of the list of questions. My mind spun in circles for a bit longer before I did the only thing I could settle on.

I took off my helmet.

I couldn't quite place the smell of the air, but it definitely didn't smell like a cave. It reminded me a bit of the smell of a self-cleaning oven. But I could breathe. I didn't have a manual monitor to tell me the oxygen level, but it felt . . . normal. No burning in the lungs. I wasn't going to exert myself to see how much it affected me, though. It definitely exceeded the 40 percent of standard that blanketed the rest of Taug. "How are we breathing?"

"I don't know," said Whiteman. "Truth be told, I'm kind of surprised that that's your first question."

"I have a lot of questions."

"I'm sure you do. And I'll do my best to answer them."

"You expect me to believe that?" I asked.

"Not really. But it's true. I've been trying to reach you ever since I heard you were coming to the planet."

I studied his face, trying to find any sign of deception. I didn't. But then again, I didn't know him. Maybe he was a good liar. I needed to keep him talking to see how well his story held up. I decided to change topics to try to catch him up with the rapid switch. "Who's the body?"

"I don't know—"

"You said you'd answer questions, but there's a lot you don't know."

"If you'd let me finish?"

I paused for a second. I could allow that maybe I was being a bit of a dick. I nodded.

"He came here to kill me. I shot first. I don't think he expected me to be armed, and he got cocky. His loss. As to who he is? Your guess is as good as mine. But who hired him? Smart money is on Caliber. But we can't rule out Omicron."

That was both interesting and plausible, especially on the surface. It also gave me a chance to force him deeper to assess how it held up. "Why do you think it's Caliber over Omicron?"

"I've had a lot of time to think about it," he said with a shrug. "Maybe it'd be easier if I started from the beginning."

"Sure," I said.

He took a moment to gather his thoughts, and then began. "I had a source here on Taug who alerted me to an anomaly in one of their scans. This happened maybe, I don't know, eight months ago?"

"That happen a lot?"

"More than you'd think. I keep contacts in a bunch of different mining companies, because they're always out looking in places that nobody else looks. They find something that flags as unusual but not valuable to them, and I check it out. Usually it's nothing. I either get their scan or send somebody out to do one of my own, do the analysis, and that's the end of it. But once in a while? Something shows up that's worth me checking out in person."

"So you came."

"Right."

"Was Jorge Ramiro with you?"

"Not initially, but yes. He's dead. I'll get to that." He said it matter-of-factly, and it felt cold. I took a few things from that. First, the man I was looking for was indeed dead. Whiteman wasn't lying about that. But second, the fact that he could casually dismiss it as something he'd get to as it fit his story told me a lot about Whiteman. He might be sharing information with me, but he was at least as heartless as the dead man on the floor.

"Caliber owned the land I wanted to search on," he continued.

"Leased, right?"

"Technically. Sure, though I promise you that neither company looks at it like that. Either way, I had to talk to them to get permission to do my thing. That part was easy. I'm well enough known that people are usually happy to work with me in hopes that they'll get some good press out of it. After all, if I make a find, it's going to be news. That's always worked in my favor until now. Because you know these companies. There's always paperwork. Except they never enforce it—at least they haven't in the past. I find something, we do a couple years of research, publish some academic papers, and, if it's interesting, hit some mainstream news. It's good for funding. Expeditions like this aren't cheap, and academic papers don't really pay."

"It's always about the money," I agreed.

"Oh. More than you know. Because once I found this"—he gestured around—"all of a sudden Caliber got really interested."

"What is"—I copied his gesture—"this?"

"I still don't completely know. But here's what I can tell you. It's old. Really old. The rock that we cut through to get to it dates to somewhere around eleven thousand years ago."

Old science classes started flipping through my head. I didn't know much, but that was impossible. Space travel began less than five hundred years ago, which meant that this . . . whatever it was . . . shouldn't be here. No way could something have gotten to this moon millennia ago. Nothing human anyway. And while I'd met aliens, they were behind us in developing that technology. Something didn't add up. "Any chance something here is throwing off your dating equipment?"

"Checked that. No. It's accurate."

"That would mean . . ."

"That would mean that whatever this is, it predates human space exploration."

I got a chill, which, oddly, made me realize that it wasn't from the environment. Not only could I breathe, but the temperature in the room was comfortable. "That's impossible."

"There's more."

I stood there, unsure what to say to that. "Tell me."

"First, there's power here. Over a hundred centuries later, whatever is here has a power source. We haven't found it yet, but you can see the evidence for yourself. There are lights."

"Radiation signature?"

"No. None."

"That's significant."

"That alone would possibly be the most significant archaeological find in history. And it's not even the most significant part of what we've found. Somehow, this room is making oxygen. Do you see any vents? Because there aren't any. And before you ask, no, I don't know how it's working. And even that pales in comparison to the big story. Someone got here before us. Or . . . something. Very potentially, we've discovered evidence of a non-human spacefaring culture. Something nobody has ever discovered before."

"There are the Cappans."

He snorted. "Yes. The Cappans are spacefaring. But you and I can both put a pretty solid date on when that happened."

Given that I'd been mostly responsible for it, I very much could. "If they were here . . . where did they go?"

"That's a great question. Right up there with why have we not seen evidence anywhere else in all the time we've been looking?"

"It's a big galaxy," I offered.

"It is. Maybe that's it. I don't know. What I do know is that there are more answers to be found here. All we need is the equipment to dig deeper."

"Which is where Caliber comes in."

"Not exactly," he said. "When Caliber learned what I'd found, they didn't want me digging at all. They got wind of the technology involved and wanted to keep it for themselves."

I could believe that. The power source alone could be worth . . . what? Trillions? What's the number bigger than trillions? Was there even a big enough number to encompass the value? "So what did you do?"

"I did what I always do. I tried to bargain with them. I'd do the academic work, take a percentage as a finder's fee, and as we developed the situation, we'd give them first crack at the economic value outside of the academic."

"But they wanted it all," I said. Because of course they did. They wanted it so badly, they were willing to fight against the military to secure it. But there had to be more to the story. "So how did Omicron get involved?"

"When I realized that Caliber wanted to completely cut me out, I went to Omicron for help."

"The enemy of my enemy is my friend," I offered.

"Right. And the only other place with the resources to do what I needed."

"But Caliber found out."

"Right again. Which goes back to this gentleman." He pointed to the guy on the floor. "That's why I assume he's Caliber."

I had no idea what I would do with all this information. After all, with Ramiro being dead, I'd completed my mission. But . . . well, I was me. And I couldn't turn away. "Go back for a second. What was Omicron's response?"

"Supportive, initially. But I got the feeling that they were lying to me. It would be naïve to think that they wouldn't want to exploit it too. They were almost too accommodating, if you understand what I mean."

"I do." Whiteman, if I could believe him, had himself in a tight spot. But one thing didn't track in his story. I could buy that both corporations would do horrible things. Shit, I'd *seen* both do them. But I had a hard time buying *his* altruism. The potential for billions of marks would affect anybody. "Let me ask you this: What's in this for you? Why didn't you cut the deal that keeps you alive and gets you paid? I have to believe that was on the table."

"It probably was, if I trusted Caliber to hold to their deal, which . . . debatable."

"Fair."

"Look. I'm not the most moral person in the galaxy, but I've got a code. Yes, I make money doing what I do. I'm a glory whore. I love a camera. But also look at where everything that I ever discovered went."

"Where's that?"

"Museums. Academic institutions. And no deal I could make with Caliber allowed for that. I know you might have a tough time believing that, but I let you find me, right? That has to count for something."

"*Let* me find you?"

"The purchases using my own ID? The camera in the parking garage? You think those were accidents?"

I had. But I had to allow for the potential that he could have staged them. "Why me?"

"Because you're the one person on this moon who I trust to actually get the truth out. You've got a track record for doing exactly that. Who better to take my case to?"

I looked to Mac as I considered it, and as usual, he didn't shy away from sharing. "If this shit is true, they're not going to let us go. We're going to have to fight our way out. And we don't have a lot of ass left to fight with."

I nodded. Always blunt, but always practical. I could count on Mac for that.

"What are you doing here now?" I asked Whiteman.

"Hedging my bets," he said. "I can't trust anybody, so I stole a vehicle and came out here to try to steal some technology. In a lower level of the dig, I'm close to being able to extract some parts. If I can get something useful, get it out of here, and hide it somewhere, it gives me leverage."

On the surface, the plan had merit, but he hadn't considered that it probably ended with him dead and nobody to find the material he excavated. "How long would it take you?"

"With the limited equipment I have on-site? If I can get some help, twelve hours. Maybe fifteen. It's not super delicate work, but I have to at least be a little careful of damage."

"Do we have that long?" I asked Mac. I knew the answer but wanted Whiteman to hear it from him.

"Not even close. They could be on the way now. Best for us if we're not here when they get back."

I agreed with that assessment. The problem was, we didn't have a way to leave. "How do we get out?"

"You said you stole a vehicle," Mac said to Whiteman. "Where is it?"

"I don't know. Outside."

"Not anymore," I said.

Whiteman and Mac looked at me.

"Pretty sure Barnes blew it up." At least that explained that weird enemy vehicle.

"We're not going to get very far on foot," said Mac. "What is it, six hundred klicks to the nearest outpost?"

"There are some mining operations closer than that, but I'm not sure they're much better than a last resort," I said. "Especially considering who runs those."

"So we dig in here," said Mac. "Use the hill and hope that their desire to take this thing intact makes them hesitate before using heavy weapons. Prepared positions give us our best chance to hold out for help."

I nodded. He wasn't wrong, but we were on an isolated moon, and the nearest help was probably five or six days away by the fastest ship. And that assumed Parnavic even had comms to call for it. At least we had oxygen. Water, on the other hand, might be an issue. It rained here, but rarely, and it brought its own problems. "I'd like to see the rest of the excavation. You can go outside and supervise the work if you want."

Mac looked unsure, probably doing the calculus in his head about leaving me alone with someone who had killed a man not too long ago.

"I'll be fine," I promised. If I couldn't hold my own against one unarmed archaeologist, I deserved whatever I got anyway.

He relented, put on his helmet, and headed out, a rush of air going behind him, which I found more fascinating than scary. It was amazing how fast I had come to accept that this structure would provide what we needed to survive. Hopefully that wouldn't come back to bite me in the ass.

CHAPTER 17

ONCE MAC DEPARTED and the door resealed behind him, I gestured for Whiteman to lead the way deeper into the structure. He opened a portal similar to the one we'd entered through, this one opening inward. He didn't put on his helmet, so neither did I, but I wanted the spotlight, so I started to fiddle with it to make it work manually, but lights beyond the door came on as soon as Whiteman walked through it.

I followed him. The light seemed to come from nowhere and everywhere, as if the walls themselves lit up, but not like a flipping of a switch. More like the gradual light of a sunrise. It shone brightest where we were standing and dimmed along the downward-sloping passage. "Why weren't there lights in the first area we entered?"

"No idea. My working theory is that whatever this is crashed here. Maybe some things were damaged."

"What leads you to that?"

"A few observations. The biggest one is the angle. You can feel that we're moving downward, right?"

"Yes." It was more obvious here, though the low gravity and the nonstick surface of the floor made it easy enough to maneuver.

"It's thirteen degrees. Not exactly an ideal parking angle."

"You think it's a ship?"

"You think it's *not*?"

It certainly felt like a ship, though it lacked the internal features I would have expected to see, other than the bulkheads and hatches. "I don't know."

"Wait until you see the next part. You'll get why I think it's a crash." He sounded confident, but that didn't mean he was right. Sometimes people believed what they wanted to believe. In that, I had an advantage here. I didn't want to believe anything. That thought reminded me why I was there, though. I'd almost let it slip with everything else going on.

"Tell me what happened to Ramiro."

Whiteman stopped, and the lights stopped with him, keeping us in brightness and dimming a bit back the way we had come. "They killed him."

"Who?"

"Who do you think?"

"I'm going to need some specifics on this one. Not a company. Names." I'd come to solve that case, and I was going to do that, once-in-a-lifetime discovery or no once-in-a-lifetime discovery.

He didn't want to answer me. Something in the set of his shoulders, a look that played across his face. I couldn't say for sure what tipped me off, just that he wasn't giving me the whole story. But I could wait. I didn't point my weapon at him, but the fact that I had one and he didn't wouldn't be lost on him. He was a smart man, after all. "I can give you names, but they're not going to do you any good. You won't recognize them, and I can't even promise that they're real. Two people. A man and a woman. They worked for Omicron."

That could have been Bingham and his associate he'd escaped with, but I didn't want to taint Whiteman's testimony by giving him ideas. "Why'd they kill him?"

"He knew too much," said Whiteman.

"So do you. You're still alive."

He took a deep breath and blew it out through his nose, maybe trying to decide how much to tell me. Or what lie. "Once it became clear what we had here, they cut us off from communications. I had no problem with that. I don't communicate much anyway when I'm on the job. No family. No romantic attachment. Ramiro, on the other hand, couldn't abide by the restriction."

"So they cut him off permanently."

"Not immediately," he said, almost too quickly. "They just forcibly cut off his communication. But then they discovered that you were involved with his daughter, and . . . well . . . I think he became too big a liability. In their eyes." Again, the last part came too quickly, like he had rehearsed it. There was something he wasn't telling me. More to the story. I was sure of it, but I couldn't pinpoint the lie.

Maybe I just didn't want to believe it. If Whiteman was telling the truth, then Ramiro might have lived if not for his daughter reaching out for help. Specifically, reaching out to *me* for help. I thought for several seconds before gesturing for him to lead on deeper. Of all the possible outcomes I'd considered with us coming to Taug, me having a role in Ramiro's death hadn't even crossed my mind. I needed more time to process that. I didn't believe Whiteman—not fully—but he could keep his lie for now. None of it mattered unless we got to safety anyway, so I might as well keep him thinking we were at least somewhat on the same side.

We came to a T intersection where the downward slope leveled off somewhat in both directions, and he headed left without hesitating, the lights following us. After about fifteen meters we reached a door that was propped open with a crowbar. If this was a ship, it was a big one. Whiteman stepped through. "The lights don't work in here, either. That's why the door is open."

I stood in the doorway, looking in. There were tools scattered around a dark room that seemed smaller than the one we'd been in before. Shovels, buckets, and some simple machinery that I didn't recognize but fit with an archaeological dig. "This is your stuff?"

"It is." He picked up a flashlight and used it to illuminate the far side of the room, which was maybe two and a half meters from the door. Rock and gravel formed the entire far wall, as if a cave-in had crushed the entire compartment beyond.

"I see what you mean about it potentially being a crash. But I don't see anything you could excavate."

"Not with your eyes. But scans show that there's metal mixed in with this rock, and it's not deep. It might be some sort of machinery."

"Isn't the fact that the ship is here—if that's what it is—a source of metal?"

He shook his head and patted the bulkhead. "Nope. This isn't metal."

"What is it?" I asked. "Some sort of polymer?"

"No idea. The chemical composition doesn't match any known compound."

I felt like he might have led with that, as it seemed like pretty important information. But then, he was a showman as much as he was an academic—perhaps more. Maybe he wanted a big finale. It led to a natural query. "Okay. If this is a ship and it has been here as long as you say, and if it's made of something nobody has ever seen, who came in it?"

"That's the big question, right?"

"You haven't found any remains."

"We haven't found *anything*. The ship is clean, almost like it's been maintained, which is impossible since it was completely buried. But you've seen all there is. Just doors and walls and lights and, somehow, ventilation."

"Somebody had to have brought it here."

"Seems likely."

"So where did they go?" I asked.

"Impossible to say. We'd have to scour the whole moon for remains, if they died here. But with the level of technology that we're seeing, it seems likely that they would have been rescued."

I didn't know if *seemed likely* fit with anything at that moment.

"Sir," Mac's voice broke in, tinny and weak, coming from my helmet that I had in my hand. I quickly put it on.

"Go ahead."

"You probably want to get up here. We've got a ship inbound. No ID on it, but it's not responding to our hails on any military frequencies, so I'm marking it hostile."

"How close?"

"Ten klicks and closing. No fire yet."

"Roger. On my way." I didn't take my helmet off, instead

switching to speaker. "You can stay here or come with me. It looks like we've got a fight on our hands."

"I'll wait in the room where you found me," he said. "It's more stable than this one, in case there are any . . . vibrations." Vibrations. Explosions. I couldn't fault his decision.

I made it back to the exit quickly and found five wounded soldiers sitting—or lying, in two cases—in the excavated area at the entrance to what I was now thinking of as the alien ship. That was smart, getting them out of the way of a potential fight, and I said a small thanks that we'd at least had the time to recover this many. I didn't know how many more we still had out there in harm's way.

When I reached the outside, my night vision was shot, so I flipped to enhanced mode on my visor. The platoon—if you could still call us that—was scrambling to improve the position, though they could do only so much with just a few multitools for digging. A couple of soldiers were maneuvering a large rock to create a firing position—one they'd never have been able to manage in regular gravity. Just another way that one had to adjust their thought processes in new environments. With the high ground and the rocks, we had at least a semi-defensible position. To attack us without crossing open ground, the enemy would have to come up from the other side of the hill and work their way around. Mac would have thought about that and had a plan to counter it.

He walked up to me, even though he could have talked over our private net from anywhere. "The ship set down three klicks out."

"That makes no sense," I said.

"Maybe they thought we had anti-air weapons."

"Maybe. What's your plan?"

"Fight," he said. "Whatever comes at us, that's all we can do. Retreat is pointless. Falling back into the cave gets us trapped and mopped up at their leisure. We'd never get back out. All we can do is hope that their assets are as limited as ours and that the military finds some sort of miracle in a hurry."

As plans go, it left a lot to be desired, but Mac knew that, so I didn't say anything. "How's ammo?"

"We're okay. Our team didn't use much. The other team shot up a lot of theirs but consolidated from the dead and wounded. With the enemy landing that far out, I'm not sure it matters. We've got nothing that can range them."

Shit. That was it. They were coming in with something with more range than we had. On the one hand, that was good in that if they had enough force to swarm us, they probably would have. But enduring a siege while being raked at long range wouldn't be a whole lot of fun either. Maybe we needed to reconsider the cave as an option.

I pulled C into the net. "Castellano. What's your range from here?"

"Tailwind helps. With confidence, nine hundred. I'd take a shot out to twelve."

"Roger. Thanks." He didn't have the 13mm, but even with his lighter weapon he outranged anything else we had. But I'd guessed right. He couldn't counter rockets or mortars, which the enemy probably had.

I flipped to the platoon net. "Alanson, what've you got up?"

"Two. One high over our position and hard for them to get at. One en route to their landing spot. We'll probably lose that one."

"Roger. Call out bogeys as you see them right up until they splash it." He didn't need me to tell him that, but I had another motive. I broadcast it over the platoon net because everyone else needed to hear it. We had some bad moments coming, and knowing the plan—hearing me talk calmly about it—would help morale. I'd stood back and let others take charge up until now, but we'd reached our final stand. No way was I going down without giving everything I could. Mac would understand. He wouldn't want to leave any card unplayed either.

I moved around from position to position—not checking on sectors of fire or fighting positions—the non-coms would have done that already and they knew better than me. I focused on the people. I knelt down next to them, made eye contact, put a hand on the occasional shoulder. Our survival depended a lot on willpower—the ability to take fire and keep fighting—and I wanted to bolster that. Plus, really, there's not much else to do in that final minute before everything goes to shit. It feels like it takes forever.

"Wheeled vehicles coming out of the ship. Armor-plated front panels. First victor has a heavy gun. Looks like projectile," reported Alanson.

"Roger. Numbers?"

"At least two. There's three. Shit."

"Lose it?" I asked.

"Roger. Down to the one drone. Holding it back so we've at least got something."

The standard helmet has a problem with depth perception, which makes it tough to judge range. Unless the enemy lit up, we'd have a tough time picking up even something as big as a vehicle from three klicks in these light conditions. Thermals would be more effective, but they'd show us blobs of heat rather than specific forms at this distance. The open terrain mitigated some of that. Contrast would be easier than picking out specifics, and now that Alanson had identified what we faced, those blobs became pictures in my mind.

Three streaks flashed out of the darkness, screaming toward us at high speed, followed almost immediately by four pops from our line. Starbursts lit the air maybe two hundred meters in front of us as 40mm anti-rocket rounds exploded, followed by two brighter, more intense explosions as they did their job, detonating the enemy rockets. The third rocket slipped through the screen and zipped a couple meters over our heads at twice the speed of sound before slamming into the hill behind us. I flinched, trying to get lower to the ground as gravel rained down. My helmet dampened the sound, but it couldn't dampen the shock wave or moon shaking like it wanted to come apart.

The whole thing probably took four seconds, start to finish, but each moment seemed to stretch. Training had paid off, as our soldiers reacted by the book. We'd fired one more anti-rocket round than rockets fired by the enemy. But we had only fifteen total, so if they had more rockets, they could bleed us dry of ways to stop them pretty quickly.

Another rocket streaked toward us, met by two more starburst rounds from our side. My visor dimmed for a second to mute the flash and save my vision, the sound coming a second later. Maybe that rocket was supposed to be part of the first volley, but maybe they'd adjusted their plan, which might indicate that they'd come to the same conclusion I had a moment before: If they fired one at a time, we'd waste more starburst rounds trying to stop them. Mac apparently had the same thought as me, as he came on the net.

"Fire the same number of starbursts as rockets. Conserve ammo."

I searched the dark in front of me, trying to tell if the heat signatures were moving forward. "They're not moving," I said to Mac on private.

"Nope."

Except they should have been. Their rockets flew at about seven hundred meters per second, give or take. Firing from three klicks, they gave us time to respond—albeit not much. What they should be doing is closing the distance. If they fired from half their current range, they'd still outrange us, and we'd struggle to stop the rockets from getting through. Maybe they thought we had longer-range weapons than we did. Maybe they were just making a mistake. I didn't believe either of those things.

Two more rockets lit to my front. One flashed, and in the brief moment that my visor dimmed the other slammed into the ground in front of me. Dirt and debris pelted my helmet and back. That one had been Holy Fuck Close. That's a technical military term. I promise. Nobody called in hit, which was a miracle. We wouldn't stay that lucky.

The problem at the back of my mind solved itself, though I hadn't known I'd been thinking about it. This wasn't the attack. "They're distracting us," I said to Mac.

"Yeah," he agreed. Unfortunately, we couldn't do much about it. They had the firepower to keep us pinned down as long as they had rockets. Even after that, they had other weapons they could fire at range that wouldn't let us get up from our fighting positions. Their other force, whatever form it took, would maneuver on us.

"Where will it come from?"

"Unless they can drop behind us—which would be some high-level shit—they'll probably come from our right flank. It has the best cover and concealment. The left flank is pretty open."

"Tell me you've got it covered."

"As well as we could. I've got four covering the right, two covering the left. It's gonna depend on what they come with. If they have more vehicles with heavy weapons, we're in fucking trouble."

For about the twentieth time, I appreciated having Mac with me. With the threat of an enemy flanking movement settled as well as it could be, I turned my mind to why. Why attack us directly when we had no way out of here? They'd cut our comms back to base—or someone had—and without that, we were stranded. They didn't have to attack us in our semi-fortified position on good terrain. They could wait until we inevitably had to move out of here or until we died of dehydration. Them attacking now meant something.

Another rocket sliced through the dark toward us. Another starburst met it, successful this time.

Time. It had to be time. They didn't have it. They couldn't wait us out because . . . something . . . had them on a clock. I didn't know what it was, but I didn't care. Their deadline changed the way we had to think about this. We didn't have to survive forever, because they didn't have forever. We just had to survive *for now*. On the surface, that wasn't much, faced with what we had in front of us. But it was also everything. Because the more you can think in situations where things are chaotic, the better chance you have of finding that one thing that might give you enough of an edge to snatch victory. Unwittingly, the enemy had given us that time. As silly as it sounds, they'd have been better off rushing at us in a quick attack. We'd have been able to fight back, but we wouldn't have had time to think.

As if they could read my mind, they charged, coming fast enough to make it obvious, even through thermal sights.

"Look alive," said someone over the net. I didn't catch who broadcast, as I kept my focus on the enemy vics.

Which made me think again. I was focused on the vehicles. We all were. A perfect time for an enemy assault. "Watch the flanks," I said over the net.

They fired four rockets at once, one from each vehicle, closer this time. Only three starbursts responded, and one of those too late.

The world exploded and everything went to shit.

Debris engulfed my entire field of vision, falling slowly in the low gravity and turning the entire battlefield into a fuzzy cloud. Voices trampled each other on the net for a moment, making it hard to parse information. Someone screamed that they'd been hit. Injured. More than one.

A pulse burst whined over my head. A few seconds later, heavy projectile fire chewed into the rocks and ground around us, kicking up more dirt, sparking as tracers skipped into the sky. In retrospect, this was the sign that the flank assault was coming.

In the moment, I hugged the ground.

"Movement, right front." A voice cut through the clutter on the net, shutting up all other talk. "Ten. No, fifteen soldiers. A hundred fifty meters and closing."

Another pulse burst sizzled into a rock two meters to my right, leaving it cracked and smoking. We needed to shift to meet the assault force, but I couldn't make myself move.

I glanced to my left, looking for Castellano. He wasn't moving. For a minute, I thought he had been hit. I checked my HUD. He was alive. Aiming his weapon. His muzzle flashed once.

One of the approaching heavy projectile weapons went silent. I looked to the front, trying to get a range. Fourteen hundred meters. It seems ridiculous that in that moment I stopped to marvel at that incredible shot, made while under heavy fire. But I did. It may have been only a second, but wow. The enemy weapon started up again, joining the other and the two pulse weapons as they continued to suppress our position. C had probably hit the gunner, and they'd replaced him. But the new gunner would at least have something to think about.

Two crunching explosions went off to my right, pulling my attention back to the fight. Grenades.

The assault force.

Fuck it. I had to move. I could sit there and die or move and die in a different way. Better to die trying.

I rolled right in case someone had a bead on me and pushed up to my feet. Something punched me in the side, and I found myself on my face in the dirt again.

I took a second. My HUD didn't show air loss, so nothing had penetrated, but my ribs on the left side started to throb.

I forced myself up again, staying lower, and crouch-ran toward our right flank, the awkward posture making my ribs scream. I half expected something to hit me again, but it didn't. After about ten steps I knew why.

An enemy soldier ran toward me, weapon raised, pointed to his right, looking for a target. I shot him center of mass from ten meters away. From that distance, I couldn't miss. The impact launched him backward, his feet flying out from under him.

I dropped to a knee, looking for more enemy inside of our position. A foot came from the right and connected with my weapon, wrenching it from my hands. I turned and launched myself into the attacker before they could hit me again.

In my mind, I was going for a double leg takedown while keeping myself inside of their weapon, which, again in my mind, they had in their hands. I forgot about the lack of gravity. I hit them and they flew back and away from me before I could wrap my hands around them. I started to dive out of the way of the inevitable gunshot, then realized they didn't have a weapon, but before I could do anything else something hit me and spun me away from them and they disappeared. I dropped to my knees and looked around, locating my weapon after a few seconds. I scrambled toward it, staying low, unsure when the enemy might open up with heavy weapons again or who might be inside the perimeter looking for a target.

As if on cue, a clear voice on the net cut through the chaos in my helmet. "Everyone drop. Anyone standing is enemy." I made it to my weapon and rolled to my back, searching for any standing personnel I could shoot. Someone raced by, a couple meters in front of me but so fast that I couldn't bring my weapon to bear, and by the time I whipped around, they'd disappeared.

A flurry of shots rang out, and then, for a few heartbeats, everything went silent, except somebody had keyed their microphone and was breathing heavily. Even that cut out after a couple of seconds, and I cautiously rolled to my stomach, protecting my ribs as best I could, and then raised up slightly to get a better look around. My HUD didn't show anybody left alive, and for a second, I panicked, until I realized that it didn't show any data at all, and maybe I'd shorted something in my helmet in the scuffle. The helmet wasn't completely dead, as I had comms and night vision, and not everybody was dead because I could still see heat sources across our position.

"Report status," I said to nobody in particular.

One by one, soldiers checked in. Castellano. Barnes. Alanson. Ezekiel. Others responded, but without my HUD to check them off against a list, I couldn't identify our losses. But two names I didn't hear. Peña, the leader from the team in the other ship, was one.

Mac was the other.

CHAPTER 18

W E NEEDED TO reconsolidate and reestablish order. Everything else had to wait. If I got focused on our losses, I'd spiral into a bad place, and we still had enemy out there. Maybe even inside the perimeter. We needed to reset the chain of command and figure out what we faced.

"Sergeant Barnes, take charge and establish squads. Once that's done, priority of work is the reassignment of defensive sectors, consolidating and treating the wounded, and ammo redistribution. Report enemy status."

"Roger," said Barnes. If she had qualms about me putting her in charge, she wouldn't mention them on the net. "Castellano, you're first squad. Walthes, you're second. C, you've got the left. Walthes, take right. I'm toggling your squadmates to your HUDs now. I'll check sectors in two minutes."

I really appreciated naked competence in a subordinate. I especially appreciated it when everything was going to shit. We had twelve or thirteen soldiers left, and no telling how many of those were in any kind of shape to fight.

"Sir, this is Mac." A private channel.

People sometimes exaggerate when they say their heart leapt.

Not here. My heart fucking *leapt*. "Where are you?" It came out a little garbled. Sue me. "Are you okay?"

"I'm hit. I've had worse. Took a shot through the shoulder but it's all the way through, and I've got the bleeding under control. Suit's fucked though. Helmet seal to the suit is busted, and I needed air, so I self-evacked back to the hill structure. Had to get my suit off to treat the wound, so I was off the net. Trying to get it fixed now so I can get back into the fight."

"Barnes has it," I said. "Go ahead and sit this one out."

He didn't respond. He probably wasn't going to listen and use that as his excuse. He'd say he didn't hear the order. I loved that fucking liar.

A pulse blast screeched by a few meters away, scorching the ground. A second later bullets from a heavy weapon ripped into the front of our position. Because of fucking course they did. They'd know we were reconsolidating, and they'd try to disrupt us. The fire cut off almost as quickly as it started, but ten seconds later, the pattern repeated itself. One pulse followed by about twenty rounds, and then silence. I low-crawled to a rock, waited for the next attack to come and go, and then looked over it to assess the situation. Three vehicles at about fifteen hundred meters. Two immediate questions came to mind. One, why were they firing slowly, and two—the more important—where was the fourth vehicle?"

Barnes low-crawled up and engaged me via private channel. She didn't need to be close, but I understood the impetus. "We're set in squads. Five in first, six in second, plus you and me."

"Mac's hit but okay. He's fallen back to the cave."

"Oh thank the Mother." Another pulse blast whizzed in, this

one passing over our heads. "What do you think they're up to? They were chewing us up before. Now it's sporadic."

"I think they're conserving ammo, just trying to hold us here," I said.

"Right. But why?"

"Could be another attack—that fourth vehicle is missing. Could be flanking."

"But they'd take two for that, right?" she asked.

"Probably. What's the status of the last enemy assault force?"

She took a second to look at her HUD. "Defeated. Estimated twelve dead or out of commission. Two prisoners, one critically wounded and unlikely to make it. One with a blown-out knee who is otherwise fine."

"Maybe they're trying to pin us here and wait for reinforcements."

"Maybe," she said.

"Where are the two wounded enemy?"

"The critical is with our own wounded, behind that big-ass rock. The other is in a fighting position, cuffed. Safest spot for him as long as the enemy keeps shooting at us. I can't spare a guard."

"Right." I waited for the chatter of the enemy projectile weapon to stop. "You made sure he can't communicate and call in our locations?"

"I couldn't take his helmet, but I told him we were monitoring him and if he talked, I'd shoot him in the other knee."

"Are we? Monitoring him?"

"No."

I snorted. That wasn't strictly legal from a law of war perspective, but given our situation, some flexibility made sense. At least on the threat. Not actually executing it if it came to that. "Maybe the fourth vehicle went for reinforcements."

"If it did, it'll take hours."

"That's the downside of taking out comms satellites. Unless they have a secret one up there that they're using and we can't, which I doubt, because it would be hard to hide."

"So what do we do?" she asked.

"Either we sit here and see what happens, or we come up with a way to get at three heavy weapons that have us outranged across a relatively open area."

"I've never really been one for waiting."

"Me either," I said. "On the other hand, I've never really been one for dying, either."

"Fair point. We could try to slip a team out the same way they came at us. Sneak around and get close enough for a shot."

"We could. But even if we got C out there close enough to take a shot, he'd be exposed as soon as he took it and in a lot of trouble when they turned the other weapons on him."

"Fuck! This sucks."

It did indeed.

THE PATTERN CONTINUED for several hours. Combat is weird, where you can go from all-out terror to near boredom in a short time. The enemy's fire never stopped, though the intervals did grow longer and longer between volleys. But they didn't hurt us. As long as we stayed down and didn't move, we had good cover. It was almost like our two sides had come to a mutual agreement. We'd stay put, and they wouldn't try to advance their position and put more effective fire on us. A stalemate, basically. More than a couple times

I caught myself nodding off. The adrenaline had worn away, and my body and mind settled into exhaustion. Unfortunately, my hand started to hurt more. I wanted to take off the tape and examine the wound, but the minute I did that something big would start up. Superstitious? Sure. Doesn't mean it wouldn't happen though.

An explosion to my front jerked me awake. It hadn't been close, but it had been big, and I peeked out around the rock in front of me to get a look. A bright light whited out my optics a bit—one of the enemy vehicles was burning. I couldn't tell for sure, but it might have been upside down. A streak flashed in from a distance and slammed into another vehicle, bright enough to dampen my visor for several seconds before my vision returned. The third vehicle took off, racing away from the new threat at a ninety-degree angle, probably not wanting to get closer to us, either.

"Anybody see anything?" I asked over the wide net.

"Eight victors. Maybe ten. It's hard to make them out at this range. Three-point-five klicks," said Castellano.

I considered the new information for a second. That might be all the time that we had. It clearly wasn't the reinforcements that our enemy had been waiting for, but that didn't necessarily mean good news for us. There had been a two-sided fight before we arrived. Maybe the second side had returned in force to finish the job. We probably stood in the way of that job. "Call them out every five hundred meters," I said. He wouldn't be accurate with thermals from this range, but even an estimate helped.

"Roger. Three thousand."

I did some quick math. They'd gone five hundred meters in about thirty seconds, which was . . . what . . . eighteen meters per second? A little over sixty klicks per hour. They weren't in a big hurry to get here. Given the rockets they'd fired at the other vehicles, they could engage us at any second, and we didn't have many starburst rounds left to defend ourselves.

It didn't look good.

I don't care what happens in the action vids. There's no good way to die. Dead is dead. Was it better to die for something that mattered? Maybe. But barely. You were still dead. *Living* for a cause that mattered, on the other hand . . . that was pretty cool. Did this one matter? I don't know what other people would say, but to me? Yeah. A girl lost her dad, and that's pretty shitty. I'm sure somebody could debate me as to degrees of shitty, but I found that in the moment, I really wanted this particular girl to know what had happened here.

"Mac."

"Roger."

"If I don't make it and you do—"

"I'll make sure the girl knows about her dad," he said. Because of course he knew. "But we're going to make it out of here."

"Yeah? You think so?"

"We always have."

I grunted. It was hard to argue that logic. Or maybe I just didn't want to. Either way, I smiled and felt better. Traffic squawked on the wider net, but it took me several seconds to recognize my name in the chatter, and another second for me to process and focus.

"Butler, this is Parnavic."

Huh. I hadn't expected that. "Butler here."

"We're coming in. Don't shoot us."

Well shit. Some good news. That seems like an understatement, but the long day and constant fire had beaten me down, and it was all the excitement I could muster.

"Roger. Weapons hold." For a split second, I considered that it might be a ruse, but it was definitely Parnavic's voice, and three minutes later he stepped out of one of the newly arrived vehicles. I met him halfway.

"What's your status?" he asked, straight to business.

"A lot better since you got here." That he'd come personally meant a lot, said a lot about him as a leader. "I didn't expect to see you."

"When we lost all our satellites, we had no visual on you and no comms. It was the only real choice."

"You must have SP'ed really quickly to get here this fast. Why didn't you fly?"

"I gave the order almost immediately after systems went down. I didn't want to risk the aerial troop carrier on an unknown LZ. It's scheduled for a flyover in about forty minutes. Now that we've got control, we'll bring it in. At a minimum, we can evac the wounded."

"Where'd you get the combat power?"

"I pulled every able-bodied soldier from the headquarters. Trust me, we look a lot more impressive right now than we are. Are we going to have to fight?"

I gave him a rundown on the day's events, from the fight between the two factions to our involvement right up until now. I kept the details to a minimum on the archaeological find and Whiteman's appearance, but that part definitely drew his attention.

"What do we do?" he asked. It was great that he wanted my opinion. Less great that I had no clue.

"I don't know."

"Are we going to have to fight to hold this?"

"Maybe. Once someone is willing to engage and attack the military, I think 'they won't do that' goes pretty much out the window."

"You can't be sure who you were fighting?"

"We've got prisoners, but they don't know their employer. Both corporations will deny it or blame it on the other. Or both."

"So we're stuck here in a defensive position forever or until we can reestablish off-moon comms and get reinforcements."

He didn't have to say that that was untenable—we both knew it. We didn't have the forces for it, and we didn't know what threats still existed out there. "Maybe not. Whiteman said that with twelve or fifteen hours, he can excavate some tech from the cave complex. If we get enough from that to prove what's here, control of the actual site matters a lot less. It's not like someone is digging up the whole thing overnight, and the evidence should be enough to put pressure on the corporations once it's made public."

Parnavic considered it. "I don't like it, but I don't have a better idea, so we'll execute that one until we come up with something else or we can get comms back."

—

It took both Barnes and I arguing for several minutes to convince Mac to get onto the bird when it came in for the wounded, but finally he relented, taking Alanson with him and leaving Castellano with us. Parnavic also kept most of his forces on site, prioritizing evac of our wounded and the POWs, though he planned to send some of his less combat-ready troops back on the second flight, about two hours later. The troopship would make constant trips, both to keep us supplied and to keep us in communication with headquarters. It wasn't ideal, but we'd work with what we had.

Parnavic took charge of increasing and improving the defensive position, in case we faced another fight, leaving me to supervise Whiteman's operation along with Barnes and a detail of half a dozen soldiers.

The first thing I learned about archaeological work is that it's *really* slow. I didn't have anything to supervise. As much as I didn't totally trust Whiteman, he couldn't run away, and we had a ton of dirt and rock between us and what we hoped to find. The soldiers pitched in, digging and carrying out buckets of scree. Part of me wanted to get a couple of grenades and see if we could speed the process along. Another part of me really wanted a nap.

I jerked awake at the sound of Mac's voice coming from a room away, asking some soldier where to find me. He'd gone back to base, so hearing him now cut through the haze of sleep. I stood and met him at the door. "What happened?"

"They've got Ganos."

My blood went cold. "Who?"

"Not sure. They'll only talk to you. We got a text message on one of her screens when we went looking for her."

I took a deep breath and blew it out, trying to calm myself. Acting irrationally played into the enemy's hands, but for a minute, my thoughts focused on making someone pay. But that could wait. First we had to get there. "Barnes, get C. We're leaving on this hop."

"Roger," she said, setting down her shovel without question.

"Let me go talk to Parnavic," I said to Mac.

Parnavic met me at the entrance to the cave, on his way in. "I heard. You go. I'll take care of things here."

I nodded and held out a hand for him to shake. "Thanks."

CHAPTER 19

PARNAVIC'S XO, MAJOR Xavier, met us when we landed. "Sir, I'm so sorry. We dropped our guards to the bare minimum—lower than that, really—to resource the mission out to relieve you."

I blew off her apology. We had to get Ganos back, and nothing else mattered. In retrospect, we should have thought of this. I should have thought of it when I left Ganos behind by herself, and Parnavic should have considered the vulnerability of his base when he came to our rescue. But we'd both made the best decisions we could at the time, and relitigating them now wouldn't help. We could worry about recriminations once we'd solved the problem. Xavier hurried to keep up with me while I spoke as I walked toward Ganos's room. "Anything on cameras?"

"Negative."

Of course not. "What do we know?"

"They came in through checkpoint four. They disabled the single guard there and left him bound and gagged in a back room."

"Injuries?"

"Bruises." That, at least, was good news. If they'd treated him humanely, it boded well for Ganos.

"Roger. Shut down all gates but one. Physically lock this place down."

"Already done, sir."

I grunted.

Ganos's room hadn't changed since the last time I saw it: crowded but organized, her monitors blinking on her makeshift desk. No signs of a struggle. That could be good news or bad. We didn't know how they'd captured her—whether they'd taken her from here or if she'd ventured out and into a waiting ambush. With Ganos, the former seemed more likely, but we couldn't rule anything out. I swept my eyes around the room looking for potential clues, though to be fair, I had no idea what to look for. The only thing I knew about detective work I'd learned from fiction. "How did you get the message?" I asked Mac.

"It was blinking in big letters on the center screen right there. It said 'Click me.' So I did."

I touched the screen to bring it to life, but that message was gone. It did give me a thought though. "Major Xavier." I waited for her to come in from where she had been hovering in the corridor. "Can you send over one of your computer techs? Maybe Ganos left us something in her system." If she could have, she would have, but I had no idea where to find it, and I didn't want to risk destroying the information with my ham-fisted attempt.

"Roger," she said, and tapped something into her device, presumably summoning somebody.

As it turned out, we hadn't needed to bother, because a few seconds later, a flashing message came up that said "Colonel Butler, click here."

I did not click here. The fact that my presence triggered the message gave us some information. They knew I'd come back. They may have simply monitored our flight, which was easy, or maybe they had this room bugged. If they took Ganos out of here, they could have easily left something behind to monitor the space. Before I did anything else, I wanted to make sure the enemy—and whoever did this *was* an enemy—didn't have access to my internal conversations with my team. Alanson seemed to come to the same realization as I had, as he began sweeping the room with a handheld sensor, looking for . . . something. Major Xavier tapped another message into her device.

"I'll bring over a full sweep with the tech."

"We're clear," said Alanson after another minute.

The link on the computer continued blinking at me. I stood up and walked away. If I sat there, I'd click it, and who knew what that might execute within the system? I was in a rush to find out information about Ganos, but a few more minutes wouldn't make a difference. To kill time, I walked over to my own room to use the latrine. Who knew when I'd get another chance once things started moving?

Mac met me when I came out, the door to my quarters closed to give us privacy. "What's the plan?"

"Get her back," I said.

"Of course. Any ideas on how?" he asked.

"Not yet. But get the team ready for anything. If they wanted Ganos dead, they could have left her here. They didn't. So whoever took her wants something, and here's what I know: They're going to fucking *get* something." In my mind, it was my boot in their ass. But I'd settle for Ganos back in one piece.

"Roger." Mac was shot through the shoulder, and he still planned to strap it on and do whatever it took. Hopefully I'd hold up my end of the deal and put him in a position to win. The enemy held a lot of the cards, but not all of them. They had Ganos. That was big. But we had the dig site. And we had a few pissed-off ex-soldiers. I was betting they hadn't accounted for exactly what that last part meant.

I took another minute to collect myself and headed back over to Ganos's room. A female tech sat at the desk, tall and thin with dark skin and hair. She didn't look up when I entered, her eyes on the screen and her fingers flying over the keys of a virtual keyboard. I stood next to Xavier and let the tech do her thing. After a few minutes that felt longer than that, she sat back and then turned to us.

"I entered through an alternate means and analyzed the link. It's a simple comms link. No tricks."

"How sure are you?" I asked.

"Completely," she said, unbothered by the question, unflinching in her demeanor.

"Any chance Ganos left us a message in there?"

"Not in an obvious fashion," she said. "I can go deeper if you want, but it seems unlikely that she'd have buried it if she wanted us to find it."

I considered it and then nodded. We could go back and search more thoroughly later. For now, we needed to move. "Okay. So I'm safe to click the link."

The soldier stood up and moved aside so I could sit. I touched the link on the screen, and it went immediately into waiting for another party to connect. Four seconds later, Francesca Alexander appeared on the screen. "Colonel Butler."

"Ms. Alexander." I kept my face as neutral as I could, but on the inside, I was seething, and it probably showed through. "You wanted to speak?"

"I do. We should meet."

"Sure. Come on over." I said it seriously, even though I knew full well she wouldn't take me up on the invitation.

"I don't think I will. You should come here. You're going to want to hear what I have to say."

"Let me see Ganos," I said.

"Who?"

I hung up.

"Was that wise?" asked Mac.

"Fuck her. I'm not dealing with that disingenuous shit. If she wants to pretend she doesn't know anything about Ganos's disappearance, that's fine. But to pretend she doesn't know who I'm talking about? Please. Anyway, she'll call back."

"If you say so."

I suppose Alexander really might not know about Ganos, but I didn't have time to consider it because a link flashed up on the screen. I looked at Mac to rub it in, and he shook his head, almost laughing. I clicked the link. "Ms. Alexander."

"We seem to have gotten disconnected," she said. I had very little patience for her games.

"Don't pretend you don't know who Ganos is. You've studied my entire team, and you sent me a message on her computer." I wanted to confront her to force her to react. If I let her stick to her script, we wouldn't learn anything.

"Fine. I know your team. Doesn't change the fact that we need to talk and I'm not going there."

"Why not? We're under the protection of the military, which guarantees your safety."

"Am I supposed to hang up on you any time you say some bullshit? Just trying to establish the rules here."

I almost cracked a smile. "Touché. So you're not coming here. I'm not going there."

"And yet we need to talk. Where else is there? Halfway between?"

"There's an old launch pad that's outside both of our facilities. I can send you the coordinates."

"And what? We both lie and say we're coming alone?" she asked.

"Nope. We both come. We meet alone, away from everybody else, if that's what you want. But there's no point in promising anything beyond that since neither of us is going to believe the other. On-site, everybody stays back a hundred meters except you, me, and one person each. You want to talk, that's how it happens."

"I do want to talk. What do *you* want, Colonel Butler?"

"I want you to bring Ganos. Because anything you want from me starts with me getting her back. If you think I'm going to negotiate any other way, you don't know me very well."

"If I run into her, I'll certainly let her know you're looking for her," she said. She was smart and wouldn't admit to a crime on the net where I could record it as evidence. She'd issue her threat in person.

"You do that," I said.

"What time?"

"Two hours from now. Fourteen hundred."

"Send the coordinates," she said.

I did. She cut the connection.

I spun in my chair to face Mac. "Get our team. Give us the room," I said to everyone else. We'd brief them all on the plan, but I didn't know this command and couldn't trust people not to talk. The fewer people who knew our plans, the fewer chances we had that someone would spill them. Keeping my discussion to our small group gave me the cleanest slate I could hope for. I had no illusions about Alexander: Her designs for me went beyond talk, and she wasn't going to all this trouble in order to invite me to a conciliatory lunch in a fine-dining establishment. We had to be prepared for everything, and we didn't have the time or resources for that. I needed people I could trust.

Mac took longer than expected, but came back in with A, B, and C and shut the door behind them. "Sorry. Couldn't find Barnes for a minute. What are you thinking?" he asked.

"Thinking that this is a setup."

"Obviously."

"Thinking about how we flip it," I said.

"You have any ideas? Because it feels like they've got us in a pretty good bind."

"I have one," I said. "It works assuming that Alexander really has Ganos. I think she does."

"Who else could?" asked Mac.

"There's some chance that it's Caliber. Less chance that the two are collaborating. And a really, really slim chance that the military has her, or an unnamed player. We can't know for sure."

"But we play the odds," said Mac.

"That's our best bet, yeah."

"This is the part of the plan where you try to use yourself as bait." Mac's tone made clear that he didn't like that. The others looked on, probably wondering what was happening between us. They didn't know all our history.

"What other option is there?" I asked.

Mac thought about it. "We plan with the assumption that Alexander has Ganos or knows who does. I'm also pretty damned sure that they won't bring Ganos to the meeting. Why would they? She's their leverage over you."

"Agreed," I said.

"But Alexander will bring proof of life. Probably video, and probably live. She wants you to negotiate, so she's got to meet your condition in some way."

"Right. She'll show me that proof to pressure me."

"So the real target isn't at your meeting. It's somewhere else. Wherever Ganos is."

A light came on in my brain. "I see where you're going. I'm willing to bet a lot of money that Ganos isn't inside the Omicron facility. Or, if she is, they'll move her before we meet. They have to."

"Right. Because if we can tie her to that location, we can make the case for the military to raid their headquarters."

"Exactly," I said. "Parnavic probably doesn't have the ass to go in there physically, but if he makes the demand and they resist, it puts them in a tough spot. They attacked the military and they want to deny that. If they resist a lawful order now, all the trouble they've gone to in order to maintain deniability goes out the window."

"It's thin," said Mac, "but it's what we've got. I still don't like using you as bait."

"Getting Ganos back is the number one priority."

"I could argue that keeping you safe is our number one priority, given that we're *your* security detachment. If it came to a choice between you and me, you know that I'd save you, right? So would Ganos."

He meant it. I knew that, even if it seemed a little difficult to admit. "This is different. I need you to give me this one."

He stared me down for several seconds, maybe still undecided. "You remember what happened the last time we used you as bait?"

"I do."

"So you remember that they had an EMP, and they drugged you, and then they dragged you away to an underground facility and forced you to fight a war against a species of native apes using illegal war robots?"

I cocked my head and stared at him. He was being a little over the top.

He kept going. "Because I need you to remember that that happened."

"I do remember. Do you remember how that ended up?" I asked.

"I came to the rescue at the last moment and we won."

"Right. See? So we'll win this time, too. We always do."

He stared for several more seconds before he cracked and laughed. "I can't believe you're going to talk me into this shit. Okay. But if we're going to do this, I'm taking the dangerous part. You're bait, but you're a decoy. You get eyes on the video. Alanson, you rig him up with a camera with every redundancy you can get."

"Can do," said Alanson.

I met Mac's eyes, and everyone else in the room faded away. "I can't let you put yourself at risk. You're wounded."

He shook his head. "You don't get to make that call. You promised me you wouldn't take unnecessary risks, so we're going to do this my way."

I hesitated before finally nodding.

"Okay," said Mac. "Once you've seen the video, you stall. Do some of that officer bullshit and keep her talking. We'll need time to find the location, get there, and get Ganos."

"Ganos won't be unguarded. You sure you're up to this?" I nodded at his shoulder.

He glared at me. Okay then. There was no way he wasn't hurting. I was hurting too. There was also no way he would admit it.

"I'll go with the colonel," said C. "I'll be his backup."

"I'd rather you go with Mac," I said. "He's got the tougher job, and he'll need your gun. I'll take Barnes with me plus a backup team from the military. Mac, you take Castellano and Alanson and some backup. That kid Ezekiel is pretty good. You don't worry about me. Just get Ganos back."

"And you don't die."

"I'll do what I can."

CHAPTER 20

WE ARRIVED BACK at the launch pad where we'd chased Bingham. The remains of the explosion and burned vehicle still scarred the ground black, visible from our position about a hundred yards short of it. We'd come in two vehicles: five soldiers, including Walthes, who led them, and Barnes and me. I'd have preferred more, but Parnavic could spare only so much, and Mac needed soldiers for the real mission.

I tested my comms with Sergeant Walthes again. He'd have the team ready to race in if we needed help. I went over hand signals as well just in case they did something to cut our comms. We couldn't plan for everything, but we'd done as much as we could. Now we had to play it out.

Right on time, three vehicles pulled up two hundred meters away. I upped the magnification in my helmet and zoomed in on them. Two people got out of the center vehicle. The other two vehicles had darkened windows, obscuring observation. Smart. We couldn't gauge their numbers, and couldn't know if they'd brought Ganos or not. I wished I had Alanson with his drones, but I might as well have wished for a cheeseburger. I had what I had.

I checked my sidearm and Barnes did the same. We were leaving our long guns behind, so as not to be provoking. I had a grenade tucked up under the back of my shirt that I hadn't told anybody about. Even Mac, who would have made me give it up. We'd call that the last resort plan. Any time *colonel* and *grenade* came up in the same sentence, it was definitely the last resort. Let's just say that I didn't plan on them taking me alive.

Their two people—Alexander and a guy I didn't recognize— started toward us as soon as they saw us moving, and slowly we came together. Both of us took our time, as if by delaying we might gain some sort of advantage. In truth, my clock didn't start until we got a picture of Ganos for Mac to analyze, but starting the pace slow now would make it less obvious when I took my time later. Neither of us spoke until we stopped, facing each other, about four paces apart. Alexander's escort was a big guy, taller than me and lean, broad at the shoulders with a square jaw. He had a sidearm at his hip and no other visible weapons. He kept his hands in front of him where we could see them. Everything about him screamed ex-military. I had no doubt that he'd be a beast in a fight if it came to that. Barnes could fight, too, but that was a scrap I didn't need to see. We took a couple of seconds to synch our comms so we could converse.

"Here we are," said Alexander.

"Here we are."

"Shall we talk alone? Have our seconds back off?"

"I'm game if you are."

"Jurvis. Wait about ten meters back," she said. "Drop off this net."

Her companion immediately fell back, though he didn't ever take his eyes off us, backing away without turning. I didn't believe for a second that he'd dropped off our net. My people wouldn't.

I nodded for Barnes to follow his lead. I didn't look back to check her compliance. She'd know what to do.

"You wanted to talk," I said. "Talk."

"You wanted information about your hacker before you'd agree to anything. As it turns out, I've learned something in that regard."

That wasn't exactly what I'd said, but I nodded my agreement. Alexander reached into a pocket on the front of her thigh, and I tensed, waiting for her to try something. She slowed her movement, reaching in with two fingers and pulling out a rolled-up flexible tablet. She made a show of unrolling it, then touched the screen a few times before turning it to face me.

"This is live," she said. A video window showed Ganos, her hands cuffed behind her back, standing outside of a vehicle with a man whom I recognized from somewhere. I moved closer to get a better look—at least that's what I tried to make it look like. In truth, I wanted to make sure that the tiny camera Alanson had fitted to my helmet was picking up the entire picture. I didn't spare any thought trying to figure out Ganos's location. We all had our jobs, and that was Mac's. Mine was stalling to facilitate that and getting all the information I could. As I got closer, though, the man's identity clicked somewhere in my brain.

Kirk Bingham.

I thought the hit man had left the moon from this very location. Shit. That complicated things. A hyper-competent killer against my guy, Mac, who was no slouch, but who had also taken a bullet recently. I tried to put that out of my head. I had to keep reminding myself to trust my team to do their jobs and focus on my own part. Control what I could control.

"That's Kirk Bingham," I said, more to make sure that my team picked up on it as they listened in than to elicit a response from Alexander. At least they'd have early warning on what they faced.

"Who?" she asked. I marked it as disingenuous. She didn't really even try to hide it. She probably knew I was recording. She almost certainly was, too. Nothing prevented either of us from doing so, which made the idea of speaking alone kind of a farce.

"Where are they?" I asked.

"I'm sure I don't know," she lied.

"Then I guess we're done," I said, moving into stalling mode. The picture hadn't changed on the screen, though the image moved enough to suggest that it *could* be live.

"We haven't even started. Surely you can hear me out."

"Is there a point to that? You're not going to tell me the truth."

"I'll be completely honest with you. I want your help, and I won't get it if I lie."

"But you aren't going to help me get Ganos back."

She shrugged. "Everything is on the table. You let me know when you're ready to get serious."

"I could say the same." I wasn't sure where she was going, but as long as we continued to waste time, Mac and his team had more opportunity to do their thing.

"We'll need to stop recording, if you want the truth," said Alexander.

"I don't suppose you're going to trust me if I say I've turned it off."

She shook her head. "Do you blame me?"

"I don't. So what do you propose?"

She reached into her other pocket. This time I didn't flinch, and she pulled out a disc-shaped device and then fished out something with a black wire. "This is a localized jammer. It'll kill transmissions in about a fifteen-meter radius. Nothing in, nothing out. You and I can hard wire."

"I'm familiar with the technology."

"With your permission, I'll turn it on."

"Why do you need my permission?" I asked, to draw out the process. Her caution was playing right into my hands.

"I assume your team back there is listening in. When they get cut off, I don't want them to overreact and come rushing to your aid. Nervous people with guns is never a good idea."

"They'll be fine," I said. I'd gone over exactly this situation with Walthes ahead of time. If we lost comms, they would stand fast unless I gave a hand signal.

"Still, do you blame me?"

"No. Do what you need to do."

She hesitated, and then bent to set the device on the ground between us, stood, and activated it with the bottom of her shoe. In the moment, that's what struck me. She was wearing regular shoes instead of boots, and somebody had modified her suit pants to seal to them. It seemed ridiculous. And ridiculous is a hard line to cross when you're already standing in a clearing, negotiating something to do with potential alien technology while one of your subordinates is held hostage. She walked to me and handed me one end of the wire, which I plugged into a jack on my helmet.

"We good now?" I asked.

"I can hear you," she said. "I'll get right to the point. You know what's in the archaeological dig on the other side of the moon."

"I'm not sure any of us *know* what's in it, but I've seen it. Yes."

"And you've surmised that both of the major corporate players on the moon have interest in claiming it."

"The shooting war in that vicinity did provide a little bit of a hint. Yes. Was it you who tried to have Whiteman killed?" The more I could change the subject from where she wanted to go, the longer it would take. Bonus, I might learn something.

"What? Somebody tried to kill him?"

For the first time I marked her surprise as genuine. "They did. At least he says they did. And the physical evidence on-site did lend some credibility to that."

"Why would we try to kill him? He was working with us."

"Was he? Because he had an office at Caliber."

"Initially, yes. And when he made his discovery, he didn't like their plan for it, so he came to us to see if we could help. We were willing to be . . . more flexible, in our arrangement with him."

Interesting. Whiteman had sold it a bit differently, but her version did fit the facts. It especially explained two different groups fighting over the site. "But when you flipped him, Caliber wouldn't let it go that easily."

"Of course they wouldn't. And because of that, the military got involved, and now they hold the site."

"Until you take it back from them."

"Which is where you come in," she said. Alexander didn't even try to hide the fact that she planned to make a play for the site. I almost respected that.

"Why do you need me? You've already directly attacked the military. Why not hit them again before reinforcements can get here from off moon?"

"Attack the military?" She put her hand to her heart and made a shocked face. "We would never."

I snorted at her act. "There's no recording. You can cut the shit."

She smirked but didn't concede the point. "That's exactly why we need your help. This whole situation has gotten out of hand, and somebody will have to answer for it."

"On that much, we can agree. You—or somebody, at least—have isolated this moon for now. But it won't stay isolated forever."

"I'm glad we both understand it the same way."

I thought I could see where she was going, but I wasn't going to make it easy on her. I still wanted to stall. "I don't see how I can change that."

"Somebody has to tell the story of what happened here. And the way I see it, your voice will be more credible than most."

"There are dead military satellites. There are dead *soldiers*. Forces literally attacked coalition troops not even a full day ago. Nothing I can say will change those facts. Every soldier involved in the fighting, every soldier who had access to satellite feeds—they're all going to tell their own story."

"Good then that we have a convenient party to take the blame, isn't it?"

"Caliber," I said. I could only be so obtuse before she'd catch on.

"Do you know they wanted to destroy the site? They wanted to obliterate it with a fission weapon."

I didn't have to fake my surprise at that revelation. "Why?"

"It's simple enough, if unimaginative. Who profits from the current energy industry?"

"Ah." They wanted to prevent new technology from emerging

that made their current businesses obsolete. "But I could say the same about Omicron."

"You could. We just have . . . a better vision."

"So let me make sure I have it straight," I said, continuing to draw things out. "You want me to cast blame on Caliber while exonerating you. What I don't see is how that helps you exploit the situation for gain, other than removing a competitor. And we both know that competitor won't stay away. Sure, they'll pay fines. But they'll find people to blame, throw their hands up in the air in consternation at the actions of those rogue elements, and buy some politicians. They'll be back in business before we can even get home."

"That part of the plan I'm going to keep to myself. Sorry, but you understand. I can't give away *all* my secrets."

"Fair enough."

"So let's cut to why we're here," she said.

"You want me to help you by spinning the story. I'm not currently inclined to do that. So go ahead. Make your pitch."

"I won't insult you by offering you money again."

"Thanks," I said, though by saying that she wouldn't, she kind of *was* offering. It hadn't worked the first time, and it wouldn't work now. "You know what I want. Ganos. Right here, right now. You bring her to me or there's no deal."

"Counteroffer. You do what I tell you or we start cutting body parts off her and bringing them here one at a time."

Wow. That got dark in a hurry. At least she'd stopped pretending that she wasn't in on the abduction anymore. That last bit was actually good news and bad. By admitting to it, she might as well have said that she had no intention of letting me walk away from this. I'd have been smart to ignore it, maybe deflect and change the subject, buy some more time for Mac. But I was done with being smart for two reasons. First, I didn't believe they'd really harm Ganos in the near term. They needed their leverage over me, and as soon as they hurt her, they lost it. Second, and more important: I really didn't like being threatened.

And if I wasn't going to be smart . . . well . . . I might as well be *really* stupid. I've always favored naked aggression. Going on the offensive created multiple ways to win. It forced your enemy to react to you, and any time they had to react created an opportunity for them to make a mistake. And even if they didn't, maybe it would sow doubt in their mind, make them think a little bit longer before they acted.

I looked Alexander straight in her eyes, and I made sure I had her attention before I spoke. "Counter-counteroffer. You bring me Ganos right now, unharmed, and we negotiate from there." I waited, letting silence hang between us.

"Or?" she asked, finally taking the bait.

"Or I burn down your company and kill every single person who had anything to do with taking her, starting with you." I paused to let it sink in. "And then I have a whiskey."

She stood there for several seconds, possibly unsure how to react. Unlike me, she probably hadn't had her life threatened before. No matter what the circumstance, it's a hell of a thing to contemplate. Maybe she was cooler than that, just considering things. Calculating my ability to actually carry out the threat. Rationally, she'd know I couldn't do what I said. Not all of it. But I could carry out part of it. I could shoot her. And she couldn't say for sure that I wasn't bluffing. She couldn't say that for sure because I wasn't completely sure myself. I wouldn't kill her. Maybe just wound her a little bit. "That's not your style," she said, after what seemed like a minute.

"I react when I'm pushed. I protect the people who matter to me."

She considered it some more. I would be hard to read, because I wasn't lying. "You're putting me in a tough spot. But you're bluffing. You're not going to kill me in cold blood."

I thought about it a bit longer than I probably should have before I ruled it out. "So you're not bringing Ganos?"

"I'll take you to her," she said.

"I'm not going anywhere."

"I think you are." Her guy put his hand on his sidearm and came forward, though he didn't draw. Behind me, I heard Barnes draw her weapon and come closer until I sensed her beside me, but I didn't take my eyes off the two people in front of me. At least not until I noticed Alexander looking at Barnes and smiling. I looked over to find Barnes with her weapon trained on *me,* using her body to shield it from the soldiers watching us from behind. They wouldn't know that she flipped—it would look totally natural for her to join me.

"Really?" I asked, even though she couldn't hear me.

"I'm sorry," she mouthed. She might have even meant it, for all the good that did me. "I need the money."

Well shit. Clearly I hadn't done enough to get to know my team, but I couldn't think about that now. I needed to act. Or at least continue to stall. The stakes had grown now, but my part in saving Ganos hadn't changed.

"As soon as we start walking away, my team will notice that

something is wrong. They know that's not the plan." That probably wasn't completely true. Barnes was the only one with a weapon out, and my team wouldn't take that as a threat. But it was the best story I could invent on the fly. I had to give Alexander credit. She had set this up perfectly.

"Don't make things harder than they already are. Come along quietly." She gestured for Barnes to get my weapon. I considered making a move for her pistol when she disarmed me, but I remembered her fighting Mac back in the gym and thought better of it. If I was going to die, I wanted it to be useful.

"Why do you want me?" I asked, trying to buy time to come up with some way out of this that ended with both Ganos and me in one piece.

"Give me your weapon. Slow." Barnes was shouting, but I could barely hear her without comms. No way did it carry back to my team.

I reached down to my sidearm and undid the clasp with two fingers, and then I pulled the weapon out, also with two fingers.

Barnes gestured for me to drop it on the ground in front of us. I thought for a second about trying to toss it to the side in the hopes that the soldiers behind me would see it and catch on. In the end, the risk wasn't worth it for the small chance that they'd recognize it as a cry for help, so I dropped it as instructed.

"I have another weapon," I said.

Alexander looked at me and then at Barnes. Only she could hear me, and we stood in silence for several seconds as she tried to figure out the awkward communication situation. She looked at the jammer, as if debating turning it off. If she did, I wondered if I should call for help. Barnes could shoot me before my team reacted. No doubt about that. But would she? I didn't know how fully she'd gone over to the other side or what that deal included. Finally, Alexander gave up on that thought and gestured for Barnes to watch me. "Let's have it," she said.

I reached to the small of my back and detached the grenade I had hidden there under a flap. I think I had some design on using it to threaten to blow all of us up if they didn't let me go. As I brought out the grenade, the air snapped in front of me and something cracked beside me almost simultaneously. I instinctively dropped into a crouch—someone was shooting at us. Barnes slumped to the ground, her neck at an awkward angle. Time seemed to slow as my mind processed things in that way where you somehow understand things even though they're happening so fast that it should be impossible. The shot had come from my left and had hit Barnes in the helmet. There was no blood yet, and no way to know if the person who took the shot was on my side or against me and hadn't realized Barnes had flipped. Alexander's bodyguard reached for his sidearm.

I tossed my grenade to him.

I hadn't activated it, but he didn't know that, and for a second, he froze. I dove over Barnes, intending to use her for cover. I forgot the low gravity and sailed a good meter and a half too far, leaving me exposed and without a weapon. I started to crawl back to her. If I could get to her pistol, I could even the odds.

Alexander's man moved faster. He'd recovered, tossed the grenade away, and had his weapon trained on me.

Shit.

Sometimes I really hate competence.

I stopped moving, but my mind didn't stop working. Walthes

and his team might open fire, but we'd gone way off plan and I couldn't count on that. I needed to buy time. "You really think that's a good idea when my sniper is out there?" Except nobody could hear me, because when I dove, I'd ripped the comms wire out of my helmet. I kept my hands visible as I moved to retrieve it. I crouched slowly, not wanting to give the man any reason to shoot. Once I plugged back in I said, "Have your man stand down or my team will engage."

"Call them off or my shooter will fire." said Alexander.

A round skipped off the ground directly in front of my adversaries, kicking up a puff of dirt. I take back what I said about competence. I kind of liked it now. "Looks like mine's better." Part of me thought that it had to be Castellano, but he'd gone with Mac. If Walthes had put a person out there, he'd done it without telling me, though I'd be willing to forgive him at this point.

Alexander and her bodyguard turned as one and ran.

I had no idea what Walthes would do with Barnes down and people running away, and I couldn't contact him because of the jammer. Part of me didn't want to stand since that would make me a bigger target, but I needed to signal my team not to shoot. As much as I wanted to take Alexander down, I didn't want them to shoot her in the back.

I pushed up to my feet and put my thumb and two fingers up, our signal not to shoot. Two members of the support team were already halfway to me, and another figure was running toward me from my left.

The latter carried a weapon which was longer than a standard military rifle. Castellano. What the hell was he doing here?

For a split second, I had a horrific vision of the support team engaging him as a hostile, and I really hoped my signal would calm them.

It didn't. One of the charging soldiers dropped to a knee, sighted in, and fired.

Time stopped as I tried to process everything happening. The soldier hadn't aimed to the left. They shot someone behind me. I turned to see Alexander's crony with his hands pressed to his gut. Alexander herself was face down in the dirt, not even halfway to her vehicles. A second later, the vehicles sped away, kicking up dirt and rock in their wake. Rats fleeing a sinking ship.

Everyone arrived at once, and for a few seconds we yelled until Sergeant Walthes got control and sent two of his people out to secure Alexander and provide first aid to her badly wounded compatriot. For my part, I reached down and turned off the jammer.

"What the fuck just happened?" Walthes asked me, once he had security established.

I looked to Castellano, who stood a step back. If anyone could explain, it would be him.

"You remember how you told me to watch people that you couldn't see? Barnes was acting funny."

"Funny how?"

"She snuck away before we went out to the dig site and met with some dude, which . . . normally, I'd think that was a private thing . . . you know."

"I get it," I said.

"But here? Something seemed off. I wanted to keep an eye on her, so when we broke up into teams, I told Mac that I wanted to go out in secret and provide cover. I didn't tell him about Barnes, because if I say something and I'm wrong, I'm an asshole, you know?"

"Sure. But why did Mac let you go then?"

"Countersniper. I told him that if I was the enemy, I'd have a shooter out, and that I should go handle that."

"Alexander did mention that they had a shooter."

Castellano snorted. "Fucking amateur. The kind of person who thinks they're the only danger on the battlefield. Surprise, asshole. He set up in the most obvious spot and didn't check his six. I took him out and slipped right into his hide."

"So you saw Barnes draw on me."

"Yeah. Suspicion confirmed. I wasn't really sure what to do, but I figured that dropping the person who had a gun trained on you was justified."

"Who shot the other guy?"

"That was my team," said Walthes. "Corporal Vania. The guy with the handgun turned and pointed his weapon back at you, and she reacted and drilled him center of mass."

"Thank her for that." I hadn't even considered him to still be a threat when they'd turned to run. "Why'd Alexander—the woman—go down?"

"She did that on her own," said Walthes. "I guess when her boy got hit, she thought we were shooting at her too. But she's fine. What do you want me to do with her?"

"Treat her with respect, but don't let her out of your sight. I doubt she'll be a problem physically, but she'll be manipulative if you let her. She'll threaten, bribe, or do whatever else she can. Make sure you trust the people you put on her. She bought Barnes.

We'll let your boss figure out if we can hold her or not." Probably not. Not for long anyway. The military had limited powers in that regard, and this fiasco would be her word against mine, given that Barnes was dead and the other guy might be joining her.

"Roger, sir. What now?"

"Now we've got to hope that Mac was able to do his part of the job. Or we've got to figure out where he's at and help him."

WE DIDN'T GO back to base. We had the vehicles, so I commandeered my team and cut overland to the location that Mac had sent us forty-one minutes prior. Forty-one minutes. It hadn't seemed like that long. It never does. That Mac wasn't responding to calls weighed heavy on me as we drove. I try not to catastrophize, but it's hard when you know there are probably bullets flying. Bad things can happen even on the most successful operation. Our recent encounter proved that. Barnes was dead. That had me reevaluating some things.

I'd always kept a running tally of the people who'd lost their lives on my watch. It wasn't a physical list anymore, and I debated with myself often about who I should keep on it. I'd caused a lot of Cappan deaths back on their home planet. The fact that they'd mostly forgiven me didn't erase my culpability. When I start thinking about that, I'm not in a good place mentally, but even seeing the warning signs, I couldn't turn back. Did Barnes belong on the list? In the end, she'd shown herself as an enemy, and I didn't keep track of those. Even if I wanted to, many of the dead were nameless and even faceless in my mind. But Barnes had started out on my team, and I had every reason to believe that at the time, she'd been at least reasonably loyal.

I needed to stop. Maybe once we got through this, Mac and I could sit down over a beer and talk it out. If he was okay. Mac. He fucking had to be okay. Him and Ganos. They both had to be. I wanted to distract myself by talking about something—anything—but every thought that came to mind turned dark, and the last thing I needed to do was put that shit on a team of soldiers that hadn't signed up for this ride. If they knew me better, maybe they'd have known to chatter. Would have sensed my trauma and filled the void to distract me. But even that thought wasn't fair. It wasn't their job.

Mac's voice on the radio broke me out of it. I didn't even hear what he said. I heard the voice and stopped processing. Walthes had turned around in the front passenger seat, staring at me, waiting. After he realized I wasn't going to say anything, he prompted me. "Change of plan, sir?"

"I missed it. What did he say?"

"Ganos is secure. They took casualties and they're headed back to base."

"That's it? That's all he said?"

He hesitated. "We can be there in twelve minutes."

"Yeah. Change of plan. Go."

"YOU'RE SHOT." IT was the first thing I said when I saw Mac. He was standing in the reception area of the base medical facility, motionless amid the rush of people around him, a bloodstain soaking a damaged vac suit just above his right hip.

He turned to meet my eyes and walked gingerly over to me, so he didn't have to use the same raised voice I had. "I was shot before we started."

"You're shot *again*."

"You should see the other guy. And is that really what you want to focus on right now? It's not bad."

He was right. We had more important concerns. "How's Ganos?"

"Physically she's fine. Mentally . . . not sure. She's always been a hard one to figure out. She's been quiet, but I can't tell if that's an 'I'm traumatized' quiet or an 'I'm thinking about how to destroy the entire moon' quiet."

"What happened out there?" I asked.

"Long story," said Mac.

Mac had . . . well, maybe I should let him tell it. There would be an investigation, and no matter how much the bad guy deserved it, we would have to answer for killing a man. I wanted to record Mac's thoughts as close to the event as I could, so they'd be as accurate as possible.

"So . . . what?" asked Mac. "I just talk into the recorder?"

"Yeah," I said. "Pretend you're telling the story to someone in a bar that doesn't know anything about it."

Mac thought about it. "That's fucking weird."

"Humor me."

He stared me down for a few seconds. "Yeah, okay."

CHAPTER 21

MAC'S STORY

So I talked the boss into being a decoy, which was no easy thing. I honestly didn't think he'd go for it. Butler kind of has a death wish. Not the kind where he's going to jump off a cliff or slit his wrists or anything like that. He just doesn't give a shit if he lives or dies sometimes, and that can affect his decision-making. That's not great if you're his security detail. Pretty obvious when you think about it. I need to remember how I got him to agree so I can use it in the future. Not that a situation like this will come up again. Okay, who am I kidding? This shit'll come up again.

The minute he and I agreed on the plan, and he took off to prep his part, Castellano grabbed me.

"I should be with the colonel," he said.

I considered it. Castellano wasn't the kind of guy who wanted to be near the boss because he thought it would look good. I've known guys like that. He's not one of them. "Why? Barnes has him."

He hesitated. "I think they'll try to take him out. If they've got a shooter, I can work countersniper. If not, I can provide overwatch from a distance and see the whole scene. Deal with whatever comes up."

I studied him. He was full of shit. He had another motive, but I had my own shit to do and didn't have enough time to wring it out of him. I decided to let him go. Whatever his motive, his made-up reason actually made a lot of sense. "Yeah. Make it happen."

That left me and Alanson to find Ganos and get her back. Oh, and to kill whoever had her. Can't forget that part. Politically, I should probably say that nothing mattered as long as we got our lady back safely. But fuck that. Somebody needed to pay.

But that was the easy part: Making them pay. First we had to find them. We had a plan, but it relied on a lot of things going right and a lot of luck. It also relied on me having access to some high-level intel, and if I knew one thing about intel types, it was that they didn't like to share their toys with grunts like me. I had to get past that, and I had to do it fast. If I did it the proper way, through official channels, there'd be paperwork and delays as we waited for whoever had the right authority to clear us. Leave that to the officers. I took a minute to brief the team leader of the crew that would go with us, and then I went to see the sergeant major about a shortcut.

Davenport was standing in the door of his office as we came up the hall, talking to the XO, who was in her own office. "Look at this. It's the walking wounded," he said, referencing Alanson's broken arm and my messed-up shoulder.

"Can I talk to you for a minute, Sergeant Major?" I asked.

"Oh, shit. This is serious." He must have read that in my demeanor. "Yeah. Come on in."

"Thanks."

Alanson shut the door behind us.

"What do you need?" he asked, before we even had a chance to sit.

"Well, my boss has us in a bit of a jam." Sure, it was mostly my idea, but I didn't figure he'd be as sympathetic to that. Somewhere in his career, some officer had given him something ridiculous to do. Probably a lot of times. I wanted to play to that feeling.

"Ain't that always the way?"

"Yeah. The only way I pull it off is with a lot of help from intel. But if I go down there"—I shrugged—"they're going to send me away."

Davenport studied me for a while, sizing me up. Apparently he liked what he saw, because he said, "Okay. I got you."

"Thanks," I said.

He picked up the comm and waited a few seconds. "Ma'am. Sergeant Major. I'm sending McCann and Alanson down to see you. Give them anything they want." He waited. "Roger. They're on the way." He hung up and met my eyes. "Captain Nixon will take care of you. She's all right."

"Thanks, Sergeant Major," I said. Him tabbing Nixon as all right was a high compliment. I could respect a sergeant major who called captains, told them what to do, and they did it. That meant the colonel had his back. I'd have liked to stay around and talk to the man, but we had to hurry.

True to the CSM's word, Captain Nixon was waiting for us outside the Two Shop. She was tall. A lot of people are tall, compared with me, but she was taller than most. She palmed both of us through the door without a word. Was that legal? Probably not.

But it's only illegal if somebody reports it. Either way, it got me what I needed.

"Sergeant Josephs is going to assist you," said Nixon. Josephs waited on the other side of the room, dry washing his hands and looking like someone had taken a shit in his bed. Great. Just what I needed.

I didn't wait for him to say anything, instead headed for the inner door. I assumed that was where they kept the good secrets. Josephs stepped in front of me. He said something about this not being authorized under his breath, but then he opened the door, so I let it go.

"Corporal Sevilla will help you," said Josephs when we got inside. It was starting to get a little nerve-racking, being passed along to the next person—like they were giving me the runaround.

"You didn't ask what we needed," I said. Sevilla was a sharp-looking soldier, but I had no idea who had the skills to help me. Neither did Josephs.

"They said I had to help you," said Josephs. "This is what that help looks like."

Okay. This was going to be a problem. Because if the NCO in charge didn't give a shit, nobody else would either. I stepped close to him and spoke low, so only he could hear. "Listen, mother-fucker. There are lives on the line here. Your boss said you'd help, and this only goes one of two ways. One, you cut the attitude and help us, or two, I beat your ass right here in front of your soldiers . . . and then you help us."

I know it sounds like I'm a bully, that I can't be polite. But go easy on me. I can play nice. But right then, I had a hard mission and no time. Ganos's life was on the line. Maybe Butler's too.

If I had to threaten a sergeant to save them? I could apologize later.

He looked at me, maybe wondering if I was serious. I was. "What do you need?" he asked, after a couple of seconds. I guess he got the message.

"I need some black magic." I said it loud enough so all the analysts could hear. I didn't trust Josephs to get it right. "Someone who can get stuff from the system that it wasn't designed to give. In a little bit, I'm going to get a video. I need to identify the location of the people in the video based on what we see."

"That's impossible," said Josephs.

Sevilla's face scrunched up, thinking, but she didn't contradict her boss. That wasn't good.

"I'll give it a shot." A private had turned around in his seat to look at us. He was a bit sloppy looking, but if he could do the job, I didn't care.

"You think you can do it?"

"Maybe," he said.

"If anyone can, it's Torrens," said Sevilla. That settled it. Peers always knew, and she had no reason to lie.

"Okay. You're it." I moved over to Torrens. Alanson pulled out a rolled-up screen that would get the video and handed it to me.

"You can't have that in here," said Josephs.

I glared at him, and after a few seconds he backed away to sulk.

"Is it okay if I take some time to set my stuff up?" asked Torrens.

"You do whatever you need to in order to give us the best chance to get an answer when this video shows up." I said it like I was confident that it would show. Personally, I was maybe fifty-fifty that we'd get anything at all. The whole plan was sketchy, but

Torrens didn't need to know that. He needed to believe. If it didn't work . . . well . . . I didn't even want to think about that. A ton of things could go wrong, and we needed every single one of them to go right. We needed to find Ganos, but we also needed the colonel to be safe. I had to trust that to Barnes and Castellano, though. All I could do was handle my part.

We got a video feed pretty quick. Problem was, there was nothing on it except open land. We had sound, but only wind and footsteps and the whir of respirators. They were talking on comms, but our feed was an external camera. We couldn't hear them. If we'd had longer to prep, I'd have probably thought of that. But there was no sense in wishing for shit you didn't have. We'd have to watch close and hope we saw what we needed.

When it happened, I almost missed it. The camera didn't give us the big picture, making it hard to follow the action. Like trying to watch a video through a soda straw. Alanson caught it when it came. He fiddled with the screen some after that, trying to get us the best possible still frame from it. When he got that done, he showed it to me before sending it to Torrens. It showed Ganos, hands behind her back—probably cuffed—standing outside of a parked vehicle with someone holding her hostage. From the angle, it seemed like maybe her captor was holding the camera himself, which might mean it was just the two of them. That would certainly help.

I recognized the guy. At least I thought I did. One look at Alanson told me I had it right. Kurt Bingham.

Well, shit. Guy was supposed to be some kind of badass. That would certainly *not* help.

Being honest, I probably wasn't a match for the dude at my

best, and with a hole in my shoulder and very little rest, well . . . let's just say I wasn't at my best. But he had Ganos, so that made Bingham an obstacle we'd have to deal with. He'd fucked with our team. If Torrens could give us a location, we were going. Consequences be damned.

"You got it?" I asked Torrens.

He nodded without looking up, his fingers moving across his keyboard, pictures flashing on his screen for split seconds before switching to another scene. If I asked questions, I'd slow him down, so I let him work. The colonel was on the clock, and I had to get moving. Even if we got an accurate location on Bingham, there was no saying he'd stay there. But he might. I needed *something*. Josephs thought it was impossible that we'd find him from this video, and I got that. But maybe impossible helped us. We had no current satellite feeds, and the enemy knew it. Maybe Bingham would think like Josephs. That we couldn't find him. If he thought that, maybe he wouldn't move.

"We're heading for our vehicles. Send us the grid when you get it." I spoke like it was going to happen, as if I could will it into existence. If *I* didn't believe, who would?

A bunch of shit happened all at once, so you'll have to forgive me if I get things a little out of order. We reached our vehicles, Torrens sent us a grid location, and Alanson called for my attention before handing me the video screen. He'd cued up a clip that I assumed had just happened. I got in the front seat of the lead vehicle as Alanson got in the back. I flashed the grid to Ezekiel, who was driving, and motioned for him to go. I hit play.

The video quality hadn't improved and was hard to make out.

But it got worse. The whole thing tumbled, as if the colonel had been knocked down or dropped the camera. For several seconds, the screen blurred into a mush of nothing before finally coming to a rest and clearing. The last frame was impossible to miss. It was Barnes's head, lying in the dirt. The weird angle of her neck made it clear: She was dead.

That was bad. Really fucking bad.

For a few seconds, I panicked. We had a grid to Ganos that might or might not be accurate. But we *knew* the colonel's location, and it looked like he needed help too. We couldn't go to both. I'd told the boss that if it came down to it, I'd save him over myself. But this wasn't about me. I'd like to say that I made a rational decision here, that I'd thought it through and decided that there was a chance the colonel could save himself, but Ganos was screwed without help. But that would be a lie. We kept going to Ganos for one reason and one reason only. That was the plan, and I couldn't function well enough to change it.

It took twelve minutes to get there at top speed. Somewhere during that time, I got my shit together and looked at a digital map to see how we wanted to approach the place. That he'd see us coming was a given—he'd picked a spot where he had fields of view and fire. He was a pro. Of course he did. He probably had cameras up as well. I sent a message to our second vehicle to keep going while we looped around to the left on an unimproved road. That was our advantage—that we could come at him from two directions. Hopefully they'd tie him down and suppress him while we got in close. One problem with that, of course. He had Ganos.

He wouldn't kill her. Him being a pro helped us in that one way.

He wouldn't throw away an advantage. As long as he had her, we had to be careful firing into his position. We couldn't just open up. He had no such restrictions.

As if to prove that, he was already firing by the time I got a visual on him. He'd put his own vehicle—presumably with Ganos inside—between us and him as he engaged our other team from long range.

A second later, the comm blared, "We're hit! Vehicle's dead. Trying to get out to establish a base of fire, but he's keeping us pinned inside." He'd disabled them 250 meters out, but he kept up his fire.

"Get as close as you can," I told Ezekiel on internal comms. We'd either close on him or force him to engage us, freeing up the other team. We couldn't shoot from inside, so we'd have to dismount at some point. For a split second, I regretted letting C go, but I dismissed that thought as quick as it came, because it served no purpose now.

"I'll use my taser drones once we stop," said Alanson. "It'll be hard to take him out with them from this distance, but they should at least keep him busy."

The windscreen shattered. Not going to lie, I flinched. The round didn't penetrate. In theory, it was bulletproof, but it had spiderwebbed, cutting my ability to see. I didn't want to test if it would hold up to another shot.

"Full stop," I said to the driver, a little too loud. I had the door open before we'd ceased moving, going out low and rolling away into a prone firing position. I forgot how bad that would hurt. Fucking shoulder.

I couldn't see Alanson, but three small discs zipping away

to the front indicated that he was out on the other side. "Tasers away," he said. How he could control them all at once I had no clue. I couldn't worry about it.

I crept toward the front of the vehicle. Bingham had the high ground, and I couldn't get a sight line with him behind his vehicle. That meant he couldn't see me, either, but he had plenty of other targets. I only had the one. If he didn't have Ganos, I'd have hit his vehicle with explosive rounds and hoped to take him out that way. As it stood, I needed a clear shot. If I got it, from ninety meters I wouldn't miss.

He wouldn't either.

"Drones are almost there. Twenty me—" Alanson's broadcast cut out as rounds cracked on the other side of the vehicle.

That caught my attention like a punch in the gut.

I had one chance. I stood and put two rounds into Bingham's faceplate, and then I was on one knee, half turned away. It took me a second to process, and another second for the pain to register. Something had punched me in the hip and spun me. I'd like to tell you how it all happened. That I'd sensed Bingham focusing on Alanson, knew he'd be exposed, and that I got my shots off faster than his return fire. But that would all be bullshit. It happened in a second and it was all instinct. I got my shots off. But beyond that, it's hard to say now what I knew in that moment and what I pieced together after the fact from the results.

Things went silent. It's eerie how quiet things get when there's been a lot of shooting and then it stops. I didn't have time to enjoy it.

"Ezekiel, dismount and check on Alanson. I'm going to secure the target." I took off, trying to run, but stopped, my hip throbbing.

There was a gash in my suit, and I stopped for a second to slap a patch over it. I'd worry about the flesh beneath it once Ganos was safe. I half ran, half limped the rest of the way, watching in case Bingham popped back up again.

He didn't. I circled wide of his vehicle and came at it from twenty meters out. He was on the ground, slumped against the front quarter panel. I walked up to him, doing my best to hide my limp.

As far as you know, he was dead when I got there.

He's sure as fuck dead now.

I jerked open the front door to the vehicle, standing back, my weapon in my other hand in case Ganos wasn't alone inside. She sat there by herself in the backseat, handcuffed to the headrest of the seat in front of her. I searched Bingham's body and found the keys and got her free of her restraints.

"Hey," she said. That's it. Just *hey*. She might have been in shock. Hell, I might have been too. She didn't have a suit or helmet, which wasn't an issue inside the vehicle but would be soon.

"Stay here," I told her, and shut the door. No way did I want to save her just to have her die from radiation poisoning.

CHAPTER 22

MAC HIT STOP on the recorder. "Can I stop there? The rest of it is cleanup. We got Alanson evacked along with a wounded soldier from the other vehicle."

"Yeah, you can stop."

I gave him a look that asked the next question without words. Mac shrugged. "I don't know. It's bad though. Not sure he's going to make it."

Shit. First Barnes, now Alanson potentially lost. Mac wasn't doing so well himself. "I'll find the doc and get an update once they get through triage. I'm sure they're not staffed for the number of wounded we've brought them in the last couple days. Where's Ganos?"

"I got her into a suit and back to her room with guards on the door to keep anybody from getting to her. What about Barnes?" he asked. "I saw her in the video feed. It didn't look good."

"Barnes flipped sides."

"No shit?" Mac's expression barely changed, as if that kind of thing happened every day. Funny that so much has happened to us that even the biggest twist barely registers.

"C drilled her in the head after taking out the enemy sniper." I filled him in on the rest of our operation.

"Good man. I guess two out of three of my hires paid off," said Mac.

"Yeah," I agreed. "It's unfortunate that Bingham is dead. I'd have liked to question him."

"Not as unfortunate for us as it was for him," said Mac.

I couldn't argue with that. "Do me a favor?"

"What's that?"

"Get medical treatment. This thing might not be over yet."

"It has to be. Over. We've got nothing left in the tank."

"We don't necessarily get to decide that. The enemy gets a vote."

Mac stared at me, made sure I was meeting his eyes. "Listen to me. You need to end this. So do that thing you do, whatever it is—talk to people, manipulate them, whatever—and get us out of here."

I gave it some thought. Could I do that? I had to try. I owed Mac that much. "Yeah. Okay. I'm going to go see Ganos."

"Good. She'll do better with you than she does with me. I'll stay here and give you a call when there's a good time to engage the docs regarding Alanson's medical status." He paused, and then gestured to his hip. "And I'll see about getting this thing cleaned up."

"Thanks," I said.

"Keep C with you," said Mac.

"Wouldn't dream of leaving him behind." I signaled to C, who was waiting in a corner, out of the way, but before we got to the door, Parnavic entered through it and looked around, finding me quickly.

"We need to talk, sir."

He'd added the honorific. This was formal. "In a bit of a hurry. What's on your mind?"

"You can't go around killing people extrajudicially."

I looked around to see who might have heard him. He wasn't yelling, but he hadn't been quiet about it either, and while he had a point, the way he said it made it sound a lot worse than it was.

I almost snapped on him. On the outside, maybe I seemed calm. But people were dead, and while I act flippantly about that as a defense mechanism, I was barely holding it together. C coming up on my right side saved me from an unprofessional outburst. I didn't want him to think badly of me. I took a deep breath to compose myself. "You sure you want to talk about this here?"

He took a second to glance around, and then nodded and headed for the door with me right behind him and C hurrying to join us.

Outside in the empty corridor, Parnavic glanced at C, as if asking for him to give us privacy.

"He stays with me," I said. "I promised a friend."

Parnavic's mouth narrowed into a flat line, but he didn't really have a choice. I didn't work for him. Legally he could probably have me hauled in. But practically, given what had happened, that was a technicality at best. Part of me wanted him to try it just to see how C would react. He'd probably run and get Mac, which, on the surface, would be the right thing to do, but in practice would escalate things even further given Mac's current mindset. Finally, Parnavic spoke. "I apologize for my tone inside. But you've put me in a terrible spot."

I snorted. I'd done no such thing, and it irked me a little that he couldn't see it. Or maybe he could, and he was playing out the game at a higher level. Either way, I needed to get to Ganos, and I didn't have time for this shit. "I helped you, and I think you know it."

The confusion on his face said he *didn't* know it, so I took a second to try to see it from his perspective. He *had* come to my rescue, so I guess I owed him one. I could take the time to explain.

"You've got a problem, and I'm your solution. Two corporations were . . . *are* . . . doing bad stuff here, right under your nose."

"And I've got no authority to regulate that."

"True," I said. "But when it comes out that this stuff happened on your moon—and it *will* come out, because it always does—how much do you think that's going to matter to the people above you? Especially when some of the politicians above *them* are potentially bought and paid for?"

"Good point," he said without hesitating.

"With me, you have a built-in excuse." I didn't elaborate. I didn't need to. His face said he saw it now, and he was probably already crafting his story about how the rogue colonel came to town and started a war with the corporations that ended with a lot of dead people. He'd conveniently leave out the part about a known killer gaining access to the moon and roaming around and kidnapping a mostly innocent hacker.

"What do we do now?" he asked.

"I need to get to the rest of my team and see how they're doing. You need to get us communication off moon. I guarantee you one or both of the corporations have it and they're already shaping the narrative. If we leave them time to do that, by the time we catch up, there will be enough shit to bury both of us."

"I'll get on it," he said.

Something in that exchange was tickling at my brain. Mac was right. I had to end this, and right then I couldn't see how to do it. I needed to sit down and think before I acted. But Ganos had to come first.

AS PROMISED, TWO soldiers stood outside Ganos's door when C and I arrived. They watched us as we approached, and one of them stepped out to bar our way. I hesitated for a second, not knowing how to deal with that, which seems stupid, given the mundanity, but I hadn't slept nearly enough to puzzle through my next action. I couldn't yell at them. Mac had given them orders to protect Ganos and probably threatened their lives if they failed. I couldn't ask *Do you know who I am?* because only assholes do that, and while I *am* an asshole, I'm not *that kind* of asshole.

C saved me the trouble. "This is Colonel Butler. Get the fuck out of his way."

While he had no authority to order them around, something in his tone snapped the two into action and they stepped to either side of the door. I buzzed, but Ganos didn't answer.

"She's in there?" I asked.

"Yes, sir," one of them answered.

I tried the pad and the door slid open. I don't know what I expected to find. I guess maybe I thought Ganos would be face down on her bed, crying into her pillow or something. I should have known better. She sat in front of her screens, fingers flying across virtual keys. I guess that answered Mac's question from before about whether she would turtle up or burn the moon down. This was how Ganos started a fire.

I almost wanted to let her. Shit, I almost wanted to hand her a can of gasoline. But revenge isn't a great motive. No, check that. It works as a motive, but it made for a trash plan. And we needed to plan our fire carefully.

"Ganos," I said.

She didn't answer, but her fingers slowed, indicating she'd

heard me. I gave her a few seconds, and eventually she stopped working and turned to me.

"Whatcha doin'?" I asked, falsely casual.

She snort-laughed. "You know fuck well what I'm doing."

"You want to talk about it?"

"What's to talk about? They laid hands on me. Now they pay."

"We could talk about the specifics."

A smile crept onto her face, which made me smile in return. Hers was a murderous smile, to be sure, but the fact that she could smile in any way told me she might be okay eventually. "You think I don't have a plan?"

I gave her a wry look. "Do you?"

"What's the most important thing that Omicron has right now?"

"The ability to communicate off moon." I said it without hesitation. I didn't know for sure that they had it, but I assumed that they did, and if they did, then that topped the list.

"Exactly. They don't have it anymore."

That silenced me for several seconds, because, well . . . what could I say? "So . . . they did have it . . ."

"Oh yeah. *Did* being the operative word."

"What'd you do?"

"I locked them out of it."

"Can we use it?" Screw caution. If we could communicate off moon, I'd take the risk.

It took Ganos a second to parse that I was now fully on board before she answered. "Unfortunately not. I've got it locked down with a thousand different . . . never mind. You don't want the specifics. Bottom line, nobody can use that system to talk until they get through all the shit I've lobbed in there. Not unless they want to melt their entire system . . . That's not a technical term, but you get the idea."

"How'd you break through? I thought they had too much defense." I wasn't surprised as much as amazed. I'd never considered it as an option, but now through it I could see a potential way out.

She pointed to herself. "Super genius. Remember?"

"Yeah, yeah. I know. What I meant was, if we could get that deep into their system, why didn't we do it before?"

"Before we were worried about being caught."

"Now we're not?" I asked.

"What are they going to do? Send an intergalactic hit man after me? I feel like maybe they're out of those. Nope. They'll know exactly who did this. I hope they *do* come after me. Let them fucking come!" Her voice had gone up to the point where she was almost yelling. "I've got my two boys outside the door and Mac is absolutely pissed, in case you didn't catch that. Plus this guy." She gestured to C, who stood just inside the door. "I like my odds."

I had to admit, I liked them too, if it came to that. But I hoped it wouldn't, and I still had some worries about taking on a corporate computer network. "But how did you do it? I wouldn't think you'd have enough computing power to take them on so directly."

She looked away exaggeratedly. "Yeah, uh . . . so here's the part you're not going to like."

As if there was only one part I wouldn't like. I gave her the sarcastic look that she expected. "Tell me."

"You're right. I don't have enough computing power to go up against big corporations in this environment. Not that it's all about brute force. There's skill involved, too, and—"

"What did you do?" I interrupted.

"I borrowed some computing power."

I thought about that. "Please tell me that you didn't *borrow* resources from the military."

"I could *tell* you that, if it makes you feel better," she said.

I sighed. "This isn't one of those times where you can tell me that I don't want to know. I *have* to know."

"You sure? Plausible deniability is right there."

That *did* sound good. Parnavic didn't know about it yet—he couldn't—because if he did, I'd have heard about it. As if the universe were reading my mind, my comm buzzed. I let Parnavic go to voicemail. "I have to know."

"Okay. But you have to promise to help cover up my mole."

"You had a mole?" This was getting better and better.

"Yeah. Couldn't have done it without her. I *told you* I had fans. Plus, it turns out that soldiers really don't like what the corporations get away with on remote stations like this and want to see them get smacked."

"So you convinced a soldier to commit a crime that's going to send her to prison."

"That's why we have to cover up her involvement."

"So only *you* go to prison?" That was optimistic. If I was a pessimist, I'd have said that I'd be there with her. I probably should have chosen plausible deniability.

"You'll talk them out of pressing charges. You always do."

I stared at her, and I couldn't help it. I laughed. "You've got a lot of faith that I don't share."

"That's right. I do. Was that the commander on the comm?"

"Yup."

"Wow. You sure have your work cut out for you. You should really keep better control of your people."

"All that aside . . . you've got Omicron locked down?"

"Yeah. I'll only be able to handle it until the military cuts me off, which, if that call is any indication, could happen any second. So . . . you better get to work."

I thought for a bit about my next statement, because once I said it, it would be hard to get it back. If I could have, I'd have thought longer, run through all the possible outcomes. But with Parnavic calling, time was a luxury I didn't have. "Can we lock Caliber out of off-moon communications too?"

Ganos looked at me for about two seconds before responding. "Yes. I won't even need the military for that. I still have that back door that we installed."

"Do it," I said.

"You sure? What's your play?"

"We can't fight anymore. Not physically. This conflict is going to be won by talking. If nobody can talk off moon, then we're all on a level playing field. And if we control the means to get the comms back, well . . . that's our advantage."

"They've got to come to us," she said.

"Exactly."

"Until the military commander cuts you off."

"Right."

"Like I said. You better get on that."

CHAPTER 23

MY COMM BUZZED again as C and I left Ganos in her room with her security detail. I almost ignored it, assuming it was Parnavic calling back and I was heading to see him anyway. It was Mac, though, saying that Alanson's doctor was available, and could I get over there before he punched the dude in the neck? I texted Parnavic, telling him I'd get with him as soon as I handled the higher priority.

We got back to the medical facility just in time, as I could hear Mac's raised voice before I even went through the door. Inside, he stood face-to-face—or more like face-to-chest—with a tall, thin man in a white coat. Mac's face was red as a sunset as two orderlies looked on, probably hoping they wouldn't have to step in to try to control the angry ex-infantryman. His multiple wounds made him more of a terror, not less.

"What seems to be the problem?" I said, before Mac could make things any worse.

"Dr. Dickless here won't give me an update on Alanson," said Mac.

Dickless—probably not his real name—turned to face me, trying his best to ignore Mac, which was a little akin to trying to ignore an angry badger locked in a closet with you. "I'm Dr. Steven Lassiter. Can I assume that you're Colonel Butler?"

"I am."

"You're the one who, and I quote, 'is going to show up here and shove your fist so far up my ass that it might dislodge the stick'?"

I looked at Mac.

He at least had the courtesy to look embarrassed. "Maybe I got a little carried away."

"As I told the gentleman," said Lassiter, "I can only inform his next of kin or his commander."

"He's got no next of kin here, and I'm his boss. It'll have to do."

"It will not *have to do*," said the doctor.

I could see why Mac had threatened him. I kind of wanted to do that too, even though technically, the doc was probably right. While I felt very responsible for Alanson, legally I had no standing. Or none I could prove, anyway. It made me wonder who got notified in a situation where someone who worked for one of the corporations got hurt. But they probably had their own doctors, and doctors could share information with other doctors. Then I started thinking about doctors becoming like lawyers as my mind continued to drift. I really needed sleep. And I *really* wanted to walk out and leave Mac to deal with him, but I didn't. Who says I'm not making progress? There had to be a way around the impasse. "Is he alive?"

"Yes." No hesitation. Apparently not against the rules.

"Is he going to be alive tomorrow?"

This time he didn't immediately answer. Okay. We were closer to the line. "Most likely."

"Let me ask you a hypothetical logistical question."

The doc eyed me as if it might be a trick, but said, "Okay."

"If a patient required follow-on care at an off-moon medical facility, would you arrange the transportation?"

The doctor smiled, catching on. "We wouldn't. Since he's not a military member, a government employee, or an authorized veteran, it would be the responsibility of the employer to provide medically suitable transportation to another facility."

"Great. As his employer, what day should I charter that flight for and what level of care is required for transportation?"

He considered that. "I'd be comfortable releasing him in three days. He'll need a flight that can support level three medical care. That's one step down from ICU," he added, helpfully.

"Thank you, Doctor. Let's go, Mac."

"Your hand is bleeding. It also appears to be . . . what is that? Duct tape? You want us to take care of that?"

I looked down at the brown stain that had crusted into my glove and part of my sleeve and the makeshift bandage that I hadn't taken time to fix. I'd almost forgotten about it. Must not have been too serious. "I'll get it looked at. I promise."

Outside, Mac said, "That was pretty smooth. How did you know to ask it that way?"

"I'm fluent in all forms of asshole," I said. "The doc there is a very specific kind. He was right, and he would never budge on not telling us even though a reasonable person would see that events warranted some discretion."

"Fuck him."

"He'll probably be your doc when you go for treatment," I said, only half joking. Mac had, after all, still been shot. Twice.

"I'll find an army medic," he said, seriously. "Where are we headed?"

"I have to go see Parnavic."

"Again?"

"Yeah. Ganos did some stuff."

"That's our girl," he said.

"And besides," I continued, "he holds all the cards we need right now. He's got Alexander, and he's got Whiteman. I need to talk to both of them if we're going to get through this."

"You make any progress on getting us out of here?"

"I just left you like fifteen minutes ago."

"A man can hope."

"We'll go. I promise. As soon as we're done."

"I've been thinking about it," he said. "The man we came to find is dead. We can go home and give the girl the bad news. It sucks, but it is what it is."

I understood why he thought that way, and I took a second to think about it. To make sure I had my motives correct, and that it really was about Eliza, and not me selfishly wanting to get back at Omicron. It's hard to know, but in this case, Mac being there helped. Because I'd lie to myself, but I wouldn't lie to him. "We owe her more. The girl."

"What more is there?"

"Someone killed her dad. Whoever that is deserves to pay for it. We owe her *that*."

Mac considered it, but I had him. He wasn't thinking about *if* someone needed to pay. He was thinking about *how*. "We've got no evidence. There *is* no evidence. So how do we pin it on somebody?"

"*Someone* knows who did it. At least one person, right?"

"Someone pulled the trigger. Or swung the shovel. Whatever. Yeah. But there are a lot of suspects."

"Right. So we look at motive, opportunity, and means."

"That sounds official. Did you read that in a 'how to be a detective' book?"

"No." My face heated. I absolutely *had* read it in a book. "Maybe."

Mac laughed, which made me smile. "Seriously, though. How do we do it?"

I thought about it for a few seconds. "We get the fuckers to turn on each other."

He considered it. "Yeah. Okay. But do it fast."

"I will. But first I have to convince the commander."

PARNAVIC WAS WAITING for me by the front door of his headquarters this time. I'm not sure why, since we couldn't talk until we got to his office. Maybe he thought if he didn't escort me, I wouldn't come. But I was always coming. He might want to chew me out about Ganos, but he also had Whiteman and Alexander, and I needed to talk to them. Unfortunately, I didn't have much to offer him in return. My only course was to appeal to his sense of decency and justice. Fortunately, he had one. How much he'd go out on a limb for it remained to be seen.

I didn't speak when we entered his office. If I let him speak first, I didn't give anything away that he didn't already know.

And while I *assumed* that he had Ganos dead to rights on her system incursion, no way did I want to give the damning evidence myself.

Finally, one of us had to break the silence, and he did it. "You know why you're here."

"You called. I'm trying to be amenable."

"Cut the shit." No *sir* on that. That was telling.

"If you've got something, lay it out," I said.

He hesitated, probably knowing that he was giving up an advantage. "You broke into my computer system."

I almost said, *Did I?* I could make him work for every centimeter of ground. But something in the moment told me to play it friendlier. So instead I said, "Okay. Sure."

If it surprised him to hear me almost admit it, he didn't show it. "Care to tell me what that's about?"

"We've locked up Omicron's capability to communicate off moon. That keeps them from telling a story before we get to tell it, but significantly, it also keeps them from calling for reinforcements before we get them."

"That's not a good excuse," he said.

"It's what I've got. It's also true. These folks attacked your soldiers. They kidnapped my associate. They're bad people."

"You're not exactly a shining beacon of morality and ethics."

"No argument there."

He took some time to think about that. "What do you want?" he said, finally.

"I want to know who killed Jorge Ramiro. It's what I came here for, and I really don't want to leave without it."

"How does your associate breaking into Omicron's network get you that?"

"They were involved. Their desire to exploit Whiteman's find is at the root of the whole thing."

"And you think you're going to find the answer in their network? I doubt they'll have a confession there."

"The network isn't about answers," I said. "It's about pressure."

Parnavic walked around his desk and took a seat as he pondered that. "So you took their network hostage to force them to negotiate."

"It's one piece. It also buys us time—they can't contact anyone off moon, which means they can't have someone order us to stand down. I intend to use that time to get answers."

"Why wouldn't they just wait you out?"

"They would if they could," I said. "But I'm not going to let them. I'm going to force them to act."

He thought about it. "You're going to use Alexander."

I nodded, glad that he understood. He needed to if I expected him to help. "You got it. Whiteman too, but she's the key."

"We could probably get prison time for Alexander."

"We could *absolutely* do that," I said. "In fact, if we went to Omicron right now and told them that if they'd give evidence against her, we'd drop everything we had against them, they'd hang her themselves."

"Just another price."

"Just another price," I agreed. "And to them, not a high one. They've got a hundred of her."

"She has to know that," said Parnavic. "What makes someone like her do the kind of thing she does? There's no world where she thinks a kidnapping is ethical."

I shrugged. "People convince themselves about all kinds of things to get what they want. Whether it's money, power . . . whatever. But I don't think the reason is the key point here."

"What is it?"

"You said it yourself: She knows they'll sell her down the river. And if she forgets that, well, we can remind her."

"You think she'll turn evidence?"

"Probably. But even if she doesn't, we can make Omicron believe she will."

Parnavic nodded. "I need to think." I gave him time. I'd stated my case, and now Parnavic had to make the decision on his own. Ganos using military assets to break into a corporation's network was absolutely against the rules. He had to decide whether to follow the rules or do what was right, and that's no easy thing. Parnavic hadn't made a promise to Eliza Ramiro. I had. That he seemed to be truly considering letting me fulfill that promise was all that I could ask.

"Okay. I'm in."

It was my turn to be silent. He'd given me what I wanted, but now I found that I couldn't take it. I had to make sure that he understood the potential cost. "I'll do what I can to protect you, but I need you to know the risks."

He shook his head. "No, sir. There's no protection."

I raised my eyebrows. "No?"

"I'm not going to lie. I'm not going to hide anything. By not immediately shutting down your hacker's operation, I own it. I know what's going on. I'm not going to pretend I don't."

I nodded. Good man. Whether the decision would be *smart* or not, well . . . we'd have to see. But I respected it. "Okay then."

"I am, however, open to your suggestions for what's next. Kind of my first time going off the reservation. We can keep jamming the off-moon transmissions for as long as that works or until someone higher than me tells me to knock it off. Of course, it's a shame that we don't have off-moon communications ourselves so that nobody can order me to stop."

"Someone will pressure you on that soon, I'm sure. One of the corporations. Or both. They'll threaten you. Try to scare you."

"I can handle that," he said. I hoped he was right. It's a lot easier to say than to do, and they'd be very persuasive. "What do *we* do?"

"I threaten them back. The one thing we've got going for us is that there are two of them. They're working against us, but they're also never going to work together. I'll start by talking to Whiteman."

Parnavic considered that. "I don't know that I can hold him. We don't have him on a crime. Why do you need him?"

"He can give us stuff we can use against Caliber and Omicron. And I'm not convinced he doesn't know more about Ramiro's death than he told me."

"What do I detain him on?"

"He shot a man. It was probably self-defense, but I'm sure you've got some paperwork that you've got to do regarding that. But more than that, you're keeping him for his own good."

"I don't get that second part."

"Someone kidnapped Ganos. Corporations have definitely killed people on this moon. We can tell him that we're worried about what they might do if they got their hands on him." Once I said it, I recognized the truth of it. "In fact—you can let him make the decision himself. Give him the choice of staying here in protective custody or you can drop him off outside of Caliber's headquarters."

"You think he'll choose to stay?"

"Almost positive. At least here, he's alive."

"I can definitely ask him, but if he calls the bluff, once I get through looking into his self-defense shooting, I'll have to let him go."

"Sure. That's fine." It would have to be enough time. I'd make sure of it, even if I didn't know exactly how yet.

"You want to talk to him now?" he asked.

"First, I'm going to go to sleep for four hours."

"Really?"

"Yeah. Ganos says she can hold comms hostage with your support. I'm a mess. I'll be worth more if I get a little bit of rest before I dive back into the fight."

"You know best. I'll try not to let things fall apart in the meantime."

CHAPTER 24

REALLY DID SLEEP. I woke a bit disoriented, and I definitely didn't feel refreshed. I almost felt worse, but it wasn't about how I felt. It was about cognitive function. Sleep is a weapon, and given that I couldn't go into another actual fight, I needed to arm myself for the only kind of battle I could manage right now. A fight with words. Had my enemies slept? Probably not. In theory, that gave them a four-hour head start on me. But I still had the advantage of knowing the chaos I planned to unleash. I could afford to wait, because *they* were going to have to react to *me*. At least in theory. One never wants to get too caught up in the brilliance of his own plans, after all.

I checked in with Parnavic and found that Whiteman had taken him up on staying on base, and within a couple of minutes I'd secured an agreement from the archaeologist to meet for coffee at the military dining facility. It was an open space. Maybe he'd feel safe, being in public. He wasn't. But he didn't have to know that.

I took twenty minutes to get a medic to clean up my hand and put some medi-strips on it to speed the healing, and then I met Mac. Surprisingly, he'd actually gone for medical assistance too, and they'd patched him up. He wouldn't be winning any fitness competitions, but he was moving a bit better, and he, C, and I headed for the DFAC, where we found Whiteman already seated. I gave Mac and C instructions to hang back and watch over us from a distance. They could be in sight: I needed security, and I was fine if Whiteman knew that. But I wanted him to feel comfortable. I went to the machine and got a coffee and then took a seat across from him.

"How did it go? With the excavation?" I asked.

He shook his head. "Still no luck. I stayed out there as long as they'd let me, but it's not as close as I'd hoped. We're going to need more equipment."

"Are you going to be able to get there?"

"I'm hoping. The military has the place secured right now, but they don't have what I need to do the job. One of the corporations could provide the tools, but something tells me the two sides won't be working together anytime soon."

"A couple of major firefights will definitely put a damper on the cooperative spirit. I'm surprised to still see you here," I lied.

"Yeah. Well. It's a fluid situation."

"I can see that." I waited for him to take a sip of his coffee. "Where's Ramiro's body?"

Whiteman choked. It took him a few seconds to recover and set down his cup. "How would I know?"

"You do know." I didn't know that for sure, but it stood to reason that he might. It was *his* assistant, after all. "I'm not saying you killed him. But you know who did, and you know where they did it."

"You're not saying I *killed* him? Do I need a lawyer?"

"I'm not law enforcement. I don't even work for the government anymore. I'm also pretty sure the only lawyers on the moon work for companies who might not have your best interests at heart."

Whiteman thought about his situation for a bit. "I think I want to leave."

"Go ahead." I waited for him to stand. Mac made eye contact with me, asking in unspoken terms if I wanted him to make the guy stay. I shook my head slightly. I had another idea. I let Whiteman take three steps before I said, "But if you do leave, it's not going to go well for you."

He stopped. It was several seconds before he turned to face me. I can only imagine that his mind was racing, weighing his options. But he didn't even know the game, let alone the rules. "That feels like a threat."

"Oh. Good. I got my point across then." I smiled. "Have a seat."

"I'm not sure I'm going to do that."

"Then I don't think you quite understand the situation. Let me explain. Here's what's going to happen. You're going to sit, and you're going to tell me where to find Ramiro's body so that we can recover it, do an autopsy, and get it back to his family." I paused. "Go ahead. Ask why. Ask why you'd do that."

"Why would I do that?"

"Because if you leave this room without doing that, I'm going to go to the commander and have you expelled from the military facility. Then I'm going to get on the comm to my contacts at both Caliber and Omicron and tell them that you gave us a full deposition of every meeting you had with them and everything you did with them."

"That's a lie!"

"Yes, it is," I agreed.

"You can't do that."

I glanced around in an exaggerated manner, as if maybe he was talking to someone else. "Wait. I can't?"

He stormed back to the table, and for a second, I thought he might lunge across it and hit me. That would have sucked for the embarrassment of it more than anything else. But he pulled himself up short, rested his weight on his hands, and leaned down so he could stare at me directly. "You wouldn't. That would be a death sentence."

"Good. It's nice that we both understand things the same way. And as far as whether I would or wouldn't . . . I've been responsible for the deaths of much better people than you. Now sit."

Yes, I was being a total dick. A bully. But one thing had struck me in the exchange that justified that in my mind: Never once had he said that he didn't know where the body was. I'm not going to throw around legal terms like *accessory* or *accomplice*. I'll leave that to people who know the law better than me. All I know is that morally, that made him guilty, and practically, that made him a person who could give me an answer that got me closer to recovering Ramiro's remains and closer to figuring out who was responsible for his death.

Also, he was an asshole. That counts for something in my book.

He sat. "I'm listening. What do you want?"

"The real question is, what do *you* want?"

His face scrunched in confusion. "Can you stop with the games? I don't follow."

"Your endgame. Given everything that's happened, how do you want this to end?" If I were him, I'd have been thinking, *Not in prison*. But I didn't expect him to admit anything so candid as that.

To his credit, he took some time to think about it. "I want to be able to continue to dig here on Taug."

"That's it?" I didn't believe him, and I implied that with my tone.

"Okay, no. I want to dig, but I also want to be in charge. I want my name at the top of the research documents."

"You want the notoriety."

"Notoriety. Legacy. Compensation. Call it what you want. This is a huge find, and yeah, I want my name on it. It would be the culmination of my career. And, if we're being totally honest, it would mean I'd never have to work again."

Fame and money. I could believe that. I was calibrating my ability to read him, and knowing this was the truth might help me spot a lie when it came. And something about Whiteman told me that lie was coming. "Okay. And what's your path to get there from where we are right now?"

He thought some more. "It depends on who controls the site. Currently that seems like it's a little up in the air. The government has physical control, but legally, the land is leased to Caliber."

"We can see how that is going to go, though. Right? Regardless of what happens, the whole galaxy is going to know what's at that site. Too many people here know to keep it quiet. So how's it play out? Maybe Caliber takes it to court. Maybe they even tie it up for a while. But knowing what's there, does the government relinquish the site?"

"No," he said.

I wasn't as sure about that. When it came to powerful corporations and the government, a lot of variables came into play. But him believing what he did fit my agenda, so I didn't correct him. "Exactly. So if you want access, the only way you get it is to be commissioned by the government. Now—how do you get that?"

He smirked. "You're implying that if I want that, I have to work with you. That you have some control if that happens or not."

"Are you saying I don't?" I smiled. I had to make him believe it. Leading him to it on his own would be more persuasive than saying it, though.

"You don't control the site," he said.

"I don't. But then again, nobody here does. Which means we're talking about appealing off moon. You know someone else on Taug who gives you a better shot than me?"

"I can make a direct appeal. You're not the only one with connections."

"I'm not. And I'm going to straight-up admit that I can't get you the job."

"That much was clear when you resorted to a threat." He made like he was going to stand.

"A threat that I'll absolutely follow through on." I waited for him to settle back into his seat, which he did. "And I'll go one step further. I can't get you the job. But I can absolutely make sure you *don't* get it, and I won't even have to lie to do it. I'll make it very clear that you have allegiances not to one corporation, but to two, and how you betrayed one for the other in order to further your own personal glory. That'll be enough to end whatever hope you have of continuing here on Taug. The corporations have a lot of options and a lot of pull. You have none."

His shoulders slumped as the fight went out of him. He could have been faking that—letting me see what I wanted to see—but probably not. His wants were real, and even if I'd embellished my story a little, it rang true enough. "What do you want from me?"

"The same thing I asked from the start. Where's Jorge Ramiro's body?"

He spoke so softly I could barely hear him. "Buried on the southwest side of the hill near the dig site."

I almost asked him the obvious question—who killed him? But I caught myself and thought it through a little before speaking. "Who put it there?"

His eyes went a little wider at that. He could see the trap. He could deny knowing who killed the man, but if he knew the body's location, he couldn't very well deny knowing how it got there. Hopefully he didn't see the rest of the pitfall yet so I could still catch him out. "I don't know who it was. Someone from one of the corporations. They don't wear name tags."

"How many people?"

"Two."

"Men or women?"

"Men."

"What did they look like?" I asked, not giving him time to think.

He hesitated. "I don't know."

"How can you not know? You saw them. Old or young?"

"I don't know . . . thirties?"

"Describe them."

"One guy was tall. Dark hair. Looked like he was ex-military. The other guy was shorter and more muscular. Lighter hair."

"How'd you see their hair?"

"Excuse me?"

"The men. They'd have to have been in suits and helmets in order to breathe, right?"

He went for the obvious lie. "We were inside the excavation site. There's oxygen there. You've been there, you know that."

"I do. I wonder though . . ."

His eyes darted to the entrance of the DFAC, as if someone might show up to save him. Nobody came. "Wonder what?"

"I wonder why, if someone was showing up to kill someone, that they'd take the time to remove their helmets before doing it. Unless they were already there, and you knew them." I smiled, narrow and fake, and waited for him to realize the trap he'd stepped into. If he said they were already there, he couldn't deny knowing them. If he didn't, he had to come up with a plausible reason for them removing their helmets. After he didn't answer for several seconds, I pushed him. "When did you decide to kill him?"

He took a quick breath, and I could see the panic in him. "I'm leaving." He started to rise, but he hadn't noticed Mac, who had come up behind him, and now put a hand on his shoulder, forcing him back down into his seat.

"Nope," said Mac.

"You can't keep me here. You have no right."

"I probably don't," I agreed. Mac didn't take his hand off the man's shoulder, however, and he wasn't being subtle about the pressure. I didn't have any authority to keep him there other than the authority of force, but I wasn't going to let a murderer just walk out. Maybe Whiteman hadn't been the one to pull the trigger, but he'd been in on it. I was sure of it, and he wasn't denying it. None of what I had so far would hold up in a court, but it was enough for me to ensure that he got to someone who *did* have the authority to hold him and question him further. How to do that? Well . . . I hadn't thought that part through yet. It meant getting him to law enforcement off moon, though, which we currently couldn't do. So I texted Parnavic to tell him what I'd learned and my suspicions. If I took a little longer than absolutely necessary so that Whiteman could sit there, impotent in Mac's grasp . . . well . . . I never said I wasn't a little petty.

"So you admit it?" he asked, finally. "You can't keep me."

"That's not what I said. I said I probably don't have the right. But then again, you had no right to turn Ramiro's daughter into an orphan. So . . . here we are."

AFTER PARNAVIC SENT guards to pick up Whiteman and put him under house arrest—basically putting him in a room and telling him not to leave it—I headed to find Alexander, who was already in the same situation. She wouldn't be as easy to crack as Whiteman. She had more experience with manipulation and pressure, and she also had a corporation—with all its lawyers—demanding her back. So far, Parnavic had resisted those calls, but the pressure would increase, and while he had said he'd support me, he had limits. So, in theory, I had less time. In practice, it didn't matter much. I'd get her to turn, or I wouldn't, and it would happen quickly either way.

Alexander had absolutely participated in a serious crime, which made it different than questioning Whiteman. She'd been part of a kidnapping, and she'd proven that by showing me video of Bingham holding Ganos. I didn't have any living witnesses, and the low-quality video didn't prove much, but *I'd* seen it, and that established her guilt beyond a doubt in my mind. But she also had the weight of the legal department of a major corporation behind her—at least, she would as soon as she could get in touch with them. That meant that my belief about her guilt or innocence meant nothing, because they could bring to bear every technicality of the law.

I wasn't big on technicalities.

A single guard stood outside the door of the room, and she moved aside when I approached. I'd turned Mac free to get a nap (he argued for only a minute, a personal record for him), and I gestured for C to wait outside with the guard before I pressed the button on the door.

"Come in," said Alexander from inside. I have to admit, I love the pure balls of someone in detention giving her jailer permission to enter. Once more, I almost respected her.

The door opened into a small room with a narrow bed on the right and a desk against the left wall. Alexander was seated in the room's only chair, her back to the far wall. She had both feet on the floor, her hands on her knees. Somehow, her hair was perfect, and the whole scene gave the feel of me walking into her office even though she still wore a soiled vac suit. I almost smiled. She was trying to set the terms for the coming negotiation. As I'd expected, she'd be a tougher nut to crack than Whiteman. But I wasn't really planning to negotiate. You don't negotiate with criminals unless you absolutely have no other options.

"Colonel Butler. So nice of you to stop in to say good-bye."

"Oh. Are you going somewhere?" I shut the door behind me and leaned back against it to bring myself down closer to her eye level. We had maybe two meters between us, and I didn't feel the need to close the distance. I wanted to intimidate her, but not physically.

"I'm sure I am. My employer will undoubtedly be sending attorneys to secure my release at any moment."

"Oh. About that." I paused, letting it sit for a moment. She didn't react, but it would wear on her. The unknown was my ally here. "Your employer came and went. We turned them away."

She frowned, but it was probably performative. I assumed she'd prepared a script in her mind of how this would go and how she would respond to whatever I said. It's what I would have done in her place. "They'll be back. You can only stall for so long."

"They weren't attorneys, though."

No response, but her eyes didn't leave mine. Time to take her off her script.

"It was two security guards. At least that's what they *said*— they seemed a little smooth for that in my estimation. You get a feel for things like that in my line of work—who's a common grunt and who is more of a . . . what's the right term . . . higher-level operative?" I let her sit with that for a little bit. She may or may not believe me about who showed up, but she'd know exactly what I was implying. Now it came down to how safe she felt with her employer. But given that she absolutely knew that her employer would hire an assassin and take part in a kidnapping, she had to question whether these two men would take her back to her office or to an unmarked grave somewhere else on the desolate moon. It didn't matter that I'd invented the two men.

"What do you want from me?"

"Evidence," I said without hesitating. No sense in lying about it. She already knew.

"Which means you don't have anything."

"Which means we have plenty on you, which you already know. You don't walk into a meeting with a sniper in a hide position observing it and come out clean. And you also know that since we have that on you, your employer will heap everything else on your shoulders as well. They'll sell you out and wash their hands of the whole thing." I waited for her to respond, and when she didn't, I prompted her. "You disagree?"

"That's not the question here. And *you* know it."

I *did* know it, but I didn't know where she was going with it. "So what's the question?"

"Where do I get the best deal?"

"Ah." Purely mercenary. That I understood. "So you're going to turn on your company. Just maybe not to me."

"Nobody on this moon has the authority to prosecute me. It's debatable if they even have the authority to hold me."

"We could let you go to Omicron," I offered. She didn't seem to want to talk with me, so the threat seemed necessary.

"You won't." She had that right, unfortunately. They'd make her disappear and I'd lose my tool to get at them. Plus I wouldn't actually send her to a sure death. Well . . . probably not. "You've got nothing. You can't give me the immunity I want. You can't even guarantee me a reduced charge. So save your time and don't bother telling me that you'll put in a good word for me. We both know what that's worth."

"I had to try," I said.

"I understand. But you're out of your league here."

I smiled. "Can I get you anything to make your stay more comfortable?"

"A change of clothes would be nice."

I looked again at her vac suit and almost laughed at how out of place it seemed on her. "I think I can make that happen."

"I have to say—you're taking this pretty well. I expected more threats."

I gave an exaggerated shrug. "What can I say? Like you said, I'm out of my league." I smiled again and left.

Outside the door, I leaned against the wall. I probably shouldn't have had that last exchange with her. She'd underestimated me. It happens a lot. People dealing with military officers think that we're all action and no brain, that we'll go into every problem trying to use a hammer. I should have let her keep that illusion instead of putting doubt about it in her mind. But let her doubt. She'd be in that room for a while, and over time, who knew what that doubt might lead to?

In the meantime, she'd missed the obvious. She didn't even consider that I'd be recording the conversation. She'd given me exactly what I wanted. I didn't need her to give me evidence. I just had to be able to make Omicron believe that she *would*.

CHAPTER 25

I TOOK TIME TO update Parnavic on the events so far. He caught on quickly to my overall plan, which was, admittedly, banking on a lot of good fortune. But what choice did we have? We didn't have the force to storm a corporate compound and demand answers, and we didn't have the time to wait them out while we controlled comms off moon. When your two best tools are out of your toolbox, you use what you've got. What I had was a lot of bullshit and an absolute belief in corporate greed. What can I say? Not everything can end in a spectacular gunfight.

Hopefully not, anyway.

Parnavic dispatched a recovery team to search for Ramiro's body, and having secured the commander's help, I got ready to make a video call. We agreed that Parnavic would be there but stay off screen. He had more legal vulnerability than I did, and while we wouldn't be able to deny his knowledge of the situation, we didn't need to advertise it to our adversaries. Besides, I wanted them focused on me. Classic misdirection. Go ahead and watch the man, not what he's doing.

Part of that meant keeping things tight to the vest, so when I sent a message to Omicron, I told them I wanted a video call with Madeleine Blaylock, the head of local operations and Alexander's boss. I didn't tell them why. They could probably guess, but let them. Any doubt they had worked in my favor. They set the call quickly, which probably meant they'd been planning for it. I wasn't going up against an individual here. I was going against a full team that included high-priced lawyers, which meant I wouldn't get away with any of the tricks I'd used up until now.

As I expected, Blaylock took the call with her team present, flanked by a man and a woman whom she didn't introduce. Probably her legal team. She sat at a small conference table, and she didn't bother with small talk once the call connected.

"I assume you're calling to try to undo the damage you've done with your illegal incursion into our network."

"I'm sure I don't know what you're talking about," I lied. But it was nice of her to confirm the effectiveness of our efforts. "I'm calling about your company kidnapping my associate and trying to murder me."

"I've heard about those incidents. Rogue actors with nothing to do with our organization. I do hope you're all well, though. Very unfortunate the kind of people who make it to an outpost like this."

I hit play on the recording of my conversation with Alexander. Just the good parts. Nobody on the other end gave even a single reaction as they listened. When it finished, the man leaned over and whispered something into Blaylock's ear.

"You're illegally holding an employee of our corporation. Of course she'll tell lies to save herself. Any court will see that for exactly what it is."

"You want to bet on that? What if I offered you a way to be sure?"

Blaylock started to respond, but the woman next to her put her hand on the table and she stopped. I didn't mind. I had her interest. The two women conferred in voices too low to hear.

"I'll meet with you, but only in person."

"Sure. Come on over," I offered.

"We do it here or we don't do it."

She cut the connection.

Well, that didn't go how I'd hoped.

"So what now?" asked Parnavic.

"Now . . . I go to a meeting."

"That seems like a really bad idea," he said.

"It does."

"I mean, they've basically tried to kill you."

"More than once," I said, though he wouldn't know about the previous time.

"What makes you think that they won't try again?"

"Motive? Killing me doesn't help them now. If anything, it puts them in a worse spot."

"Pure vindictiveness isn't a motive?"

"For someone like Blaylock? She can't afford that. She has to look out for the bottom line."

"Okay. Well, I'll send a team with you. I sure hope you know what you're doing."

I sure hoped so too.

I HEADED TO check in with Ganos and get a feel for her part of the operation. Mac was still asleep, and I didn't look forward to breaking the news to him about my plan to go to the meeting at Omicron. Saying that he was going to lose his shit was probably an understatement. I arrived at her room to find two new guards.

This time, they immediately stood aside for me, and I went in. At some point they'd dragged another computer in, and a soldier in uniform pants and a T-shirt sat in front of two monitors. I took the only free space and stood in a corner.

"Who's this?" I asked.

"That's Dobkins. Dobkins, say hello to the colonel."

"Hello, sir." He didn't look up from his screens.

"How's it going?"

"We're holding," said Ganos. "They're kind of in a bind, because they don't want to go after the military network, and that's causing them to hold back. We can keep them locked up for a while yet. Their only short-term option is to build a new system. We're in about the same status with Caliber. Bottom line, nothing's getting off this rock today unless we say it does."

"How long will that take? Building another network?"

"Depends on how good they are. They have the hardware. But it's not like I'm going to sit here and make it easy on them. I'm in their satellite, but more important, I'm in their heads. I'm the thing that goes bump in the night."

"You're making some enemies, I'm sure," I said.

"Worth it."

"Best guess for me on the timeline?"

"They might restore their capability by the end of the day. Probably tomorrow. Day after at the latest," said Ganos.

I sighed and nodded. I had to take the worst case, and that didn't give me long. I'd have to wake Mac and get moving.

MAC WAS AWAKE and ready when I entered his room, cleaning one of his weapons. I wanted to ask if he'd slept, but I didn't want to push him, especially when I had to tell him that I was reneging on our agreement. Besides, if I enquired too much about his health, I'd be implying that he didn't know his own limitations. Being honest, a lot of us don't, and Mac is no different. But now wasn't the time to deal with that. He had on fresh clothes that weren't caked with blood, and maybe that was enough.

"How are the wounds?" I could ask that much.

"Doc said that they should heal to a hundred percent."

"That all the doc said?" I asked.

Mac gave me a flat smile. "Said I should avoid strenuous activity. You know—like docs do."

"Be honest. You good?"

"I'm not quitting, if that's what you're asking. Now . . . why don't you go ahead and say the thing you came here to say instead of dancing around it."

I half chuckled without really making a sound. "Someone come tell you?"

"Didn't need to. It's written on your face."

I sighed and nodded. "I need to go to a meeting at Omicron. I wouldn't go, but—"

Mac held up his hand to cut me off. "How soon?"

"Soon," I said. "As soon as we can manage."

Mac stood there, silent, his hands putting his weapon back together from muscle memory.

"You want to say something?" I asked, once it got unbearable.

"Just thinking through what we need to make it work. I assume we wouldn't be going to their place if there was any way to avoid it."

That he'd said *we* made me feel better instantly. That there had been any doubt in my mind made me feel like shit for thinking it.

"Yeah. Only option. But I figure that this time it's very public. They can't do anything to me because Parnavic knows we're going in there and is sending people with us, so if we don't come out, they won't be able to hide it."

"We'll take four vehicles if we can get support from the command here. We don't enter their parking facility. We stop outside and we go in on foot. We don't surrender weapons."

"You're okay with this?" I asked. "You don't want to talk about the decision to go?"

"You told me before we came on the mission that you weren't going to needlessly put yourself at risk. You know the situation here."

"That's right."

"Going back on that promise isn't something you'd do lightly. So I trust that you've thought it through and don't see another way."

I let that soak in. Had I truly thought through all the options, or had I defaulted to my comfort zone? Was I thinking clearly enough to know the difference? "The only other thing I can think of is to walk away."

"We both know that was never a real option," said Mac.

"Right," I said.

He snapped his weapon closed and performed a function check. "Let's get to it."

WE PARKED IN a defensive posture about seventy-five meters from a service entrance. Given the environment, the building had no "front door" per se. Normal humans entered through the parking garage where they had important things like shelter from the elements. And oxygen. If it surprised anybody at Omicron when we'd called to say that we'd be entering from the surface, they hadn't said anything about it. So we wore full environment suits and moved to the big commercial door in a small wedge formation with C on point, three soldiers making up each wing, and Mac and I walking in the somewhat protected center.

The building looked different from this vantage, long and low, rising to maybe fifteen meters in height along its entire front. The utilitarian construction gave it a look that more resembled a warehouse than a corporate headquarters. The soldiers would escort us to the entrance, and then Mac, C, and I would enter the facility on our own. We'd considered taking more people inside, but two or three extra soldiers wouldn't save us from an ambush. I had to trust our hosts, as hard as that was given our history. It did make me feel better that I'd have Mac with me. Something about that seemed to make it less likely that they'd try anything. Kidnapping—or even killing—one person . . . maybe they'd do that. But three? That seemed less likely. I was probably being naïve about it.

The large vehicle door—the only door in the vicinity—opened as we approached. Mac checked in with the escort team leader for a few seconds, and then he moved forward to join C and lead me in. I patted the sidearm on my right thigh to make sure I still had it. It wouldn't do a ton of good in a fight, but psychologically it helped. I didn't want to carry a long gun into the building. Mac and C had theirs though. They'd asked to bring grenades, but I'd vetoed that. Seemed like a bad idea.

Never mind that I'd brought one to my own adventure a day before. It had been a bad idea then, too.

Inside, the huge airlock reminded me of something in a space-port, as befit a facility designed to accommodate all manner of delivery vehicle. A single person in a vac suit waited for us in the center of the otherwise empty space. They held a whiteboard that said "follow me," which conveniently showed that their hands held no weapons. Not that I expected to be attacked in the airlock. But still, I appreciated the gesture.

The big door shut behind us as we made our way to the back of the facility and through a human-sized door into a second airlock. Once inside, it sealed, and the rush of air into it vibrated me in my suit. A light turned green, and our host took off her helmet, at which point Mac and I did the same. C kept his on for now, waiting for Mac to give him a signal.

"Welcome to Omicron," said the woman. "I'm Tahani Kapono. You can leave your suits and helmets here if you'd like."

"We'll keep them with us," said Mac. Kapono stared awkwardly for a second, but Mac didn't budge. He was worried about poten-tially having to leave in a hurry from another exit. Personally I'd have argued for running out into the atmosphere, where we could survive for a few minutes without suits until help arrived. But I didn't want to challenge Mac on it, so we stayed in the uncomfort-able suits and carried our helmets.

Kapono adjusted to that reality and turned to lead the way through another door, which led to an industrial-looking hallway with ribbed aluminum walls. A moment later we reached more corporate-looking corridors and soon stopped at a thick glass door that sported a huge company logo. Two guards waited outside, armed, but with their weapons—just sidearms—in holsters. It was about as unthreatening as they could get while still providing any sort of security. Mac didn't relax, holding the tension in his shoulders and the set of his feet.

"We need to search you before entering the director's suite," said one of the guards, a tall man of maybe fifty with a bit of a paunch.

"We're keeping our weapons," said Mac.

"I don't care about your weapons," said the man. "I need to scan you for recording devices." It was an interesting priority. It also was impossible, since we had our helmets, which all had transmitters.

Mac seemed to understand the issue as well. "The meeting is right in here?"

"Second door on the right," said the man. We could see it well enough through the glass door and wall.

"We'll leave our helmets here. C, you stay and guard them."

The guards searched us with wands in the thorough way of people whose jobs depended on it, and then they let us through. Madeleine Blaylock emerged from the first door on the right to greet us as soon as we entered.

"Colonel Butler."

"Ms. Blaylock."

"I thought the two of us would talk. No lawyers."

Mac ignored her and pushed on to the second door on the right. "I'd like to check the meeting room."

I nodded at Blaylock, hoping she'd get the point to let him do his thing and that it would be fine as long as she didn't have a hit team in there.

"Door's unlocked," she said.

Mac triggered the door open and disappeared inside for at least a minute while Blaylock and I stood there in silence, unsure what to do until he reappeared. "Good to go." Mac took up a position outside the door, his back to the wall on the same side of the hallway. I drew my sidearm and handed it to Mac as I followed Blaylock into a small conference room. It had a nice table with eight high-quality chairs around it. A rolling cart with glasses, some bottles, and a bucket that I assumed held ice sat against one wall.

"Take any seat you like," said Blaylock, as she went to the drink cart. "Is he going to be okay if I close the door?"

Mac reached his hand into the room with his thumb up, which answered that. I took a seat on the long side of the table on the opposite side from the drink cart. The door closed.

"Can I get you a drink? Water, coffee, whiskey? I've got Ferra Three, fifteen-year."

"I probably shouldn't," I said, a little concerned that they knew me well enough to even know my brand.

"You sure? I'm having one." She poured a finger and a half into one of the heavy glasses.

"Sure. One won't hurt."

She poured a second and added two cubes to each glass. She passed me one and then took a seat across from me. She took a sip of her whiskey before speaking, and I followed suit. It had been a rough couple of days, and it went down smoothly with just the right amount of bite.

"You have good taste," I said.

"Thanks. It's from my private stash."

I didn't necessarily believe that. It could easily be a gambit to try to convince me that we had things in common before jumping into what she wanted to talk about. Whatever. It was good whiskey.

"I'm going to get straight to the point and not bullshit you."

Again, I didn't believe her, but it didn't make sense to say so. "I'd appreciate that."

"We're in trouble here and I'm looking for the best way out."

Okay. At least *part* of that was true. "And you want me to help . . . how?"

"You want to know who killed Jorge Ramiro. What's that worth to you?"

"You can provide that?"

"What's it worth?" she asked again.

"A lot."

She took a device out of her pocket, set it on the table, and hit play on an audio recording.

"I need help," said a familiar male voice.

"What do you need?" asked a woman's voice, also familiar.

"Hit pause," I said. After Blaylock did, I asked, "Is that Whiteman's voice?"

"It is."

"And the woman is . . ."

"Francesca Alexander."

I'd thought so. "It's real?" There was no point to the question. It's not like she'd tell me if it wasn't. But a forensic data agent would be able to tell the truth, so she had little motivation to lie.

"You have my word." She hit play, and I listened to Whiteman say that there was a dead body and that he needed help hiding it and Alexander promise to send somebody to deal with it. I sat with it for a bit once it ended. It painted a different picture from what Whiteman had told me. It might not prove his guilt in court, but it removed all doubt in my eyes.

"Why share this with me?"

"It's what you wanted, right? To know who killed Ramiro."

"And you gave it to me for free." I needed to think that through. Her giving it to me meant that she saw benefit in it for her and her company. That she hadn't offered to trade the information or tried to tie me into a deal was the confusing part.

"I still have the recording," she said, which implied that she might withhold it. That didn't present as big of a problem for me as she might have thought. Having heard it, I could probably wring a confession out of Whiteman, but we didn't need to go there. She wanted something. I might as well find out what.

"What do you want in return?"

"I want you to go home on the next thing flying out of here."

"I'm not sure when that is," I said, intentionally skirting her point.

"As soon as we have communication off planet, I'll make it available to the authorities here and they can schedule it."

So she wanted *two* things. Me to go home, and for me to call off Ganos so they could get their comms back. That she didn't accuse me personally for the system incursion meant something, but I didn't know what. There was a lot I didn't understand, but one thing I did: Even if I gave her nothing, me having the recording helped Omicron. It specifically implicated two people, both of whom would likely be a problem for her. Alexander could potentially testify to . . . something. Whiteman probably would too.

If I, as a neutral source, put this recording into the hands of the authorities, it would greatly undermine both of their testimonies when it came to implicating Omicron. This was how Omicron got out of trouble—or how they thought they did.

But I still wanted the recording. I'd come to identify the killer and make him pay, and that hadn't changed. But now I wanted to know why she wanted me off Taug. "You're not doing this out of the goodness of your heart. What do you get out of me leaving?"

"A lot of stuff has happened here. A lot we're going to have to answer for."

"That's for sure." I almost listed their offenses but telling her that gave away free information. We all knew about the combat, but I didn't need to share *how much* I knew about it. Let her guess.

"I'm just going to say it bluntly. We'd rather you weren't here for the investigation."

That *was* blunt. And very believable, since I could counter their lies and cover-ups. But so could other people. "There are dozens of people who know what happened. They're not all going to leave."

"We control what we can control," she said. "We live with the rest."

I resisted the urge to shake my head, trying to keep my features neutral instead. It still didn't make sense. I could leave and still file a report. I had the contacts for it, and she had to know that. It was so obvious, I decided to broach it. "You didn't say that I had to stay quiet. Just leave."

"Obviously we'd prefer if you did keep quiet. I won't insult you by making an offer . . . I assume you recognize that there's one to be had if you decide you want it."

I almost laughed. She said she wouldn't insult me with an offer and then basically made one. I decided to make it clear. "I'm not for sale."

"The offer doesn't have to be for you."

She lost me with that one. "What's that mean?"

"There's a little girl back on Ridia who has lost a father. You don't need anything from us, but maybe she does. Funeral expenses. A university education fund. Use your imagination."

Ah. I had to hand it to her. That was actually a good play. Money wouldn't bring her father back, but it sure could make a lot of other things easier. How much easier, I didn't know. I didn't know the Ramiro family's situation. I had a sneaking suspicion that Blaylock did. I smiled.

"We understand each other." Blaylock finished her whiskey.

I swirled the final sip of mine around in the bottom of the glass. "We do."

She slid the recording across the table to me. "That's for free. The rest is contingent on how hard you make things."

I nodded.

"Any thought as to which way you'll go?"

I polished off my whiskey, set the glass down, and stood. I gave her a fake smile. "It's hard to tell with me. I'm known to be a bit unpredictable."

She didn't speak as I went to the door, opened it, and left. Part of me expected her to snap. Maybe she'd have her guards hold me up. Maybe she'd rage and call me an asshole, which would be totally fair. But Mac and I left, joined C, and were back in the airlock just a couple of minutes later without incident. I looked back over my shoulder, but nobody had followed us.

"What's wrong?" asked Mac. We were alone now, though probably being monitored.

"I wasn't sure they'd let us go. I didn't exactly give her what she wanted."

"We'll talk about it in the vehicles," he said. "I don't trust this place."

We sealed into our suits, and for a second, I worried that the door wouldn't open, but it did. Our team was waiting for us outside to lead us to the vehicles. C took up a position just behind me, walking backward, keeping his eyes on the building in case anybody tried to follow us. I'd almost reached my vehicle when he shouted, "Down!"

I dove to the ground to my right, and at almost that exact instant, the crack of a bullet cut the thin atmosphere close to my head. A headlight on one of the waiting vehicles exploded into shards. C was on one knee and his rifle barked. I scrambled to get behind the vehicle, not turning to look at the result.

"Inside!" said Mac across the net.

I stayed low and fumbled with the door before getting it open. C ran by me, heading for his own vehicle, and a few seconds later we raced away at top speed.

"What happened?" I asked over the net, once we were safely out of range.

"Gunman," said C. "On the roof. I caught a flash off his optics."

"You were looking for it," I said.

"When you said you didn't give her what she wanted, it gave me the idea that maybe they'd try something," C responded. "Lucky for us the person they sent wasn't very good. Everyone who can hold a weapon thinks they can be a sniper, like there's no skill involved, and it's some sort of video game. That guy learned."

"Not soon enough," said Mac.

They'd tried to shoot me. Maybe Blaylock had been planning to have me killed all along. Maybe she'd made the decision when I played coy with her in the meeting and refused to tell her my plans. I considered that maybe Caliber had sent the shooter, but I dismissed it. Omicron's security was too good to allow for that. I settled on a single thought: *Fuck her.* I stayed on that the entire way back, stuck in my own head, dreaming up ways to make Omicron, and specifically Blaylock, pay.

CHAPTER 26

AFTER WE CLEARED the airlock, I got out of my vac suit and headed to Parnavic's office, where I played the recording for him. He whistled. "That's enough for me to hold them. Obviously Omicron thought it was in their best interest to cut those two loose."

"Yeah," I said. "You know they took a shot at me."

"I do. They'll deny it, of course. We'll never find the body."

"I'm sorry we couldn't go back for it," I said. I meant it.

"I know it. That leaves us with very few options, and all of them have drawbacks. What do you want to do?"

"Can you give me thirty minutes? I need to talk it through with my team." I wanted to act, to get after Omicron any way I could, but I didn't know what that looked like, and now that I'd had some time to cool off, I needed to talk to Mac about it.

"Sure. What's another half hour in the scheme of things?"

I didn't have to look for Mac. He was right outside, chatting with the sergeant major, talking up Private Torrens and his role in our success. I appreciated that. I should have thought of it myself.

"You ready?" I asked him.

He shook the sergeant major's hand and joined me on the way out. We didn't speak until we got outside of the military compound. "What's the plan?" he asked.

"I don't have one. Not yet."

He looked at me like he didn't believe it and stopped walking. "You're going to go after them. They took a shot at you."

"What if I didn't?"

He snorted. "Yeah. Right."

"Seriously. What if we walked away?"

"Doesn't sound like you."

"I promised you at the start that I wouldn't take unnecessary risks," I said. "Maybe walking away is how I hold to that. We know who killed Ramiro, and we've got enough to at least make sure Whiteman faces a trial somewhere. We're recovering Ramiro's body. We could call that mission complete."

"But they need to pay. Right?"

"Do they though? Will they?"

"What do you mean?" he asked.

"What am I going to do that will actually hurt them?"

"I don't know. You'll come up with a plan though."

I thought about it some more, but nothing he had said changed it in my mind. "Here's a plan. We get on a ship, we get Alanson to a med facility, and we get Ramiro's body home to his daughter. We answer whatever questions the investigators have for us, and then we go on about our lives. Alive."

He stared at me without speaking.

"You don't believe me," I said.

"You're not wired that way. You think that you need to right all the wrongs in the galaxy." That would have stung more if there was bitterness in it. Or if he was wrong.

"Maybe this is growth. Blaylock made me an offer, you know. They'll pay off Ramiro's family."

Mac shrugged. "That wouldn't be the worst thing, but she wouldn't have done it unless it'll help them get away with it."

"They're going to get away with it regardless. You saw what Caliber did on Eccasis. That should have shut them down, but they're still here. These corporations pay the fines—even the really big ones—and they keep on going. They shouldn't be allowed to, but they do."

He snorted. "What's *should* or *shouldn't* got to do with anything in the real world?"

"So you think it's okay if we let it go?"

"Nobody would expect that. You'll shock everyone." Mac started walking again. "I wish we could do both. Get out of here *and* make them pay."

"I'll give it some thought," I said.

I had the beginning of an idea that might do just that.

I SAT ALONE in my room. Or as alone as anyone would let me be right then. I had guards at the door, and someone would poke their head in every ten or fifteen minutes to ask a question, or, more often, to use the excuse of a question to check on my mental state. I didn't know what to tell them. I wanted to punish the corporations for their activities on Taug, but no matter how I tried to work it out, I couldn't see a way where they both went down. After about two hours, I made my decision and went to a video terminal.

I called Andrew Toney at Caliber.

"You asshole," he said, by way of greeting. "You've got me in a lot of hot water."

I understood his attitude. We *had* hacked his device to give us a way to shut down his company's network, and they'd surely traced it back to him. I hadn't really thought about it, but he was lucky he still had a job. I was lucky, too, since I wanted to use him as an asset. "Let me make it up to you," I said.

"Yeah. Right. How are you going to do that?"

"I'm going to give you back control of your network."

"Sure you are. What's the catch? There has to be one."

"Of course there is. But the catch is what helps you. You're the guy who is going to make the deal that gets you back control of your system."

He didn't show anything on his face, but he hadn't hung up. That was enough. "Forgive me if I still think you're trying to screw me."

"Totally understandable. Here's what I want. Right now, nobody has communication off moon. Not you, not Omicron, not the military. What I can do is give you a head start over your competitor. It won't be forever, but I can get you six hours."

"Six hours," he said, as if it wasn't much. I'd have to spell it out for him.

"Six hours where you can get ahead of the story. You can get all the evidence out about the things that Omicron has done here. By the time they get on the line, they'll be playing catch-up." What I didn't say—didn't *need* to say—was that it was six hours where they could make themselves seem like the good guys.

"That's something," he admitted.

"It's more than something, but let me sweeten it. I'm about to send you a file with everything we've got on Omicron. Every illegal action we can tie them to, including accessory to the murder of Jorge Ramiro, the kidnapping of Maria Ganos, as well as other crimes."

He thought about it. "Yeah. We could use that. But again I ask: What's the catch?"

"Three catches. One: You promise that you'll use the information and get it out there. No making a deal with Omicron and burying it. You make sure that the entire galaxy knows what those assholes did here."

"There's no way for you to ensure that I follow through on that."

"You're right. You tell me right now that you're going to do it and I have to take you at your word. Number two, you give the military use of your off-moon comms."

"So they can counter what we're doing?"

"Obviously not. I'll give them restrictions. But they need to call for reinforcements, start an investigation, and coordinate space traffic. It's your network, so you'll be able to monitor everything they send."

"Done," he said. "What's the last catch?"

"You make financial restitution to Ramiro's daughter. Funeral expenses. Higher education fund. She wants for nothing."

"*We* didn't kill him."

I could have argued that. Could have said that their initial grab at the find was what drove Whiteman to Omicron in the first place. I could have said a lot of things, but I was sick of their shit. "That's the price. Take it or leave it."

"I need to run this up the chain."

"No, you don't. And I don't have a ton of time," I said. "Just say yes."

He thought about it for a good while before responding. "Okay. Yes."

CHAPTER 27

RIDIA 2 IS, objectively, not a good-looking planet. From space, it's all dull green and brown in its landmasses, and the blue of the oceans often looks almost gray. But my part of the planet—home—looked good. It was mostly trees and farms and scattered buildings—residences and small businesses. But it was familiar, and it had nice things like gravity and air. Air that smelled like autumn with just enough bite in it to wake you up in the morning. We'd said good-bye to Ganos at the shuttle landing port. She was home with her husband by now, and probably glad to be rid of us. Mac and C spent the night at my place, both for convenience and because they still thought someone might come for us.

I had my doubts but didn't object to the company.

That we would escort the body of Jorge Ramiro across the planet to his daughter was never in question. How exactly we'd do it—the logistics of the thing and the etiquette—we debated. Mac thought we shouldn't talk to the family at all. They'd suffered enough, and he favored leaving them to grieve in their own way. We could drop the body off with a funeral home and be done with it. But that seemed too much like the coward's way out to sit well with me. We hashed it out over some good whiskey at my house, and in the end, he gave in. C didn't drink, but he sat with us anyway. He'd earned his spot—there was no doubt about that.

C was flipping through stuff on his device while Mac and I poured another round when something brought him up short. "Did you see this? About Whiteman?" When we assured him that we hadn't, he passed the device. "Take a look."

Mac and I crowded together and watched a video of Whiteman being walked into prison by an angry-looking guard. The grainy video appeared to have been taken by an internal security camera at the facility.

"This is great," said Mac.

"Wait for it. It gets better," said C, smiling.

The video ended with a still frame of a particularly unflattering mug shot.

I chuckled, but it got me thinking. That video shouldn't have been public. I took out my own device and sent a quick message to Ganos.

Did you do that?

She responded almost immediately.

Do what?

Never mind

If you mean did I hack into the network of a prison and route the video of an asshole

> *being processed to a somewhat dodgy*
> *media site, then no, I didn't do it. Because*
> *that would be illegal.*

I laughed. Mac and C looked at me like I was nuts, but hey, maybe I was.

We were about four drinks in when Mac said, "You know what bothers me about the whole thing, still?"

"What's that?" I asked.

"Barnes."

"How so?"

"How I could miss on her so badly?" he asked. Which wasn't really about Barnes at all, but about doubting himself.

"You know what it's like?" I asked, and then continued without waiting for an answer. "It's like when somebody sees combat for the first time. You never know how they're going to respond until the bullets start flying, right?"

"Sure," said Mac, and C nodded along with him. They knew.

"Maybe it's the same way with a bribe," I said. "Nobody sits there on their sofa and says, 'Yeah, I'd definitely take a bribe.' We all want to think that we wouldn't. But that's the thing . . . you never know until someone actually offers you one."

"Hmm," said Mac, considering the bottom of his glass. Thankfully, he let it go, because if I'm being honest, I still hadn't resolved my own questions about Barnes and her place on my list of dead. Maybe we *should* have seen the signs. Maybe if we had, we could have addressed them, and she'd still be here. But who knows? What I *do* know is that this is why I shouldn't sit around drinking after a tough mission. At least I wasn't drinking alone.

There were parts of the mission I could be proud of. A team had arrived on Taug to conduct an investigation, and Parnavic was, from all accounts, doing a bang-up job managing it and pushing for repercussions against the two corporations. Omicron had taken a huge public relations hit, and they faced a long legal battle. But for me, the good always seemed to fade into the back while the regrets pushed to the forefront. Maybe a healthy person didn't have that problem. But then, maybe not resting on your wins and remembering your failures *was* the healthy option. Either way, I'd still be thinking about it for a long time.

—

When the three of us boarded a sub-orbital flight for New Gaston the next day, I still hadn't decided exactly what I intended to say to the Ramiro family. *Sorry for your loss* didn't feel like it would cut it. We flew light, carrying only small overnight bags and one casket. We didn't really need C along—I doubted we'd be fighting it out with someone trying to keep us from reaching our destination—but Mac wanted him, and since I'd overruled him about meeting with Eliza, I let him have this one without an argument. We didn't have weapons, but the way the two of them glared at anybody who got anywhere near me probably made me 40 percent safer.

I'd contacted Eliza's aunt Sophia to tell her we were coming, both because I needed an address and because it would have been weird to just show up. This isn't the kind of thing that one should spring as a surprise, even if that's pretty much exactly how this had started in reverse. Regardless, my message also allowed her to break the news to Eliza however she saw fit. I also passed on to

Sophia the news about the funeral costs being covered by Caliber, though I didn't explain why. I'd tell her eventually, but it could wait. In all honesty, I think part of me hoped that she would tell me not to come to their apartment. Call it cowardly, but I would have been truly grateful if she'd relieved me of the burden I'd placed on myself.

It *was* a burden, too. Because while we'd done the job we'd been hired to do, it wasn't a happy ending. Rare, those. No matter what we'd done or hadn't, Eliza's father was still dead. Whether any of the other stuff mattered to Eliza, well . . . it probably didn't. All I could do was relay the information if given the opportunity. In the end, Sophia didn't stop me from coming.

Not going to lie, the thought of seeing that little girl again made me nervous.

True to the plan, the funeral director met our flight. He'd arranged for us to be first to debark, which the flight attendant announced to the entire cabin of passengers. As Mac, C, and I rose from our seats to move to the front of the plane, people started clapping like we were some kind of heroes. They didn't know anything more than that we were escorting a body. I have no idea why someone started the applause. I can say this though: It made me feel like shit.

We most definitely were not heroes.

We met Eliza and her aunt at their home, which sat on the end of a set of four attached two-story apartments with its own front door. Sophia ushered us in, offered us cold beverages, which were welcome as it was a warm day and the air conditioner in the vehicle that brought us from the airport had left a little to be desired. Eliza appeared a few moments later, and she and I moved to the other side of the room so that we could talk in semi-privacy. Everything I planned to say, everything I hadn't planned to say—it all went out the window at the sight of her earnest face. Thankfully she spoke first.

"Thank you for bringing my father home."

"I'm sorry that we couldn't do more," I said.

"Do you know who was responsible?"

"I do."

"Will they pay for what they did?"

I hesitated for a second at that. There were a lot of different things I could say. Jacob Whiteman was in custody and likely to face trial—the authorities had the recording and everything else we could provide. But was he solely responsible? Was the small measure of vengeance that I'd pointed at Omicron enough to say that they were paying for what they did? Who was truly guilty and innocent? Could I be the judge of that? Was I even innocent myself? Maybe in this case, but certainly not across the scope of my life.

I had to tell her something.

"The man responsible is in custody and he's very likely to stand trial. There's a lot of evidence against him, and I think—I hope—justice will see him in prison for a long time."

She considered that for a moment, considered me. I think those young eyes saw through me; I think she knew there was more to say. Part of me was sad that she had to grow up this fast. But she didn't ask anything else, and I didn't offer. She was young. I could let her keep her belief that there's justice in the galaxy a little longer.

Finally, she nodded, having received at least that little bit of peace.

I envied her for that.

ACKNOWLEDGMENTS

As with all my books, I could not have created this one alone, and I'd like to recognize some of the people who helped bring it into existence. But I'd be remiss if I didn't first thank the fans of the Planetside series for their support, because without them buying the early books, there never would have been a fourth book in the series. I'd also like to thank R. C. Bray, who narrates the series, for all the attention that he brought to the audio versions of the books, as that's how a lot of people discovered Carl Butler.

Thanks to my beta readers for this book, Ernie Chiara and P. K. Torrens, who gave me a feel early on for what was working and what wasn't, which helped me figure out where I could stand pat and where I needed to ramp things up. Thanks to J. C. Nelson for his notes on the book, and especially on the parts related to Ganos and her shenanigans. I've said this before, but Ganos probably doesn't exist without J. C.'s involvement with this entire series. Dan Koboldt is another person who has had input on all my work, and I'm forever indebted to him.

Thanks to my agent, Lisa Rodgers, who is a fantastic advocate (and a solid editor, too) who helps me choose my projects and gets the deals done to see them to print. Thanks also to David Pomerico, my editor at Harper Voyager, for buying the book and his keen insight and great notes. I really enjoy working with both of them. Nancy Tan was the copyeditor, and she's outstanding. I can't possibly emphasize enough how much smoother that makes the process of finishing the book.

Lastly, and most important, thanks to my wife, Melody, for her unending support. Being a writer means spending a lot of time alone, which means a lot of time not with your family. Having a supportive partner is a huge part of why I'm able to keep at this writing dream. I love you, honey.

ABOUT THE AUTHOR

Michael Mammay is a retired army officer and a graduate of the U.S. Military Academy. He has a master's degree in military history and is a veteran of more wars than he cares to remember. He lives with his wife in Georgia.

www.michaelmammay.com

DELVE INTO THE PLANETSIDE SERIES
FROM ACCLAIMED SCIENCE FICTION AUTHOR
MICHAEL MAMMAY

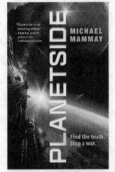

A military lifer is pulled into the kind of investigation that ends careers . . . or lives . . .

War heroes aren't usually called out of semi-retirement and sent to the far reaches of the galaxy for a routine investigation. So when Colonel Carl Butler answers the call from an old and powerful friend, he knows it's something big—and he's not being told the whole story.

A military legend is caught in the web between alien intrigue and human subterfuge...

Following his mission on Cappa, Colonel Carl Butler returns to a mixed reception. To some he is a do-or-die war hero. To the other half of the galaxy he's a pariah. Forced into retirement, he has resettled on Talca Four where he's now Deputy VP of Corporate Security, protecting a high-tech military company on the corporate battlefield—at least, that's what the job description says.

A military hero is coming out of disgrace—straight into the line of fire...

Carl Butler was once a decorated colonel. Now he's a disgraced recluse, hoping to live out the rest of his life on a backwater planet where no one cares about his "crimes" and everyone leaves him alone.

It's never that easy.